WRITTEN IN THE WIND:

A WORLDSMYTHS ANTHOLOGY

TABLE OF CONTENTS

LETTER FROM THE EDITORS

In this collection we asked our authors to explore the theme of names, the power they have over us and our world, but also the relation of a name to one's identity. The answers they came up with awed and delighted us! From tales that wax nostalgic for Celtic legend and trapped Djinn, to stories set in an uncertain future with portals to hidden realms, our authors delivered. There were many more we wanted to include, but simply didn't have the space or funds to do so.

We really feel this is our strongest collection to date, but getting it put together has been harder than usual. 2023 was an exhausting year and it gave us a lot of time to think and a lot of things to think about. Ultimately, we decided to make a very big change going forward; we'll be putting the fifth anthology on hold while we focus our publishing efforts on novels and novellas. Submissions are open!

It's 2024, which is our eighth year of a writing community and third year as a publisher, a fact we are extremely proud of! Our community is thriving with over 800 members and lots of activities to participate in. We've created a House Cup challenge where writers can take a short survey to be sorted into House Kraken, Gnome, Dragon, or Pegasus. We also have casual write-ins, editing sprints, and a growing book club with live readings and discussions every week.

Remember, if you are interested in publishing (either independently or through Worldsmyths), you can connect with us through a variety of channels (see our socials listed in the back of this book). Or, if you just love hanging out with a kind and welcoming community, we're always happy to have more readers around too.

Finally, we would like to thank our volunteer ARC readers who put in the time and effort to read this book for free before publication, as well as our editor, Aaron, who was fantastic to work with. We'd also like to thank Odessa Silver for creating our beautiful cover art.

We hope you enjoy this wonderful collection of stories!

TRIGGER WARNINGS

Some stories may contain subject matter that is extremely upsetting to some individuals including, but not limited to the following topics:

General death
Guns
Murder
Child abuse
Domestic abuse
Violence

THE GIFT YOU GAVE AWAY

BY ALEX MASSE

Tiffany stood at the edge of the wood, a pan flute in hand and an alias on her tongue. They weren't her only weapons: she kept honey in her bag as a straightforward peace offering, and—if all else failed—iron stakes hanging from her belt. They were her favourites.

This wasn't her first foray into the fey courts, but as she'd learned early on, each and every one had its own ... quirks. Some courts liked toying with humans, some courts liked trading with humans, and some courts liked eating them.

She hoped she wasn't walking into one of the third. Still, none of them would be getting her name. That was a kind of power she'd rather die than hand over.

She'd learned a lot about names. After all, she was looking for one.

Tiffany sucked in a breath as she crossed the forest's threshold, shuddering at the immediate temperature drop. The glamour fell soon after: trees parted like curtains, and the world went dark. When some light returned, she found herself under the glow of a new sky.

It never failed to be beautiful. It never failed to be haunting.

She wanted to be angry that she was still here, taking this trip, and hadn't seen home in years. That her son had run away, shed his name like old clothes, and vanished without a trace. She wanted to be furious—but she couldn't. How could she feel anything but guilty?

In the months after, she'd looked for signs. Perhaps, with hindsight, she'd get some sign as to why he'd done this, where he'd gone, who he might've gone with—but found nothing. Worse, the loss of his name was spreading. She'd long forgotten his face, and the memories of their sixteen years shared were blurring away with it. One night, in a fit of terror, she'd carved his name into the hilt of her iron stake. It was the only way she'd remember it, and no fey was bold enough to grab the one thing that could kill them.

Not yet, at least.

A pang of hunger struck, and Tiffany pulled the last of her rations from her coat pocket. It was pitiful, really: some nuts and herbs, with a ghost of some spice. Meant to be chewed more than swallowed, to distract more than feed. In a realm where meals were offered on shining platters, their ambrosial scents a siren song, she learned to keep her mouth full.

If only every fey trap had such a simple solution.

She'd come in during some kind of celebration. Of course she had—it was the only time a fey court opened up, hoping to lure in oblivious travellers with all its glitz and revelry. Banners and lights were strung amongst the branches, stands at the edge of the clearing offered food and goods, and the music seemed to come from everywhere at once. A hypnotic wind quartet was complemented by a low, percussive beat that gave it a sense of hysterical glee.

Tiffany had heard the stories: people dancing themselves

to death, being drowned by "gifted" horses, their own children being snatched from their hands. Of course, avoiding *these* traps wasn't as simple as it seemed. Saying yes was a death sentence, but saying no had to be done with surgical precision. If she said "No, *thank you*," the bastards took that as meaning she owed them something, and wouldn't let her go until she'd paid it off. If she was rude, that, too, was an unforgivable slight against their pride that would be swiftly dealt with.

A fey man offered her a steed, one he promised would take her across the realms. Tiffany shook her head, tried a smile, and simply said, "That is lovely, but not for me."

She ignored the glimmering lights, the hollers about free food, and the laughter of children. She ignored the dancers and their outstretched hands.

But not all of them ignored *her*.

"Oh, what darling hair, all streaked with silver," cooed a dancer, taking her by the arm. "And what *striking* features, in that strong jaw and those bright brown eyes."

Tiffany smiled in acknowledgement, lightly tugging out of her grasp, but the fey persisted.

"I think you would make a lovely constellation," she went on, "strung up in the sky. Dance with me, you stellar specimen."

It wasn't the first time a fey had made an advance on her. Tiffany had to admit, she was pretty: vibrant blue skin, flowers of every hue blooming from her dark locks, pointed ears and antennae both perked up and alert. But what drew Tiffany's attention the most was the clawed hand still digging into her coat sleeve.

"I am afraid I have a previous appointment. Perhaps some honey could make up for my absence," Tiffany offered, reaching for her satchel. The fey grabbed her other hand by the wrist. They made an odd couple—Tiffany in her long black skirt and old brown trenchcoat, the fey in a glimmering white piece that left little to the imagination.

"Honey's become such a bore," whined the fey. She slid her hands down, interlocking her fingers with Tiffany's. "I want to taste something else. I want to taste *you*."

"I have someone expecting me," Tiffany pressed, even as her cheeks grew hot. "You are lovely, but I have to go." Not a lie in the slightest; she *was* lovely.

The fey dancer winced as if struck. "Ah, I see how it is. You've made up your mind, haven't you?"

"It was made up from the start."

"Well." The dancer checked her nails, a mischievous glimmer in her eye. "How about a deal?"

Tiffany bit back a retort, smiled demurely. She wasn't new to this. "I really should be going."

"Oh, it will be wholly beneficial. You'll give me a show ..." She grinned, a row of fangs poking out from beneath violet lips. "And *I* won't kill you if it's a good one. It's more than any of my sisters would've offered you, so take it in stride." She snapped her fingers.

Tiffany felt the beast's approach before she saw it, a rumbling in the earth beneath her feet. Its howl pierced the air, confirming her worst fears.

A Black Dog.

The other fey heard it too. Their faces split into fanged grins, and they gathered around like it was a dancing circle, and Tiffany was their star.

The Black Dog leapt over them like it was nothing, skidding to a stop mere feet away from where Tiffany stood. It towered over her, a low growl in its throat, saliva dripping from between bared teeth, sizzling where it hit the forest floor.

Tiffany reached for an iron stake.

Spurred on by the cheers of the crowd, the Black Dog

lunged, jaw open, eyes burning red. She rolled out of the way, leaving the creature to fumble, its legs folded under its massive weight. Its muscles rippled beneath an ink-dark coat, and she knew immediately that taking even one blow would end the show and, with it, her life.

The Black Dog recovered, and Tiffany ducked a swiping paw. Mercifully, it wasn't blessed with agility on top of strength and bloodlust. On top of that, like everything else from this realm, a good iron staking would probably do it in —or at least stop its rampage.

She could manage that. In one decisive movement, she slid between the beast's legs, each thick as trunks, stake at the ready, aimed for that dark, hanging underbelly, and plunged.

The screaming came from all around. It wasn't the creature—it was the crowd.

"Stop!" shrieked the dancer. At once, Tiffany scrambled out from under the Black Dog, chucking her stake to the ground. She had others, but it was good manners to at least *appear* unarmed in situations like this.

"You were supposed to put on a show," the fey woman snapped, her face tight with disgust, "not *kill my hound.*"

The crowd around her murmured in agreement, staring down at Tiffany through narrowed, shimmering slits of eyes. Their rage came down on her like a fog, heavy and permeating.

"I can still put on a show," Tiffany blurted out, "if you'll allow me. And then I'll be gone. Is that a fair deal?"

The fey murmured amongst themselves. As they did, Tiffany reached into her coat, pulling out her pan flute. After all, it had saved her from worse.

"Please," she insisted. "Let me show you what I can do."

The dancer stared her down then, eyes narrowed. "If we

deem your performance worthy, you may go. If not, I will tear you apart with my bare hands."

Tiffany smiled. "Very well. It is a deal."

She held the flute to her lips, took in a breath …

And played.

Tiffany had never seen herself as an artist, performer, or musician—no, the title she identified most with was that of "alchemist." Every piece she played began as a pang in her chest, low and mournful, seeping into the bones, and her gift was to transform this into breath and melody. The pain she carried was ripe, and when it became music, even the fey fell silent. The Black Dog lay down, whimpering, the last of its fight surrendered as its whines melted into snores.

"Consider us even," Tiffany said, sliding the pan flute back into her coat. She spun on her heel and walked on, the crowd parting before her in that uncanny silence only fey could have. "I have a meeting to attend to."

* * *

The burrow was exactly as Tiffany had heard it described, and so she had no trouble finding it: a humble stone cave, framed by the swaying branches of a willow tree.

Tiffany leaned forward into the unyielding darkness of the cave, which allowed not even the faintest silhouette of the space before her.

"I'm looking for the one called Calla," she said into the black. "I was told they could help me."

Nothing. Tiffany sighed, though she had expected as much.

"I am willing to bargain," she added.

The shadows parted like a curtain, and she shielded her

eyes from the glow that broke through. Gradually, her eyes adjusted to the figure before her and the desk it perched at.

"Hello, little one," they cooed with a voice like the northern wind.

Tiffany had long grown accustomed to fey and their various glamours, though there was no escaping the primal, possibly vestigial dread of seeing one so old and powerful. Calla towered over her, all four deep, violet eyes aglow, dark against their alabaster skin. A single golden horn poked through their reddish hair.

They could kill her in an instant, in so many ways. This was their domain, the very earth beneath them and the pointed stones above—the latter of which Tiffany was suddenly, keenly aware–ready to move at their will.

Calla cleared their throat. "What are you seeking?"

You have a script, Tiffany reminded herself, shaking her head to clear it. "I am looking for my child, whose name was taken." A lifetime ago, she'd said she was looking for her son, but that'd gotten her laughed out of the burrow immediately. "I was told you could help me—that you hold names nobody else will, names so thoroughly erased, this is the only place they persist. I am willing to pay in honey, fruit, or herbs." When Calla didn't react, she added, "I am also willing to pay in song."

"Why do you seek your child's name?"

"I ache for the lack of it," she replied. That was the simplest answer, and any fey would know the many truths it held. Not only did she miss her child, but the remaining memories warped in such an absence. She could barely hold onto herself.

Calla tilted their head to the side, peach-pink lips curling in a smirk. "I can feel it on you, sweet mother. And I happen to know where your child is. You should be proud of her."

Her? Is this some kind of trick? Tiffany knew better than to question the fey aloud, but the surprise must have been clear on her face, because Calla laughed.

"Would you like your daughter's name?" they asked.

"Please." Her voice cracked as she said it, the desperation breaking through. This was the closest she'd ever been, and it'd been so long since she'd heard—

"Cecilia Rose."

Tiffany hardly even caught the name over the roaring in her ears, but her body knew before her mind had even registered it. The memories flowed free and violent, like the torrent from a burst dam: years of holding her child, from a bundle in her arms to a stubborn, gangly mess of limbs, and then years of feeding her child, from breast to bottle to homecooked family dinners.

Ten years of arguing with the father of her child that there was nothing wrong, that it was alright that sometimes he stole her dresses, that it was alright that he took little interest in courting women or hunting with his uncles.

Five years of pleading for her child to just tell her what was wrong, because surely *something* was. Why else did he and his father always scream at each other? Why else was he trying to bury his own body in layers and shawls, with Tiffany promising she wouldn't be mad, pressing to understand the storm beneath the skin.

He'd always said he wanted to be a girl, Tiffany thought. It made her stomach twist into knots, even through the haze of reminiscence. *He—she is. Now, I can't even remember what I named her in the first place.*

Calla's head cocked to the side, eyes narrowed. "Have you learned what happened?"

"She's still my child." The ease at which the words left her lips surprised even her. "I still want to take her home."

"Fascinating," Calla purred. "Do you think she *wants* to come home, after trying so hard to leave? To be forgotten?"

"Maybe if I can make her realize I've loved her all along."

The arguments with the man who'd been her husband rattled around her brain: the accusations that she was keeping their child from him, that the son she'd supposedly given him was nothing but a mirage. In a sense, he was right—and Tiffany yearned to meet the girl who'd been there all along.

"Please, let me show her that." Tiffany knew that begging was generally frowned upon amongst the fey, viewed as pitiful and, worse, self-involved. They preferred a good bargain. When Calla didn't budge, Tiffany added, "Just tell me what you want."

This set the fey in motion. They leaned forward, all four eyes boring into Tiffany's own. "What is it you have?" Before Tiffany could open her mouth, they went on, "That is a rhetorical question. I can check right now."

Long, clawed fingers wove their way into Tiffany's hair, settling along the side of her skull. Tiffany tried not to flinch; the fey was frigid.

After the shock of having over a decade's worth of memories restored, Calla's probing was feather-light, surface-level, almost pleasant. In fact, she only noticed the fey had let go when they leaned back and declared, "I know what I want: your skill on the pan flute."

"What?" Tiffany murmured. On instinct, her hands flew into her coat, to the pocket where her instrument—her foremost companion all these years—rested.

"I think it would impress my friends in the court," Calla said with a lazy shrug. "That seems a fair trade, no? I mean, you can always learn a new instrument, but you'll never have a new Cecilia."

This was true. It terrified her, the idea of the flute becoming alien in her hands. "What would that look like?"

"On your end, mostly a loss of muscle memory," Calla explained, checking their nails. "You'd forget where your fingers go, how to shape your mouth, and you won't likely ever remember again."

Tiffany shuddered. The pan flute was embedded into her —Calla was right about that much. Her body had changed around it: her fingers folded around the reeds easier than any lover's embrace, her lips knew the shapes of notes as well as any word, not to mention every breath-holding contest she'd won with her limber lungs. With the knowledge sapped away, would any of that still be true?

But Cecilia was *so close*.

"I have some questions," Tiffany said shakily. "If the answers are satisfactory, I will allow this trade."

"You really have been doing this a while," Calla purred. "I'll allow one question."

"Is my daughter alive and in a state where she can, if she chooses, forgive me and come home with me?" It came out slow and staggered, each word chosen with surgical precision. After all, she had to be careful with the fey. Tiffany had heard stories of so-called "reunions" leading parents to graves or trapping both parties within a fey court for the rest of their lives.

"That feels like a few questions disguised as one," Calla remarked, "but I'll allow it. The answer, after all, is yes. Now that that's all said and done ..." The fey held out their hands, spindly fingers slightly curled. "Give me your skills, and I will conjure a door to your daughter. The next time you walk through it, you will be sent to a place of your choosing."

Tiffany raised a brow. *This sounds too good to be true.* "No tricks?"

"Of course not. You've made an adequate offering." Calla inched their hands forward. "Come, now, before I change my mind."

Tiffany took the pan flute from her coat, studying it one last time before everything changed. The round wooden tubes. The nicks and knots it had earned from years in and out of fey courts. The soft, earthy green band of fabric that bound it together.

"You can keep that," Calla added, smiling. "I'd much prefer one that fits my hands better."

Tiffany slid it back into its pocket. "Thank you." She placed her hands in the fey's.

"I'll try to make it quick," Calla assured her.

Tiffany tensed, expecting it to hurt. But, if anything, the sensation was pleasurable after being bogged down by so many new memories. She didn't forget all the times she'd played, but the visions held less weight now, as if the recollection of a story, rather than the life she lived.

One in particular stood out: sitting by Cecilia's bed, lulling her to sleep with a light, lilting melody, like that of a songbird.

She's worth it, Tiffany reminded herself, even as her eyes burned with tears. *Even if she doesn't forgive you yet. Even if she never forgives you, she's worth it.*

Calla let go. Tiffany slumped where she stood, drained by the ordeal, and the fey caught her by her shoulders.

"It is done," they said. "The door awaits behind you."

Tiffany spun on her heel and, sure enough, there lay an old wooden door, embedded into the cavern wall as though it'd been built and waiting this whole time. It even bore the same moss and water damage as the rest of the area.

"Thank you," she whispered.

"You humans really love that phrase," Calla said with a laugh. "In my eyes, there is no need. An adequate trade was made. You go see your daughter. I'm going to get a pan flute."

Tiffany had never been one to overstay her welcome, especially when the thing she'd been searching for this whole time lay a mere door away. Without hesitation, she marched straight to the door, flung it open, strode through, and ...

The sun was what she noticed first, and not just because it was blinding, especially after so long in the eternal twilight of the courts, but *warm*, caressing the exposed skin of her hands, of her face.

And as she did this, a small voice murmured, "Is that her?"

Even by the time her eyes had fully adjusted, Tiffany couldn't understand what lay before her, and—the sight was overwhelming.

She was in a meadow, surrounded by all kinds of wildflowers of all kinds of hues. And not ten feet away lay her daughter, wrapped in the arms of a fey.

Tiffany had always known she'd recognize her child's face anywhere, but something in her heart sang at how uncanny the resemblance was: the strong jaw, the dusting of freckles, the shiny brown eyes.

She looked like her mother.

It took Tiffany a moment to realize that those shiny brown eyes so identical to her own were gleaming with fury.

"It seems I can't even run away properly," Cecilia murmured, soft but simmering. The fey lying beside her drew back, startled. "Is that why you're here? Did you come all this way, *hunt me down,* just to tell me I failed once again?"

"Cecilia," Tiffany began, and the name felt so *right* on her tongue, "I never saw you as a failure. I love you so much, and that's what compelled me to come all this way—"

"You 'love' me?" Cecilia cut her mother off. "Is that what you call it? Every time father berated me as a disappointment, as a *failure,* you were standing silently by because you 'loved' me?" An angry flush spilled swiftly across her cheeks.

The fey beside Cecilia cleared her throat. "Would you like me to do something, Cee?"

Cecilia blinked, and her features softened. Her head cocked to the side. "Excellent idea, Bramble. Do you need her name?"

Tiffany's heart skipped a beat. She tried not to let it show. "What are you doing?" She'd long ago lost the *I am your mother* tone. Now, it came out broken, foreign on her tongue.

Bramble smiled. "A name is always useful, my dearest Cee."

"Her name is Tiffany Gray," Cecilia declared, taking the fey by her hand. "Please, use that to get her out of here before she lies some more about *loving me*."

Tiffany took a step forward. "I mean everything I say, Cecilia."

"You don't get to call me that!" Her voice rose sharply.

"You have no idea how much I've endured, just for the chance to speak it."

Bramble cleared her throat. "Tiffany Gray..."

"I gave up years," Tiffany pressed, desperation breaking through. "I gave up my sanity. I wore my body to the bone. I can't even—"

Bramble cut her off, and Tiffany knew better than to fight it. The fey's voice carried the uncanny echo of magic at work. "*Tiffany Gray, leave this place and never bother your daughter again.*"

Tiffany tensed, assuming the worst was to come. But it didn't. She stayed where she was, unperturbed, as the demand rang throughout the meadow.

Bramble looked to Cecilia, frowning in puzzlement. "Why didn't that work?"

"I don't know. It should have," Cecilia huffed. "*That's her name.*"

"No, it isn't," Tiffany said. Her face split into a grin, giddy and incredulous. "Not anymore. I use my maiden name now."

"What? Why?"

Tiffany stood up straighter and took a step toward her daughter.

"I'm not Tiffany Gray anymore, because I couldn't stand

to be with the man who hurt you. I'll give you my real, name, though, if it means you'll listen for even a second longer." She held her head up high as she spoke, hoping the weight of the words would land. "I'm Tiffany Wright."

Cecilia didn't budge from her seat in the flowers, glaring up through her dark eyelashes. "Why couldn't you be *Tiffany Wright* sooner? Why didn't you do anything years ago? Why did it take me erasing myself from your life for you to lift a finger?"

"Because I didn't know how much pain you were in," Tiffany replied. Her daughter's words stung, but she couldn't let her see it. She had to be brave. "That's my fault, Cecilia. I'm owning it. I didn't know how bad it'd gotten, and that's my fault. But over these past few years, while I've been searching for you, I've been thinking of all the ways I could be better, too." She was speaking faster now, each word a bargaining chip, hoping she could get them all out before she lost her daughter yet again. "I won't dismiss you, I'll ask the right questions, I'll understand when you can't answer them, I'll do whatever it takes to be a good mother—because I know I can be, now. Just give me the chance."

Cecilia's eyes had started watering around *I could be better*, and now, tears practically poured down her cheeks. She hugged her knees to her chest, cursing under her breath.

"I hate that a part of me wants to believe you," she muttered. "But I'm even angrier that I'm crying."

Tiffany held out a hand. "It's okay, honey."

Cecilia took it and squeezed. She managed something like a smile, the tears still in her eyes. "If I'm coming back, I want to set some terms."

"I'm all ears."

"Firstly," Cecilia began, "You're never to refer to me by my birth name again."

"Already done," Tiffany replied. "The fey literally erased it from existence. Even in my memories, you're Cecilia."

Cecilia beamed, tears still spilling down her cheeks. "*You have no idea how happy that makes me.*" She wiped her eyes with joyous, fluttering hands, and laughed a high and gleeful laugh, like the ringing of a bell. "That's settled then. Secondly, I refuse to leave the fey courts behind entirely. I have friends here." She glanced at Bramble. "And more."

"Of course." Tiffany would rather be driven through with an iron stake than come back after all of this, but her daughter could do as she pleased. "You're an adult. You being in my life at all is a gift I'm not taking for granted."

Cecelia turned back to her mother. "I'm so happy to hear you say that. My final condition is this ..." She tugged Bramble, who'd been watching mutely the whole time, back into the conversation by the sleeve. "Bramble will always be welcome to come with me when I visit you."

"Hello, Miss Wright," Bramble said, waving shyly. "My apologies for trying to banish you."

"No harm done," Tiffany assured her, and she meant it. "Let's go home. And on the way back, tell me all about how you two met."

* * *

Alex K. Masse is a writer, musician, and communications specialist from what is colonially known as British Columbia. For Alex, writing is a means of connection and expression, within themself and with others, and a major source of joy and medicine—whether they're writing about their experiences as a nonbinary autistic person, songs about queer joy, or hope-filled fiction on neuroqueer resilience.

THE HUNDRED NAMES OF ATIYA DJINN

BY NICOLE L. SOPER GORDEN

Nuha set the sterling spice box on her kitchen table, flanked by the fresh pita and hard, green mangoes she had also bought at the bazaar. Grinning, she pulled a stool over to study the piece more closely. The spice box was tarnished, with scratches and a few minor dents, and in desperate need of a good polish. Spice boxes like this one were locally traditional, a marriage of beauty and function like she'd never seen back home. She had seen a million similar pieces coming through the city merchants' guild here on their way to markets and bazaars, though this one was clearly old and neglected. She ran her fingers over its faintly-pitted surface; she dearly loved old, pretty things.

The merchant had said the spice box was cursed by a djinn's ghost; maybe he had thought to scare the foreigner, or maybe he had hoped the wild story would drive up the price. She grinned, chuckling wryly. Djinn were real, though rare as golden phoenixes. But she had outgrown stories of curses and ghosts years since. Besides, no djinn (ghost or otherwise) would inhabit this spice box—it was made of silver.

The container was shaped as a desert rose, just like the

ones vining up the trellis outside her kitchen window currently scenting the air. She had loved the fragrant flowers from the moment she first moved to this country—the mix of soft petal and sharp thorn, sweet nectar and bitter sap was like an encapsulation of the city. Pretty, but not always kind.

Nuha flipped open the lid on one of the petals, revealing the dusty and tarnished silver pot once used to store some spice. She brought it to her nose, closing her eyes. Under the metallic tang, she imagined she could smell a hint of expensive saffron. Five petals total, just like a desert rose, and each opened. In the middle, an elaborate egg-shaped pot rose above the petals, decorated with flames and swirls that looked like wind, its lid firmly tarnished closed.

She did enjoy a good challenge.

Sometime later, after cleaning and polishing and oiling the spice box until it gleamed, she tackled that middle spice pot. With the help of a prying knife, she levered at the latch until finally, reluctantly, the lid creaked open.

There was a strong smell of old silver and ash and something musty from the space. Then a sudden hot wind arose and took her apart like she was made of nothing more than smoke.

* * *

*N*uha woke in a void. There was a moment of vertigo, feeling like she was on the edge of a cliff, poised to fall. She clenched her hands until her fingernails bit into her palms, using the pain to ground herself.

Not a cliff, but a space with no edges or walls, an ornate rug on the floor the only visible boundary. Even beneath the rug, the floor seemed absent, as if the rug floated in nothingness. Around her, distance faded to black nothing. It was all nothing—except for the man.

He stood over her, tall and dark skinned, black hair in waves down his back, eyes like two shiny black beetles. His bearded jaw was set, his brows drawn. Nuha felt the urge to shrink away from him, though there was nowhere to shrink to in this nothing place.

"You will attend," the man boomed. "I have moments to explain your situation, and I will not repeat myself."

Nuha swallowed hard, sitting upright to get a better look at the man. He wore a multitude of gold jewelry—earring hoops and studs, a pair of chains connecting ear to nose piercing, gold rings and chains around his neck—and two silver bands, one on each wrist.

"Who are you?" she asked, voice quieter than intended.

The man did not move, but his eyes flashed suddenly fiery red, pupils glowing as if angry flames burned just behind them, and she *knew*. This was no man; this was a djinn. For a moment, she was unable to breathe.

"You will know me," the djinn said. "You will know all 100 of my names. You will know them, and you will speak them, or the curse means an eternity trapped here."

Nuha stared, a buzzing rising deep in her spine. A curse. A real curse, and a real djinn, though he didn't appear to be a ghost. This all felt unreal. Why did she feel numb instead of terrified? Shock? Magic? Something else? Gulping down a deep breath, she got to her feet to meet the djinn's gaze. He still towered over her, but standing made her feel less like an insect beneath his heel.

"Please explain," she said shortly.

He leaned forward, lip curled until his teeth showed. "Are you not afraid, little human?"

"Terribly," she said, slightly breathless. "But you're the one who said time was limited."

For half a second more, the djinn's eyes burned. Then they turned back to shiny black. "There is a curse on this spice box," he said. "An eternity trap, with the ability to hold a soul for all of time. And you have stumbled in, like a curious little magpie, tangled in this net for the sake of something shiny." He tilted his head, studying her dispassionately. "However, the curse can be broken. I have 100 names and titles. To break this curse, you must remember and repeat each of them in order and correctly."

Nuha nodded slowly. Memorization she could do. She had an eidetic memory, useful for doing inventory and book-keeping for the city merchants' guild. It was why she had been trusted with the work, despite her young age. This seemed manageable—and that made her nervous. What was the catch?

"Once per hour, I will state one of my myriad names," the djinn continued. "Otherwise, I cannot speak. If you correctly repeat my listed names each hour, the curse will be delayed until the next name is given. But if you fail at any of these hourly waypoints to speak my names correctly or in order, the curse will take hold."

Nuha's mind was racing. One hundred names, once an hour, meant 100 hours' time. That was more than 4 days. A long time to be gone, but would anyone even miss her? Her only family was across the great salt sea. She had few acquaintances and fewer friends in the city. Would her neighbors realize she was gone? Or her supervisor? The merchants' guild were decent employers, and they'd been willing to look past Ziyad's accusations to hire her when so many others wouldn't, but Nuha wasn't sure her direct supervisor knew her from any of the other dozen bookkeepers on staff to realize she was missing.

And there were the more immediate concerns, too. How would she survive in this sparse bubble of space for 4 days? She had nothing to eat, and no water or wine.

As if sensing her thoughts, the djinn continued, "During

your time here, you will need neither food nor drink. You will not require sleep. And at the end, there is either failure and the curse or there is renewed freedom." He crossed his arms, looking down at her. "Do you understand the rules, little human?"

"Any mistake in pronunciation or memory, at any hour during this trial, and I will be cursed?" she asked, wanting confirmation of how dire her situation was.

"Any mistake calls the curse," he said, eyes narrowing.

"Can I speak to you between hours?"

He frowned, studying her. "I cannot speak except my names."

"I know," she said, pushing tawny hair out of her face. "But you can nod yes or no, or gesture with your hands, right?"

He stared at her as if she were speaking a foreign tongue. "You may speak to me, if you desire."

She hesitated for a moment, trying not to be intimidated by the djinn's stature or scowl or even the mere fact of his existence, let alone the prospect of a curse. "And what happens to you?"

His black gaze drilled through her, prompting an unease that nearly manifested in physical pain. "Time's up, little human. My first name is this: The Death of Ten Million."

The way he pronounced the name was like the drums of an army, declaring war. She shrank back a step, and almost another when he glared at her in fixed expectation. Belatedly, the fear bloomed, large and loud in her mind.

"The Death of Ten Million," she repeated, voice nothing but a rasp.

The djinn nodded in acceptance then sat on the rug cross-legged to wait.

* * *

That first hour felt like a lifetime. Nuha tried to explore the space, but the farther she got from the diffuse, sourceless light at the center, the harder it was to move. At some point, she froze in complete immobility until she made the decision to turn around again, shivering, to pace behind the djinn's still form.

This all felt so unreal. Nuha had never believed in curses, and she'd never before seen a real djinn. How had she gotten herself into this position, suffering the cruel trial of a djinn who was known, apparently, for killing ten million people? Struggling to avoid the djinn's vindictive curse? She thought of Ziyad's unfair accusations, the merchant's knife-sharp suspicion and matching tongue. Wrapping a tawny curl around a finger, she stared at the djinn's own black hair. Did this djinn also distrust pale-haired foreigners?

When, an hour later, the djinn's second name was revealed to be Drach'il'non's Demon, she believed it. Who but a demon would curse people for no reason?

Three hours later, she repeated by memory, "The Death of Ten Million, Drach'il'non's Demon, The Black Shadow of Ul, Red-Hand Atiya, Death's Flame."

The djinn nodded and settled back again, likely expecting another hour of Nuha silently pacing behind him, but she couldn't stand it any longer.

"Why are you doing this?" she asked, squatting down in front of him.

He blinked slowly at her as if she had forgotten already that he couldn't speak, stupid human that she was. But she hadn't forgotten. She had only grown desperate. Ninety-five names left to learn, and she was already vibrating with the stress and unfairness and the dire need to keep from crying. So much pent-up nervous energy; she had never been good at being still. It was barely the length of an afternoon, and she was already craving the taste of fruit, the relief of sleep.

With a sound of frustration, she stood and paced away from the djinn, only to come back a moment later. "I can do this trial," she insisted. "I have the memory for it. I memorize things for a living: inventory and shipping schedules, names and accounts, processing codes and dates. But this waiting ... it's interminable. It will drive me mad. Is there no way for me to repeat all 100 names now, at once?"

The djinn watched her for a moment, beetle-black eyes tracing her every jangled nerve with a certain cold resignation. He shook his head once, hard and sharp, then turned away from her again.

* * *

Later, after repeating a list that culminated in the djinn's ninth name, Shadow Flayer, Nuha tried a different angle. She sat on the rug across from him, folding her hands together to keep them from shaking under his black stare. She remembered the wind that had brought her here, the musty old smell, and the merchant's claims about the spice box.

"Are you a ghost?" she asked.

The djinn stared at her, unblinking, and she swallowed her fear in favor of logic.

"I didn't think ghosts were real," she continued, watching him closely. "But I also didn't think djinn could touch silver, and yet ..."

She trailed off, staring at the bands on his wrists. The djinn followed her gaze, his nostrils flaring briefly, and the look of disgust on his features was as clear as wildfire. He shook his head, crossing his arms.

"Not a ghost, then?"

He shook his head again, biting hard on his sneer.

"I want to know why you are doing this. I want to understand. Your names have been … dark, but I don't believe anyone is inherently evil. So why? Have I done something wrong? Have I broken a law? Have I offended you in some way? Tell me my mistake, and I will take ownership of it, Shadow Flayer."

The djinn seemed to flinch at hearing his name, but made no other reply. His silver wrist bands glinted, and for the first time she saw that they bore faint traces of the same flame and wind pattern that had been etched on the silver spice pot.

"Or is it truly just that the spice box was cursed?" she asked, more quietly this time. "Is that why I'm here? Random chance? Because—" She paused, grappling with the unfair possibility. "Because I have a weakness for desert roses and pretty, old things? For artifacts of local tradition?"

Despite her best efforts, Nuha's words cracked a little at the end. The djinn pinched his lips together, leaning forward slightly, hands on knees, watching her carefully. Finally, he nodded.

"I never should have bought that spice box," Nuha muttered, blinking hard against stinging eyes.

The djinn nodded again, expression carefully blank. Nuha hated that nod. It felt like he was blaming her somehow, like simply being herself was enough to invoke his curse. Ziyad had looked at her like that, too, when he falsely blamed her for selling his business secrets. In an instant, her self-pity turned to anger.

"But it's still your curse!" she accused.

There was the briefest of hesitations, but the djinn did nod again.

Nuha closed her eyes, pressing fingernails into her thighs to let the pain ground her. Maybe he was right; she had chosen to buy the spice box even after the merchant's warnings. "It doesn't matter how your victims are chosen, I suppose. I'm still cursed."

The djinn's expression hardened, arms crossing again, and Nuha got to her feet to pace once more.

* * *

*H*ours passed with Nuha jittering with both indignation and self-recrimination. Names of terror and blood and violence were added to her litany, like jagged and poisoned pearls on a string. She repeated the names to herself to pass the time, silently or out loud, to prove her memory was good. To prove she could beat this curse. She paced for miles, back and forth, behind the djinn's back.

Just as the djinn had said, she did not get hungry or thirsty or tired, even as the hours accumulated. But she still craved the sensory relief of eating and drinking and sleeping. She thought of her mangoes at home, ripening slowly towards sweetness without her there to taste them.

Wanting to know her captor, Nuha spent her time between names studying the djinn. She observed him from every angle, committing his looks and bearing and behavior to memory. He had strong features: a straight nose, sharp chin, high cheekbones, piercing eyes. The beard on his chin was as shiny and black as the hair down his back, like ebony satin. His shoulders were broad, the archaic sleeveless tunic showing the size of his biceps. He had not stood since her arrival, but she estimated he was at least six feet tall.

For the most part, he seemed disinterested in engaging with her. Sometimes when she tried to ask him questions, he ignored her entirely, though other times he would nod or shake his head, or mime answers. It took hours of questions and consistent prodding on her part, but she began to untwist the djinn a little. She started to learn more about him from the pieces he chose to share: that he had once been a goldsmith, and that he could turn into wind and fly if he wanted, that he loved to dance, and that his favorite food was mangoes.

When the djinn's twenty-third name was revealed to be a Sandsin word that meant "drinker of blood," she had to ask him. "Do you really drink blood?"

He rolled his eyes, then shook his head.

Nuha hadn't heard tales of djinn drinking blood, and it was comforting to hear he wasn't about to drain her dry. But it did lead to the next question: "Why give yourself an untrue name, then?"

The djinn shook his head again, scowling, and Nuha bit her lip in thought.

"Did someone else give the name to you?"

A bitter nod.

"Why?"

The djinn's eyes went to flame again, and he opened his mouth in a silent growl, each tooth growing pointier as she watched. He threw his arms wide, fingers clawed, like he was ready to pounce. She shrank back, startled, and was surprised again when the djinn's face returned to normal in the next instant. Was that sadness in his eyes? He looked away, shrugging, before she could be sure.

"Someone was scared of you," she whispered. Something about his hunched shoulders and turned-away face made her add: "But they shouldn't have been. Should they have?"

But the djinn didn't answer.

Later, the djinn's thirty-fifth name was Sire of the Myriad.

"Is it true that djinn can only have children with a human partner?" Nuha asked. It was what all the myths said, though how much truth was in the myths was increasingly unclear.

He studied her for a long moment before raising an eyebrow.

Nuha felt herself blush and raised her hands in front of her. "I wasn't offering. Just curious."

A hint of smile quirked the corner of his mouth, and it was strange how much that one gentle touch of happiness softened his severe face into something handsome. He nodded, answering her original question.

"And you have children? With...a human woman?"

He held up six fingers.

"Six children?"

He shook his head, and Nuha realized her mistake.

"Six women?"

Nod.

Nuha nearly commented on the number of wives, but then she remembered his twenty-ninth name: The Ancient Bane. She studied him again, trying to use this new information to interpret what she saw. "How old are you?"

He considered her for a moment, as if weighing whether to answer, but finally he held up fingers: four, then two, then seven.

"Four hundred and twenty-seven years?" she squeaked.

The look of mild amusement bloomed slightly larger, into something like smug humor, as he nodded.

"So it's true djinn live forever, then," she mused.

The djinn held out a tipping hand in a gesture that seemed to imply "sort of."

"Or at least can live a very long time."

He nodded agreement.

Nuha wondered if that was why the djinn played these games. A life that long was bound to lead to boredom eventually. It seemed inhumane to play with people's lives just because he was bored. But then, he wasn't human, was he?

* * *

The djinn's fiftieth name was The Half-Truth Lord. It seemed appropriate for the halfway point in Nuha's trial. She could feel the djinn starting to get restless, as if his own nervous energy was determined to match Nuha's. He watched her avidly every time she recited his list of names, as if expecting her to trip up somehow.

"I said I can do this," she insisted after listing through his fifty-fifth name, an Argrichish word that meant King of Fools.

He stared back, eyes flat.

"Trust me."

He scowled like she had cursed him instead of the other way around, and she scowled back. She was tired of being untrusted. The city didn't trust her. Ziyad hadn't trusted her. Even the city merchants' guild only trusted her enough for an unspecialized position, despite her eidetic memory.

"Stop expecting me to fail. I have a good memory, and you've provided ample motivation." She couldn't keep the bitterness from leaking into her voice, though she tried to clear it with a sigh.

But it was too late; the djinn's expression had already closed down, and he had already turned away.

The djinn's sixty-first name was Prisoner of Folly, and his sixty-second was Ruuwa's Dupe. Nuha found herself frowning and repeating back to herself every word the djinn had said, every bit of information he had mimed, growing uneasy in some of her assumptions.

"Who was Ruuwa?"

The djinn turned away and refused to answer, but not before Nuha caught the look of hurt and anger that darkened his expression.

The djinn's sixty-seventh name was The Untrusted, and

his sixty-eighth was The Other. Nuha felt them like darts in her mouth as she spoke each one back to him, watching him flinch when they landed.

She mulled over the entire list of names in her head between hours, realizing how sharp each one was—like barbs. The Death of Ten Million hit differently if it was a name given to the djinn rather than one he chose himself. Red-Hand Atiya. The Ancient Bane. She couldn't unsee his flinches. How many of the djinn's names were forged of distrust, sharpened and aimed and slung to cause him pain?

* * *

*H*ours later, when she whispered his seventy-fifth name, trying to launch it as softly into the air between them as she could, she thought she had figured it out.

"The Appellatively Cursed."

He vibrated in response, eyes shimmering with the glow of embers. Twenty-five names away, and he seemed cleaved halfway between hopeful and desperate, like he might come apart at the seams with anticipation before the cursed ritual came to a conclusion. Nuha sat carefully in front of the djinn, picking her words like they had the potential to explode. Maybe they did.

"Was Ruuwa the one to curse you?"

It was an accusation, of sorts: that it wasn't Nuha who was cursed, but the djinn himself. That the djinn had been the true, or at least the first, victim all along. That the djinn had been deceiving Nuha.

The djinn's eyes flamed, and he rose up before her like the demon he had been named. Somehow, he seemed twice as large as he should. His long dark hair whipped around in gales of wind, his sharp teeth bared.

Nuha swallowed hard, but did not move. If she was right, he wouldn't risk hurting her. So instead, she repeated conversations back to herself in her memory, trying to be sure.

Someone was scared of you.

But it's your curse.

And what happens to you?

"Who was she?" Nuha asked the raging djinn. "A human?"

For a second longer, he kept his threatening posture. Then he exhaled and came back to himself, though his eyes still burned with desperate embers. He watched Nuha carefully, as if trying to read her. She couldn't hide her relief as his anger passed, and knew he must see it, but she kept her expression open and earnest. She wanted him to know she had meant no harm by her questions. The djinn sagged, looking away. He nodded; a human, then. Using two fingers, he tapped twice at his chest just over his heart.

"You loved her?" Nuha guessed, voice gentle.

He nodded.

"Did she love you?"

He clenched a fist in the fabric of his shirt over his heart, closing his eyes as he shook his head slowly.

"I see. She betrayed you?"

Nod.

"Cursed you?"

Nod again.

"Why?"

For the first time, the djinn looked small. Pursing his lips, he clasped his two hands in front of himself, as if in a handshake, then shook his head and broke his hands apart.

"She ... broke a deal with you?"

He shook his head, holding a fist over his heart, head bowed.

"She didn't trust you," Nuha guessed, and the djinn's flinch was the only confirmation she needed. "Why?"

The djinn took a deep breath, expanding to a half-hearted echo of his demon-eyed vision of moments before, eyes flickering from red back to black like coals extinguished, and suddenly she understood.

"She was scared of you," Nuha breathed. "Because you're different."

The djinn stared Nuha directly in the eye, his expression a muddled mask of anger and hurt and at least a dozen other emotions she couldn't name, and despite everything, she saw herself reflected in his shiny black eyes. They were each foreigners capable of too much—djinn magic on his part, a perfect memory on hers. It bred distrust, and distrust bred malice, and malice bred pain. Ruuwa had cursed this djinn for being what he was, because it scared her. Ziyad had blamed Nuha for selling secrets because her eidetic memory and foreign heritage scared him. Ziyad had called her so many names, hung slurs around her neck like lead necklaces, trying to discredit her in the eyes of others. Was that Ruuwa's game, too? Spell out one hundred reasons for a human not to trust a djinn in the litany of names? Nuha's heart clenched in her chest, feeling like she might implode under the pressure of sudden sharp empathy, until she had to look away from the djinn or blaze to ash.

She sensed more than saw the djinn's shoulders droop.

"Just to be clear," Nuha said quietly. "The curse—you're the one that's cursed, not me?"

Hesitation. Nod.

"If I fail to list all hundred of your names accurately, what happens to me? Do I go home, or do I remain trapped with you?"

He looked up at her, eyes beetle-black once more but somehow lifeless, like hollow carapaces. With a shaking hand, he pointed up and away from himself. Freedom, then.

"I see. And if I list your names accurately, your curse is broken? You are set free?"

The djinn hunched in on himself, squatting in the middle of their carpet, arms wrapped tight around his middle—but he managed a nod. He had never looked so insubstantial. It was clear he was miserable, that he expected her to give up on the curse and go home. And why wouldn't she? It hadn't been her choice to come here. She had never agreed to 100 hours reciting names to a cursed djinn.

Nuha took a deep breath, standing and brushing her clothes. "Okay, then. We have twenty-five names left. A day until we're both out of here."

She didn't see the djinn move, but suddenly he was holding her elbow—gently, as if afraid it might shatter under his touch. He stared at her until hope kindled the glow back into the depths of his eyes, asking a question with no words. She wondered how many humans before her had been brought here, how many had abandoned this task out of fear or anger or mistrust.

"You should have been honest with me from the start," she said gently. "But I won't leave someone cursed out of spite. You can trust me."

He pulled his hand back as if burned, watching her carefully. He had loved Ruuwa; maybe she had pretended to love him, too, to gain his trust before cursing him. Softly, Nuha reached to run fingers along the silver bands around his wrists, tracing the tongues of flame and swirls of wind, feeling his pain within her own chest.

"The idea of trust should not hurt so much," she said, but she said it almost to herself, and the djinn gave no reply.

* * *

*I*t took over five minutes to recite the full list of 100 names in that final hour. His last name was maybe the simplest, but it also felt the truest. Nuha suspected it was his first name or the name that he thought of himself by. His *real* name.

The further she got in the list, the bigger the djinn seemed to get. Heat radiated from him. By the end, with the vocalization of name one hundred, he towered over her, arms spread, head tipped back, eyes blazing with fire, long hair whipping in gales of wind that almost ripped the voice from her throat.

"Atiya," she said into the wind, speaking the name with quiet care.

It was like an explosion.

Gusts and flame, light and sound, movement and fury—the world came apart around her. She came apart, too, and the djinn in front of her. Everything was wind and fire. All that remained were the two blazing embers of Atiya's eyes, the incandescent gleam of them an anchor in a world of upheaval.

And then she was in her kitchen, holding a sterling silver spice box, the middle pot open to show the tarnished and empty inside.

She blinked the memory of chaos from her eyes, but her kitchen was placid. It was late morning, and birds were singing in the lemon tree outside her open frame window. The rich fragrance of desert roses mingled with a fresh scent on the breeze, hinting that it had rained overnight—always much needed this time of year. Early light slanted across the kitchen floors in gentle, pale imitations of djinn fire.

Nuha felt disoriented and adrift. Had she been here, in her kitchen, all along? Had she been daydreaming? Sleepwalking? Surely it hadn't been real; djinn and curses were fables and nothing more.

But when she turned around, she found Atiya standing in her kitchen, looking too big for the world of humans. He rubbed at his wrists with something like wonder. The silver bands were gone, leaving only unmarred dusky skin.

"Free," he muttered, and it was strange hearing his voice say something other than a name. Holding his arms up before him, hands in fists, he grinned until the fires rekindled in his eyes. "I'm finally free." His voice vibrated with something dark and dangerous.

Nuha set the silver spice box on the table before her now-shaking hands gave away her sudden nerves. "What will you do now?"

He seemed to expand, making her already-small kitchen feel even smaller. "I have debts to repay." He made a fist, squeezing until the veins and knuckles stood out white.

She remembered again the stories about djinn: how dangerous they were, how vindictive, their fire and wind ravaging their enemies. This response had always been a possibility. She had hoped otherwise, and had tried to cultivate something more in him. During their last day, she had helped him remember the things he loved, dancing and flying and the sweetness of fruit, thinking they could dull the thirst for revenge. But this rage was stunning. She swallowed hard. She didn't want to be responsible for unleashing a dangerous djinn on the city—on the world.

"Freedom is worth more than revenge," she tried.

"Over a century and a half I have been in that spice box, little human. More than one-third of my life. There must be retribution."

"On who? Ruuwa must be dead by now."

"Her ancestors, then," he growled. "I have spent decades surviving on nothing but dreams of revenge. I could not communicate, could not eat, could not drink. My only conversation was with myself, inventing new punishments for those who wronged me. My bread was the carnage I will cause, my wine the anticipation of their fear and sorrow."

Nuha bit her lip. She could see the lust for blood in his eyes, but could see, too, that it was a mask, covering fear and hurt. *Trust is a thing that goes both ways*, she reminded herself. She stepped forward and placed a gentle hand on his forearm, where a silver band had recently been.

"You are free now," she said softly. "You no longer need dreams of revenge against a dead woman to sustain you."

For a moment, she thought she had made a mistake by coming close, worried he was too far away for hope to reach him. The wind whipped around her small apartment, sending loose items skittering to the corners: dried herbs, scraps of parchment, and her empty bag from the bazaar those four long days ago. His eyes flamed. He was clenching his teeth, every muscle in his body taut.

"I trust you to prove Ruuwa wrong," Nuha added, voice quiet.

And he unwound. Flame and wind disappeared, leaving a vacuum of quiet in their wake. His face fell, his gaze heavy with desperation.

"What, then?" he asked, tone pleading. "What else do I have?"

She let a sigh of relief escape her lips, shaping it into a smile. "Let's sate more pleasant appetites. You told me that your favorite food is mangoes." Releasing his arm, she walked to the bowl where she had put her market mangoes, green and hard four days ago but perfect and sweet now. She held one up in the air between them like an offering. "How long has it been since you've eaten, Atiya?" She took the time to savor his true name. It had none of the sharp edges or fierce shadows of his other names, and she found she quite liked it.

He smiled, his dark eyes shining not with fire but with something warmer and sweeter. He took the mango from her, fingers gentle. "Too long."

* * *

Nicole L. Soper Gorden is a fantasy and science fiction author with a not-so-secret identity as a biology professor at a small liberal arts college. When not writing or teaching, Nicole enjoys growing heirloom vegetables, baking award-winning cookies, and plotting new ways to make people appreciate how wacky plants are. She lives in the Appalachian Mountains with her affectionate black cat, playful goats, curious pigs, underfoot chickens, rescued box turtle, plump toads, shy hermit crabs, bearded husband, and dinosaur-obsessed kiddo.

BY ANY OTHER

BY ARLEN FELDMAN

"Thank you, James Barnet." The name slipped out of Dan's mouth without his thinking about it.

Dan cursed himself silently and looked away, carefully avoiding eye contact.

James Barnet was just pulling back his hand after dropping two quarters into the paper coffee cup Dan was holding out. Already Dan could see the confusion on the man's face and what he must have been thinking: Had they met before? Was he a former colleague down on his luck? Some sort of trick?

It could go many different ways. The pretend smile. The ignore-and-walk-away. The awkward laugh. Or anger. And Dan could see that James was getting angry.

"How the hell do you ..."

But then his friend (Thomas McDonald) punched him on the arm. "You're wearing a name tag, doofus!"

James looked down. There was a "Hello, my name is *Jim Barnet*" sticker on his shirt. He and Tom must have just come from a conference.

Tom was laughing hysterically. "Your face. Your face," he kept saying. James laughed too, although it was a little forced.

Dan tried to smile, as though he had read the name tag and was in on the joke.

Thomas fished out a five-dollar bill and dropped it into the cup. "Definitely worth it!" He was still laughing as the two men walked away.

Dan stood there for a moment, his cup held out in front of him. Then survival instincts took over. The five disappeared into an inside pocket of his army-surplus jacket, then he grabbed his backpack and started walking, head down, keeping his pace even so as not to draw attention.

Even on crowded New York streets people kept some distance from him, with his ragged beard, dirty hair, and tattered clothing. Like homelessness was contagious. As he walked, he whispered the names of the people he passed. *Mary Gonzales ... Eric Haynes ... Amber Gilmore ... Karen Estrada ... Bryan Jones ...*

His words were drowned out by the city noises—constant honking, sirens, construction. Dan felt almost anonymous in the crowds, although how could anyone be anonymous, really?

He got a sharp look from one man (Russell Perry) who must have caught a hint of his name on the air, but Dan kept walking, and so did Russell.

Dan was too late for his usual spot by Penn Station—a recessed doorway that was close to a vent that spewed warming diesel fumes. But he had several other decent spots and wasn't too worried. When he'd first got to Manhattan, he'd thought from TV that there were alleyways all over the place—perfect places to hide and sleep—but there were hardly any. Just a giant grid of roads.

He used change to buy two hot dogs from a street vendor (Hussain Abbas) and ate them quickly. He thought longingly about using the five-dollar bill to buy a bottle of vodka. But he'd promised Ed ...

It was still fairly early. He could hang around inside Penn for a while, until they kicked everyone out. And sometimes they never got around to it—it depended on how lazy the guards were feeling. But before he could decide, he caught sight of Ed (Edward Moss) coming towards him. Dan had that instant flight-or-fight reaction from being approached by any cop, but Ed was his friend, so he buried his anxiety.

"Dan."

Dan nodded at him. Ed was a head taller, black, and had a shaved head. He was a detective, and although he didn't wear a uniform, everything from his shoes to his stare yelled *cop*. Dan was glad that his friend never tried to go undercover.

"Have you been good?" This got another nod. It was Ed's standard question whenever they met. Dan didn't smile though. He suspected what was coming.

"We've got another one. Would you mind?"

* * *

The morgue was attached to Bellevue Hospital. They made their way into the building, Ed flashing his badge to get past security. There were probably rooms where they did autopsies and the like, but Dan had never seen those. Instead, Ed led him into a long passage with two-high rows of square doors along one wall.

Ed's partner (Kenny Blake) met them by one of the doors. He was also big—or would have been if Ed weren't there—white, and wore an expensive looking suit. He looked more like a mobster than a cop and would probably be great undercover. There was also a man (Nick Cooke) from the medical examiner's office, wearing a lab coat and looking unhappy. Kenny just sneered when he saw Dan.

"Well, if it ain't the voodoo kid."

Dan flinched, but Ed ignored him and shook hands with Nick Cooke.

"Thanks for arranging this."

"I shouldn't have," said Nick. "It is completely ... well ..." He lifted his hands, palm up.

"It's something to try," said Ed, his voice soothing. "If it doesn't work, we're out nothing."

Nick looked at Dan standing there in his raggedy clothing. This didn't seem to improve his confidence level.

"What *exactly* do you need to do?"

"Just need to see the body. That's all."

Kenny snorted, but Nick released the lock on one of the drawers and pulled it all the way open. Then he folded back the white sheet enough to show the face.

The girl was very young and far too pale. She was pretty. Had been pretty. A lock of blonde hair had fallen over her face, and Dan had to stop himself from brushing it back into place.

"Claire Dodson. Her name is ... was ... Claire Dodson."

The medical examiner's eyes went wide, but Kenny snorted again. "Bullshit. He could say any name. Twenty bucks says he couldn't come up with the names of any of the people whose name we *actually* know."

"I'll take that bet," said Ed. Dan, who'd backed up when Kenny started talking, looked at Ed, astonished. And scared.

The medical examiner seemed interested, though. He fished a tablet out of his pocket and started scrolling. Pulling open a drawer two down from Claire, he uncovered the face of an old man.

"Frank Dean," said Dan, unable to stop himself. Nick nodded, his mouth open, but Kenny scowled and checked the front of the drawer to make sure that the name wasn't written there. It wasn't—just a series of letters and numbers.

Dan didn't want to see any more dead bodies. He went to the next refrigerated door, put his hand next to it, and said, "Grace Ritter." He could tell the names of living people from across a room—hear the names screaming in his head. For dead people, it was more like a whisper. But if he concentrated hard, he could hear them without them having to open any more drawers.

"Ignacio Rice, Caylee Neal, Chung Seong, Jane Myer, Scott Lester." Dan touched each refrigerator drawer in turn as he said the names.

"Fuck me," said Nick as he checked the names. "All exactly right. Oh—" He stopped. "Except the last one. That's Reuben Conrad."

Dan froze, then touched the last drawer again and shook his head violently. "No. No. It's Scott Lester."

Nick shrugged. "I won't swear that we never make a mistake, but the system has this down as Reuben Conrad, 86, cardiac arrest after a fall."

Ed was already pulling the refrigerated drawer open. He pulled back the sheet. Despite himself, Dan had to look. The man was young, maybe twenty or thirty. It was hard to tell his age precisely, but this man was definitely *not* in his eighties. It seemed unlikely that he'd died of a heart attack either—there was a neat hole in his forehead that looked like it had come from a bullet.

"Well, Kenny, looks like you owe Dan twenty bucks."

A moment later, Dan felt himself being lifted and slammed into the tile wall.

"How the hell are you doing it, you little freak? Hacking the system? Paying someone off? Tell me." Kenny's face was inches from Dan, and he looked completely deranged. Dan just gaped at him, unable to speak. Unable to think.

"Put. Him. Down." Ed didn't raise his voice, but there was an edge to it that Dan had never heard before. For about three seconds, nothing happened. Finally, Kenny let go, and Dan dropped a couple of inches to the floor before collapsing the rest of the way.

"Hey, man. Just kidding." He pulled out his wallet and threw two twenties down at Dan's feet. "See? No hard feelings. Right?"

"No hard feelings," Dan mumbled and curled himself up into a ball. But his arm snaked out and grabbed the money.

* * *

*D*an sat across from Ed in a diner close to the morgue, a mug of coffee held in both hands. He was enjoying the heat from the mug. He got some dirty looks from the staff when they'd come in, but with Ed there, no one said anything.

Ed held up his phone to show a picture of a young woman with blonde hair. She was laughing and very much alive. Claire Dodson.

"Runaway from Wisconsin. You were right."

Dan nodded then looked down at his mug.

"Look Dan, it may not seem like much, but at least her parents will *know* what happened to her. That's important."

Dan looked up at Ed, stared at him for a moment, then nodded again, this time meaning it.

The waitress (Jane Cobar) brought over their food, and the two of them sat and ate in companionable silence. Ed liked the thought that he'd done some good—something useful. He missed that. A long time ago, he'd worked in a store, stocking shelves. He liked being surrounded by people doing things. But then he accidentally said the name of a female customer and was accused of stalking.

Before they left the diner, he gave Ed fifty-five dollars— the two twenties and the five from earlier, plus ten dollars in change. Ed was Dan's bank. Someday he'd have enough to do ... well, something. Something better. Something safe.

* * *

"Hey, Dan. Have you been good? Oh." Ed froze when he saw Dan's face, which was covered in purpling bruises.

"I'm fine," Dan mumbled.

"Who did this?"

"Dunno."

Truthfully, Dan had been on a mostly-deserted platform, trying to stay away from the station guards. A man in a white t-shirt and a backwards baseball cap walked by, and Dan quietly whispered his name (Bruno Fernando Garcia Ortiz). But Bruno heard him—accused him of being disrespectful. Bruno and his friends (Dylan James and Martin Brooks) left Dan lying on the platform.

That had been two days ago. Dan looked a lot better now. He tried to hide his limp as he went over to meet his friend.

"Who did this to you?" Ed repeated.

"Don't remember."

"Like I believe that."

"Don't need more trouble."

Ed shook his head but didn't push it. They started walking down 8th Avenue. He hesitated for a moment before speaking. "So, listen Dan. You've got a job offer."

It took a second for the words and their meaning to register. "That's nuts," he said finally.

"Serious. It's at the morgue. They were pretty freaked out about that unidentified body. They still haven't been able to figure out where it came from. So, they want you to check the morgue—all the morgues around the city, I figure—on a regular basis. To make sure everyone is, well, who they're supposed to be."

Ed didn't say anything for a while. The morgue gave him the creeps. But he'd liked helping Claire Dodson and her family. He wouldn't mind doing more of that.

"They'd actually pay me to do that?"

"Yeah. You'd only make minimum wage. But it would be full time. Benefits and shit. It's not just at Bellevue. There's morgues in most of the big hospitals. The city can handle hundreds of bodies at any time."

The word "bodies" kept spinning around in Dan's head. But the thought of having a *job*, of being *paid*, maybe even being able to afford a room somewhere ...

"Would I be working for Nick Cooke?" He'd liked Nick Cooke.

"Yeah." Ed looked relieved, like he'd expected more of an argument. "You'd technically be his intern. On paper, you'd be responsible for checking people's names on lists. It wouldn't actually mention *how* you'd be checking."

They walked a bit further before Dan said anything. He realized that he was crying. Finally, he just stopped, turned to Ed, and nodded.

* * *

On his first day, Dan found three mislabeled bodies. Two (Brian Ward and Chén Jūn) were just swapped in their drawers.

"We probably would have caught these two," said Nick. "Even *our* ME is not that blind."

It was later in the day when Dan found the third body. Nick had made Dan wait in his office while Nick's boss (Theresa Martin) was around. Apparently, she knew that Dan had been hired but hadn't seen him. Ed had bought him some new clothes, but he otherwise looked the same. He was used to staying out of the way, so it mostly didn't bother him.

The name on the tablet was Arnold James. Dan thought he was using the tablet wrong at first, because the guy in the drawer was obviously William Grant. But instead of a man dead of pancreatic cancer, opening the drawer revealed that William had been shot three times in the chest.

Nick looked really worried, but he told Dan that he'd done a good job and sent him home.

Home. Dan now had a home. Ed had found him a room in Astoria that he could now more-or-less afford. Somehow, the money that Dan had been giving to Ed for safekeeping was enough for the required down payment and deposit. Dan wasn't great at math, but he suspected that Ed had slipped in some extra.

The room was simple, just a bed and a rickety table, but Dan loved it. He loved that he could close the door, and no one would come in. There was the landlady (Margery Vale) and two other tenants (Ji-Hoon Park and Felipe Sanchez Diaz), but Dan was careful to stay in his room when they were around. Ed had come to check on him once, and Dan had shown him around excitedly, which made Ed smile. Dan didn't know why Ed was so kind to him. He'd asked Ed once, and the bald cop had mumbled something about doing what was right, then changed the subject. Maybe he was making up for the fact that his partner, Kenny Blake, was such an asshole.

Dan was getting used to the work as well. Nick Cooke had assured him that, after a while, he would get used to the bodies. That hadn't happened yet, but the job was otherwise simple: mostly just moving gurneys and other equipment around and filling in paperwork on the tablet. There were only so many bodies to check.

He got a lot of stares from the staff at the other hospitals, but after he'd discovered a dozen misplaced bodies in various morgues, they'd become a bit more accepting. These mix-ups were all just administrative errors. So far, there'd been no other mystery corpses.

Dan worked his way down the hallways with the freezers, listening to the whispered names of their occupants. There was one where he always stopped each day.

"I'm sorry, Jill Graham," he whispered, his hand on her freezer. He'd had to open this one before he'd heard her name —she'd been there a long time. Dan wondered how long before he would no longer hear someone's name at all. That would be very sad.

He went to the next freezer and started to pull it open, then froze. It was Bruno Fernando Garcia Ortiz, the man who had beaten him up. He pulled the drawer the rest of the way open and uncovered the head. Bruno's pale face stared up at him. He'd looked so angry when they'd first met. Now he looked restful. He could have been sleeping—except for the puckered red mark on his neck where a bullet had entered.

Dan had never seen the body of someone he knew before. He felt himself tearing up and blinked rapidly. He touched Bruno's cheek quickly, then covered him back up and closed the drawer. Then he pulled out his tablet to check off the name.

The tablet said this was James Haskell, thirty-five, auto accident.

* * *

"Scott Lester was an 'accountant' for the Costas," said Ed. "And by *accountant*, I mean that he helped them launder money. Still nothing on William Grant, but Bruno Ortiz was a low-level enforcer. For the Costas."

Ed and Dan were sitting in a conference room with Nick

and Theresa Martin, Nick's boss, who was a severe-looking older woman with a bun of gray hair. She stared at Ed for several moments, and it wasn't a friendly look. This was the first time she'd seen the new *intern*.

"And you think that someone here is also working for the Costas," she said finally. It wasn't a question.

"Whoever is doing this has access to your computer system as well as your freezers. They're changing profiles."

"Why are—" Dan started to say, then looked down.

"What?" asked Ed.

Staring down at the conference table, Dan mumbled, "Why are the fake people so wrong? Not just their names, but ... but the way they're described?"

"That," said Nick, "is a good question." He grabbed his tablet and started searching. The rest of the table looked on quietly, waiting for an answer. After a few minutes, Nick looked up. "It's because they're copying the reports. They're just changing the names. Reuben Conrad has the exact same notes and descriptions as Raymond Chen, right down to the age and the cause of death. Arnold James has an identical report to Andrew Jenkins."

"Same initials," said Dan.

"So, they're both clever and lazy," said Ed.

"Not necessarily." This was the first time that Theresa didn't look angry. "Unless you are a trained pathologist, creating a believable report is hard. Copying is safer."

"And the initials?"

"Okay, that's lazy."

Ed laughed, and Theresa actually smiled. She looked a lot less scary when she smiled.

* * *

The plan was terrible. Dan hated it. But Ed asked him to do it, so he had agreed.

Dan had to sit at the front desk and sign people in. He had to interact with *every single person* who came through the door. And if anyone wasn't who they said they were, or if the body they were bringing in wasn't who they were supposed to be, Dan was supposed to call Ed immediately.

They'd also made him get a haircut and shave off his beard. His face was raw and red and itched like crazy. He felt even more exposed than usual.

Dan did the job for a week. It was less painful than he'd expected—saying someone's name when they put it on a form seemed like a confirmation. Plus, there was a desk between him and the people.

It was late night when Richard Hoskins came in. He signed his name as Joe Francis and said that the body was Frederick Ho, even though Dan knew that it was Franklin Hale. Dan concentrated as hard as he could on not whispering either name.

Dan watched as Richard wheeled Franklin down the hallway, one of the cart's wheels vibrating and rattling like an unhappy shopping cart. He was proud of staying silent, only realizing that his mouth was hanging open after the cart had disappeared around the corner. Finally, he remembered to call Ed.

Now what? Just sit there? Or follow? Or run?

Running sounded really good to Dan.

Instead, he got up and headed down the hallway. He could still hear the little *ta-ta-ta* of the cart in the distance. Then he got to the hallway with the freezers, and he could once more hear the faint whispers of the dead, telling him their names.

Dan stopped before going around the corner. He couldn't hear the cart, but he could tell that Richard Hoskins was close by. Out of nowhere, there was the sound of an old-fashioned telephone. Dan had to shove his hand over his mouth to stop from screaming.

The ring came again, but it was suddenly cut off with a beep. It had been Richard's ringtone.

"Yeah, I'm here. No problems."

Dan tilted his head to the side, listening. He couldn't hear the *voice* of the person on the other end of the call, but he heard the *name*. And it was a name he already knew: Kenny Blake.

"Freezer B81," said Richard. It was the number that Dan had assigned him for Franklin Hale/Frederick Ho at the front desk. Dan wasn't always so quick, but this was pretty obvious. Kenny was going to create the fake record using the freezer number. Which meant that Kenny was working with the Costas.

He had to tell Ed. He needed to go back to the front desk. Dan started to turn, but he heard the familiar *ta-ta-ta* of the cart. A moment later, Richard came around the corner, and then it was the mobster's turn to freeze.

"Oh, ah. Yeah," Dan nearly stammered. "Just making sure you found your way, Richard Hoskins."

Richard smiled. He had a gold tooth. "My name's Joe Francis."

"Joe Francis. You're Joe Francis. Right. Sorry, I get confused sometimes."

"And you must be Dan, right? I was told I might run into you."

"Dan. I'm Dan." He was mesmerized by the gold tooth, couldn't take his eyes off it.

"Nice to meet you, Dan. I have something for you."

Dan looked down too late. The gun made a *pfutt* sound. It was disappointingly nothing like the guns Dan had heard on

TV. Something was wrong with his chest, and standing up seemed too difficult, so he fell down.

A second later, there was another sound, a much more satisfying *sboom, sboom*, and then Richard also fell. He was covered in red. Blood. Dan wondered if he was also covered in blood.

Before long, Ed appeared over him, an anguished look on his face.

"Why didn't you stay at the desk, Dan?"

"Sorry, Ed. I followed ..." It was hard to talk. "Richard was talking. To Kenny Blake. On phone."

Ed looked shocked for a second, then said something quietly into his radio.

"It's okay Dan. You did good."

Dan tried to nod but seemed to have forgotten how. Then, as Ed pushed down on the place where he'd been shot, he screamed.

"I'm sorry, Dan. I've got to apply pressure."

There was a lot of motion in the hallway. He heard Nick arrive, followed by lots of other people. They lifted him onto a gurney, and he screamed again. It was strange—he was having trouble hearing their names. But he could hear the names of the people in the freezers just fine. Almost as if they were shouting.

A pretty nurse looked down at him. "Dan," she said, "we're taking you to surgery. Don't worry."

"Thank you, Kate Harris," he murmured. He'd barely heard her name at all.

* * *

As well as writing fiction, Arlen Feldman is a software engineer, entrepreneur, maker, con-runner, and computer book author—

useful if you are in the market for some industrial-strength door stops. Some recent stories of his appear in the anthologies Museum Piece, Particular Passages 4, and Kevin J. Anderson's Gilded Glass, and in Little Blue Marble and Nocturne magazines. He lives in Colorado Springs, Colorado. His website is cowthulu.com. Mastodon: @cowthulu@mastodon.social

THE WHISPERING WOOD

BY ALLY KELLY

Cora's family home sat on the edge of the meadow, surrounded by the Whispering Wood, a name chosen by the townspeople. She'd heard stories of ghostly voices that whispered to people who entered the woods. Mama and Papa always told her they were nothing but stories to scare children, that there was no truth to them. At seven, Cora was a girl filled with curiosity and a thirst for knowledge. She wasn't about to let ghost stories scare her away from learning more about the woods.

At the edge of her bed, Cora sat staring out her bedroom window into the meadow below. Moonlight beamed down as mist rose after the summer storm. Thoughts of how angry her parents had been at her for entering the woods a few nights before plagued her mind, making sleep impossible. She'd seen them angry before, but not *that* angry—and certainly not angry enough to cancel her birthday party because she'd tried to go into the woods.

A cool breeze moved through Cora's bedroom as the mist cleared from the meadow, bringing a soft tune with it. Cora looked across her room to her sister's bed, wondering if

Anthea was singing in her sleep, but the four-year-old slept soundly. She turned back to the window as the tune grew louder, and she realized it was coming from outside.

It wasn't the first time she'd heard the music. Just a few days before, she'd snuck out of the house and made it as far as the edge of the woods before her dad had caught her from behind. Cora screamed, and Papa yanked her around to face him, his face white in the moonlight and his voice echoing angrily out across the meadow as Mama grabbed her other arm.

Standing from her bed, Cora poked her head out the window, listening for the tune. Below, dancing lights slowly appeared in the meadow, darting through the air like a thousand fireflies. She turned from the window, debating putting her boots on. They would likely make her footsteps heavier on the floorboards. *Is it worth waking Anthea up? Or even worse, Mama and Papa?* After a few moments of indecision, she tiptoed toward her bedroom door, carefully opening it. A floorboard squeaked beneath her feet. Cora froze and chewed on her lower lip, listening intently.

Only the music and normal night sounds met her ears.

Doing her best impression of a mouse, Cora tiptoed past Mama and Papa's room, glancing inside. Papa let out a loud snore, and Mama rolled over with a groan. Again, Cora froze, waiting for one of them to wake up. When neither did, she let out a sigh of relief.

Making her way down the stairs, Cora grabbed her cloak hanging by the front door. She wrapped it around herself, pulling it tight over her white nightgown. Then, she reached for the doorknob and slowly turned it, opening the door just enough to slip through and close it gently behind her.

The cool night air hit her in the face as soon as she stepped outside. She ran toward the meadow once more, the grass tickling her feet, using the full moon's light to guide her way. She knew she shouldn't be out there and was going against Mama and Papa, but the temptation was too great. Besides, tonight was different. It was her birthday!

Cora stepped into the meadow, watching as the floating lights made their appearance and danced around her in a swirl of colors. They moved around her arms and legs, tickling her skin. She giggled, her laughter echoing. She glanced back toward the house, hoping her laughter wouldn't disturb Mama and Papa, but there was no sign of them waking.

The lights moved away from Cora and toward the edge of the woods, just as they had last time. She was determined to follow them and see where they led her. Perhaps she would finally find out why the woods were given their name. Cora ran toward the tree line, her locks of curly brown hair bouncing behind her. She lifted her nightgown above her ankles, careful not to trip over it.

The glowing light at the edge of the woods dimmed, leaving only the moonlight to guide Cora as she stepped onto the dirt pathway. The dancing lights moved ahead of her into the woods, and she ran to catch up with them.

Cora followed the lights further, glancing back over her shoulder now and then. Part of her wanted to run the other way, but she'd come too far now. Laughter echoed throughout the woods, and she paused, her eyes widening. She looked around for its source but found nothing. Turning back toward the entrance, she chewed on the inside of her lower lip.

Just a little further, a voice whispered in her ear. She whirled around, coming face-to-face with a small figure with shimmering purple butterfly wings. Cora gasped, stumbling backward and falling hard to the ground. Using her hands to break her fall, Cora gritted her teeth, shaking her head and pushing herself back up as she wiped the dirt from her hands.

She heard the same echoing laughter again, this time much closer than before. A soft tune from a flute blended with the laughter. Up ahead, a bright light appeared, and she walked toward it, grabbing on to a nearby tree. The rough bark of the oak scratched Cora's fingers as she dug them in, the last of her willpower draining as she tried to fight the pull of the music.

The musicians surrounded the fire, a writing, gabbering crowd of creatures Cora had no name for. Stubby, imp-like beings with long fingers stroked harps, and gnarled stick-like things beat heavy drums.

Smaller fae hovered above in a dancing cloud while the orbs of light weaved intricate patterns through the smoke of the fire, their brightness outshining the stars.

"Welcome, child," said a voice in Cora's ear. She whipped around but was too slow to catch the ball of light that flew past her face.

The musicians stopped, freezing in place as the purple light flew into their midst. The sudden silence brought a flinch from Cora, and she could only watch as the creatures parted, revealing a small throne of driftwood and river stones.

The ball of light shimmered and became a small, child-sized figure. Cora judged her to be about her own age, perhaps a little older. An awkwardly large crown made of twigs and feathers adorned her head, and long, black hair cascaded down to her waist. She wore a gown black as midnight, its silky flared sleeves flowing with each movement.

Despite her fear, Cora's grip on the oak loosened, and she took a hesitant step toward the fire. The fae sat on the throne, hands flat against the arms. She twitched a finger, and the musicians bowed and stepped away from the fire.

The fae beckoned Cora forward, her eyes old and knowing.

"I've been expecting you," she said, her voice high like silver bells. "For quite some time."

"You have?" Cora took another step forward, hands twisting in her nightgown. "Why?"

The fae tilted her head, a small, secretive smile forming on her lips. "Why not? I have been watching you. I know what day it is, Cora. It is your birthday. The angry man said so yesterday."

"Papa? He's not angry. Well . . . not all the time. He was mad that I went into the woods. I'm not supposed to be here."

"No? But I invited you myself! Surely you are safe." The child's smile made Cora's stomach twist.

Cora looked around the clearing, watching as the creatures flew around her, and realized Mama and Papa had been wrong—the stories *were* true.

"Am I a guest?"

"A guest? Yes. I grant you guestright. For tonight only! You'll want to be home by dawn," the queen answered after a moment's consideration. The child queen stood and walked toward her, her long flowing gown moving behind her as she stopped in front of Cora. "Tonight is the night of the full moon, when the veil between the human world and ours opens and our worlds become one," she said, taking Cora's hand. "I have brought you here, Cora, to join our celebration and games. And, of course, we must celebrate your birthday!"

Cora was delighted. She would get a birthday present after all! Smiling, she let the queen take her hand, and they began dancing around the fire, joining in with the creatures serving as her subjects. The musicians started playing again. Cora laughed as they danced, tilting her head back in the air. The queen let go of her hand, and Cora spun, her nightgown whirling around her. Soon, the fear of Mama and Papa finding out what she had done faded entirely from her mind.

After what felt like hours of dancing, Cora fell to her knees, fighting to catch her breath. She looked up at the child queen, who had taken her seat on the throne once more. The queen raised a crooked finger, beckoning Cora forward.

"I have a present for you before you return to your home. Come closer, child," she said. Cora stepped forward and knelt down beside the queen's throne. The queen bent forward, leaning close to Cora's ear.

"Sorcha," she whispered.

Cora frowned as the queen pulled away. What did *Sorcha* mean? Before she could ask the queen, a sharp pain appeared.

"Ah!" she cried out, clutching her palm. She looked down as a tiny scar appeared on it, stepping away from the throne. "What did you do?" she asked, staring wide eyed at the queen.

"I gave you your gift," the queen answered with a smile. "It's almost sunrise, Cora. You'll need to hurry home before the veil between our worlds closes. My sprites will guide you back through the woods to the meadow."

"But—"

"I will tell you more about your gift the next time you visit. Now, hurry."

Still confused, Cora nodded, raising her hand to stifle a yawn. The pain had gone almost as quickly as it had come. She turned back toward the edge of the clearing, following the tiny lights down the pathway again.

* * *

Cora lay on a blanket in the meadow, a book sprawled open in front of her. Anthea lay next to her on her back, staring up at the clouds. The blanket sat only about ten feet from the edge of the woods. Their dog, Sorcha, lay on the blanket with them, her head resting in the crook of Anthea's arm.

Cora smiled, watching as Sorcha slept soundly by Anthea.

She glanced toward the woods as a vague childhood memory resurfaced: She had walked along a path in the woods late at night, entering a clearing surrounded by bright lights of different colors dancing around her.

Cora chewed on the inside of her lip as she tried to concentrate on reading. She didn't enjoy being this close to the woods anymore, but Anthea had insisted on them coming out here, and she had reluctantly caved in to her pleading. Shifting uncomfortably on the blanket, Cora looked up toward the woods as a small blue light appeared at the edge of the path.

A strand of curly brown hair fell in front of her eyes. Cora reached up to push it behind her ear as Anthea sat up on the blanket suddenly and looked at her.

"What do you suppose is in the woods?" she asked.

Cora looked up from her book, eyes wide. "What?"

"You heard me," Anthea said. "What do you think is in the woods? There must be *something* in there that makes everyone want to stay away from them. And why were they given the name Whispering Woods?"

Cora swallowed hard, lowering her gaze. "I don't know, Anthea," she answered, growing impatient. "There could be anything, I suppose. Maybe wild dogs or bears. Mama always said the name was to scare children."

Anthea shook her head. "No, that's not it."

Cora shrugged again, placing the book in her lap. Anthea was three years younger than her, coming close to her sixteenth year. Curious and adventurous, she loved to annoy Cora with questions. Cora tried to indulge her curiosity as best she could, but even she had a hard time staying patient. Anthea was her shadow, which made Cora both proud and cautious. Her blonde hair lacked Cora's curls, but they both wore their hair in braids.

"There's something about the woods that you don't like,"

Anthea continued. "You've stayed away from them for as long as I can remember. What is it that scares you so much about them?"

Cora twirled a piece of grass between her fingers, watching her sister for a moment. "You're too young to remember, but I went into the woods by myself once when I was eight. A few days later, I became so sick, Mama and Papa thought for sure I was going to die. My fever was so high, it gave me hallucinations," she explained.

Cora remembered laying on her bed, sweat pouring down her face as she fought against the fever. Images of bright balls of light floated in front of her, and she'd called them fairies. Mama sat by her and brushed her sweaty hair out of her face, telling her there weren't any bright lights. But Cora had insisted that there were fairies, and that they were in the woods and were why she was sick. The following day was when they brought Sorcha to her, hoping the puppy would be a good distraction from her hallucinations.

"So you think the woods have something to do with your sickness? Have you ever thought that there could be a cure?" Anthea asked.

Cora shook her head.

"Well . . . what if *we* go into the woods and see if we can find a cure? Maybe your sickness will be gone for good!" Anthea suggested.

Cora bit the inside of her lip so hard she could almost taste the blood. She slammed the book in her lap closed and looked up at her sister, placing a hand on hers.

"Thea, listen to me. I know you're curious about the woods, and you want to help me, but you can't go in there, not ever."

"But—"

"There *is* no cure, Anthea. I was exposed to the cold, and it made me sick, and the sickness made me weak. That's just the way it is. I want you to promise me you won't ever go into those woods."

"Why—"

"Promise it," Cora cut Anthea off, her tone firm. They made eye contact. After a moment, Anthea sighed and nodded.

"Okay, I promise it."

Cora nodded, letting go of her hand. "Thank you," she said, standing up. "I'm going inside. Come on, Sorcha."

Sorcha immediately rose from where she lay by Anthea, following close behind Cora with her tail wagging as she walked away from the blanket. Cora paused, looking back toward the woods. She saw a blue light dancing along the path and held her breath, glancing up at the sky. The clouds were darkening, and the sun had disappeared.

"Don't stay out here for much longer, Anthea. It's going to rain."

Cora turned away from her, heading back toward the house. She reached the porch steps and turned, leaning against the railing as she looked back toward the woods again. Sorcha bumped her cold nose into Cora's palm and she smiled, scratching her behind the ears before turning to walk up the stairs and into the house.

* * *

The night before Cora's eighteenth birthday came days later. She woke up with a start from another dream, looking around her bedroom, her breathing heavy as she fought to separate the nightmare in her mind from the reality around her.

Cool night air moved through the window, and she stood up, walking over to it. The moon was full once more. Sorcha whined from behind her, bumping a nose into Cora's palm. She looked behind her toward Anthea's bed, only to find it empty. Panic ran through her, turning back toward the window again. The dancing lights had entered the meadow once more. After Anthea's increasingly persistent questions about the woods, Cora didn't need to guess where she was.

Cora got dressed, pulling her boots on and quietly exiting her room, quickly heading down the stairs and to the front door. Pulling her cloak on, Cora stepped on to the porch just in time to see the same glowing light at the edge of the woods that she'd avoided for the past eleven years.

As Cora entered the woods, she felt the fae's magic pulling at her like an invisible hand, like a leaf caught in the current. Cora followed the dark pathway, unsure of where it would lead her. She flexed her fingers, feeling the sweat on her palms, becoming increasingly anxious. Was she walking into a deathtrap by entering the woods once more?

As she came closer to the end of the path, a soft tune filled the air, and Cora knew she was getting closer. She entered a large clearing as the music grew louder and found herself surrounded by impish creatures of all kinds. Some hung off tree branches while others buzzed around her with tiny wings.

A small cage hung high above an empty throne made of driftwood and river stones. The cage started swinging slowly, and Cora took a step closer. When she was able to make out what stood inside the cage, she gasped.

"Anthea!"

"Welcome back, Cora. It's been far too long," a voice said from behind her.

Cora spun around as a purple cloud filled the air around the throne. After a moment, the cloud faded, revealing a young woman about Cora's age with long black hair, sitting on the throne. She wore a crown of twigs and feathers and a long, dark gown."Who are you? What do you want with me and my sister?" Cora asked.

"You don't remember me?" the girl asked. "Perhaps I can help you with that."

The girl stood from the throne, walking toward Cora. Cora watched her carefully, uncertain what to expect as the girl placed a hand on Cora's arm.

Cora fell to her knees, gasping for air as memories flashed in her mind. She saw herself as an eight-year-old, running barefoot through the grass on the night of a full moon, mist rising from the meadow by her house. She entered the woods, and she danced with a girl with long, raven black hair framing a rounded, childlike face as musicians played on strange instruments. The last image showed Cora lying in her bed, covered in sweat as she watched bright lights floating above her, coughing and gasping for air.

"You," Cora gasped, staring up at the queen with wide eyes. "I do remember you. You're the reason I became sick and almost died."

The queen's expression changed as Cora stared up at her, and the memories became clearer. The ancient wisdom and queenly grace were just as she remembered, and they seemed no less strange now than they had then.

"What do you mean?" the queen asked. "You've been sick?"

Cora nodded. "I came down with a fever and cold that weakened my heart and lungs."

"Cora, I—" the queen began. "I hadn't realized . . . please, tell me everything." She waved a hand, and an enormous toadstool seat popped out of the ground near the throne.

"What about me?" Anthea's voice was quiet and nervous, but with a familiar stubborn note Cora knew well.

The queen shushed her. "Patience, my dear. You're in no danger. Let me speak with your sister."

Surprisingly, Anthea fell immediately quiet. Cora almost scoffed as she tentatively took the seat beside the queen and, with a little prompting, explained her sickness and lingering ailments after their last meeting. The queen's gaze sharpened with growing comprehension.

"Of course you would avoid us after suffering so terribly," she said. "And to think we were hallucinations. Not every human can see the fae as clearly as you and your sister do. Cora, you must believe, I never meant for you to suffer. If I'd known . . . We have been unable to leave the woods since that night."

Cora frowned. "What do you mean? What did you do?"

"I gave you a very special gift the night of your eighth birthday," the queen said.

"What kind of gift?" Cora asked. She remembered the pain, the queen's voice soft in her ear, but the whispered words eluded her.

"My name," the queen answered. "I was being threatened by a name thief, and was afraid I'd lose my throne. I found a spell to hide my name until it was safe to take it back. The spell called for a human vessel, and I chose you. I wanted to befriend you. You were such a sweet and curious child. I had hoped that you would continue to return to the woods, and I could take my name back once the threat to my throne and people was gone."

As the queen explained, Cora tried again to remember the night of the celebration, the whispered word in her ear. She rubbed the thumb of her other hand back and forth over the scar that word had caused in her palm.

"I tried to mitigate any effects the spell might have had on you while my name was in your possession. But the longer you stayed out of the woods, the weaker those mitigations became, which must have led to your sickness. I tried to invite you to return to the woods, but you ignored every attempt," the queen continued quietly.

"Is that why you've captured my sister?" Cora asked.

"Yes. It was never my intent to keep her," the queen answered. "She hasn't been harmed in any way. You must understand how desperate I became. I need my name back, and you. . ." She shook her head with a small bitter laugh. "Did you think we were dreams? Or perhaps nightmares?"

Corra nodded. "Why is your name so important to you? Can't you just get a new one?"

"Names hold power, especially among the fae," the queen replied. "Should the wrong person claim that power, it can change everything. My name means Queen of the Whispering Woods. Without it, the woods have begun to slip away from me."

The queen rolled up her sleeves and held her arms out, showing two withering hands that contradicted her otherwise youthful features. Her fingers were long and bony, with wrinkles crawling up her arms, making her look ancient.

"You were not the only one of us affected by the power my name holds," she said. "I have clung to my title with every ounce of power I possess, but it is killing me."

Cora gasped, her eyes wide as she stared at the queen's hands. She looked up at the queen, whose features had softened with a sadness behind her eyes, and Cora suddenly understood just how much this name meant to her. She looked over at the cage where Anthea was still trapped.

"So if you get your name back, you'll free my sister? Will that cure you? And me?"

The queen nodded, lowering her sleeves. "With time, it should," she said.

"I want to give your name back, but I—I can't remember it." Cora hung her head as tears began to blur the edges of her vision. "I can remember everything else, except that."

"Calm yourself. That is part of the ward. The name is here." Gently, the queen turned Cora's hand over, revealing the small scar on her palm. "You have to unravel the scar."

Cora frowned. How did one unravel a scar? She held her palm up closer to study it carefully. She cried out in pain as a yellow glow appeared around the scar, and she grasped at it with her other hand. It began changing shape, rearranging into six letters.

S-o-r-c-h-a.

Gritting her teeth, Cora carefully began pulling the letters from her palm, unraveling it like a thread, each pull feeling like a thousand tiny knives stabbing into her skin. Cora steadied her breathing, forcing herself to concentrate as she slowly pulled each letter out. *You can do this,* she thought.

The last of the golden letters moved into the air, and they drifted toward the queen, one at a time, circling around her into a cloud of magic. Magic lifted the queen from the ground, completely encircling her with blinding, purple light. Cora raised an arm to block her eyes from the light, stepping back as fae creatures gathered around, watching their queen. The magic faded from around the queen and placed her back on the ground.

"Sorcha," Cora said. "That's your name?"

Sorcha smiled and nodded, holding her arms out in front of her and turning them over to inspect them.

"Thank you for returning my gift, Cora," Sorcha said, smiling at her. "Now it is my turn to hold up my end of our bargain." She clapped her hands together once, and a swirl of purple lights surrounded Anthea's cage. The lights blew away from where the cage hung from the tree, sending pieces of wood scattering to the ground. Anthea stood beneath the tree branch, in her full size. Cora breathed a sigh of relief, rushing over to her sister and pulling her into a hug.

"Cora, I'm so sorry," Anthea said as they hugged. "I'm sorry I didn't listen to you about the woods."

Cora shook her head as she pulled back from her sister and smiled. "It's alright, Anthea. I should have come back here a long time ago," she said. "And you were right. There was a cure, and it was right here in the woods."

"I hope neither of you will hold any ill will against me or my court for what has happened," the queen said. "Because you have helped restore my name, I offer you and your sister both guest right to enter the woods whenever you like. None of my subjects will ever trouble you."

Cora bowed her head as Anthea gave a small curtsey with her nightgown. "Thank you, your majesty," Cora said.

Taking Anthea's hand, Cora led her sister to the edge of the clearing along the dark path of the woods. Behind her, the court musicians began playing their instruments, the familiar song of celebration filling the nighttime air. Fae traveled ahead of her and Anthea, their soft light illuminating the wood in a delicate rainbow as they marked the path home.

Cora didn't look back as she stepped out of the woods and the music faded from her ears, but Anthea slowed and lingered a moment until the last light winked out, leaving a wall of dark trees standing silent.

* * *

Ally has been writing stories for as long as she can remember. She is the admin of Worldsmyths and a co-publisher of a Worldsmyths Publishing. She loves writing stories with dragons and fairies, and is currently working on a Rapunzel retelling she hopes to debut some time in 2024-2025. She lives in an apartment in Connecticut and is owned by an orange cat named Merlin. You can subscribe to her newsletter and learn more at her website http://akfantasywriter.com

THE NAME PAINTER OF HISUI TEMPLE

BY SARA KUZUOKA

The air was a heavy blanket of humidity, the skies so achingly blue and cloudless that Asami knew she had to be dreaming. Her mother's sunlit silhouette shadowed the shoji doors, which had been thrown open to drink in the hot weather. The late summer heat pearled Asami's skin and hair with sweat, and the surrounding mountains and plains of Hisui Temple baked in the sun. Cicadas warbled and heat shimmered over the shrines and thatched roofs like iridescent fish scales.

Her mother lit several sticks of incense and placed them before the household shrine, a small wooden cabinet adorned with portraits of departed family members, belonging to Asami's aunties, grandmother, and great-grandmother. The women of Asami's family had been honored this way for generations, and would continue to be as long as the magic in their bloodline continued.

The largest shrine portrait belonged to a beautiful young woman with an ornate celestial headdress. Tengu Hime, an ancient ancestor and scholar who had won the favor of the gods with her studies in the art of calligraphy. As a gift for her work, Tengu Hime had been given the power of bringing her written name to life, and she'd spent the rest of her years devoting herself to the community of Hisui Temple—a role that the sorcerers of Asami's family were meant to emulate.

Her mother prepared her own calligraphy tools on the low wooden writing desk: a black inkstone, rice paper, and a calligraphy brush carved from shining blue gemstone. She paused to smooth back a lock of Asami's dark hair, sharing the same midnight shade and fine texture as her own. Asami leaned into her mother's touch, feeling the connection of Tengu Hime's power flowing between them.

The calligraphy brush acted as her mother's wand, a physical extension of the magic she cultivated within, the blue stone handle as vibrant and full as the deepest waters. Her mother guided the brush across the page in smooth strokes, and the cobalt blue ink rippled and glistened like the crests of the northern ocean rising, falling as her mother finished the final stroke.

水月

Mizuki. It was written in the variation of "water moon", evoking the pull of the celestial and its influence over ocean waves, water, time and light. Two elements that complemented each other in a delicate balance.

Then, soft golden light dappled through the painted brushstrokes, binding name and seal with magic. Asami watched, spellbound, as her mother stamped a red rubber seal onto the paper, bearing the surname of their family calligraphy shop. A final sealant to keep the spell bound to the caster.

"A name is our own personal seal," Mizuki said. "The kanji characters are known to be difficult to wrestle onto the page. They have minds of their own. As Name Painters, it is our duty to draw out the magic contained within, to protect Hisui Temple and its villagers."

Outside, storm clouds darkened the sky, and the chill of a coming storm breezed through the opened doorway. Thunder rumbled, promising the relief of rain. Joyous cries echoed through the temple village.

"Rain has arrived! The drought is over!"

Name Summoning, a magic inherited from Tengu Hime, was the principal magic of Name Painter sorcerers like Asami and her mother: the ability to summon the characteristics contained within the spellcaster's own name.

With Mizuki's Name Summoning spell in place, the drought would end, and Hisui Temple would have its thirst for balance and harmony sated.

* * *

*A*sami woke to rain drumming the roof of the calligraphy shop. Gusts of wind rattled the window panes and shook the entire structure of the shop and living quarters, as if something, like a restful spirit, were searching for a way inside. Asami watched the rain with tired eyes. A slow leak of water dripped onto the tatami mats next to her.

The dream had been a memory of her mother from two years ago. Only in her dreams could Asami feel the phantom heat of summer and be free of this cold, wet tempest. She shivered as she moved through the cluttered, musty calligraphy shop. Already, bits of the shop's roofing and floorboard had rotted away, ruining countless books and scrolls with water damage.

Asami had been careful to protect the household shrine and the portraits of her ancestors. She lit a stick of incense and placed it in the shrine's holder, clasping her hands in prayer. Her mother's portrait smiled back at her with warm brown eyes, joined by Asami's grandmother, great-grandmothers, and Tengu Hime.

One year ago, Mizuki's sudden death from fever and sickness had shaken the entire community. Asami still grieved with a heavy heart and tired, red-rimmed eyes. Exhaustion and heartache leached at her strength. Yet, the world still turned, and life in Hisui Temple did not slow down. In fact, life had demanded more: she had to deal with overdue bills to be paid, Governor Tadashi's debt collectors, and living by herself in a generational house for the first time in nineteen years. Asami felt like a phantom in her own home, drifting from room to room, lost and heartbroken.

Requests for spells and talismans had flooded the calligraphy shop, and Asami had struggled to keep up as sole Name Painter, a responsibility that fell heavily and awkwardly on her shoulders. She was still green, sick with grief and hardship.

Then, this storm had arrived with high winds and sheets of rain, and the entire temple village had gone dormant with its severity. The rainstorm had not stopped for four straight weeks, since the one-year anniversary of Mizuki's untimely death from fever. Just as losing her mother to sickness had been a sudden and devastating wave, so too was the storm that flashed in with lightning and heavy rain. Monsoons were common in Hisui Temple, though this storm had proved to be strange, almost uncanny. Ancient trees were uprooted near the main temple, with most of the village's connecting market roads washing away with the forces of rain. It was a relentless cold downpour that ravaged and chilled to the bone, driving all indoors.

This rainstorm, a sign of Mizuki, was smothering Hisui Temple like a curse.

Asami also held a deep secret, something that kept her

from asking The Sages, the calligraphy scholars chosen by Tengu Hime, for help and guidance.

As coils of incense smoke drifted above the family shrine, Asami prepared her own calligraphy tools and ink. A crimson red, like the glaring eye of the sun.

Outside, the storm howled and the shop shook. With her own wand in hand, Asami painted the characters of her name and anticipated that familiar thread of magic she had been taught by her mother to cultivate. The sensation was said to feel like penning a letter to a dear friend, leaving oneself vulnerable and open and loved.

Red ink spilled like blood onto the paper, the brush-strokes shimmering ever so slightly, never fully binding to Asami's name. The thread of magic danced out of reach, fleeting as the sensations faded away.

朝美

Asami. Written in the variation of "beautiful morning": wondrous daybreak, the sleepy-eyed anticipation of salmon pinks and gold painting the early morning sky. The promise of fresh beginnings.

The light on the page fizzled out like a sputtering candle flame, and Asami cast aside her calligraphy brush in frustration. It clattered against the table, throwing more blotches of red onto the rice paper.

Asami's secret was that she disliked her own name. The combination of kanji characters was an abnormal, unique variation that made the character strokes when writing it cumbersome and difficult, requiring great concentration. On top of the sudden passing of her mother, Asami found it impossible to draw out the magic from her name. And where her duty to protect Hisui Temple stemmed from her ability to Name Summon, she was rendered powerless by it. Asami didn't dare to think what fate could befall her if The Sages caught wind of her situation.

A sharp knock then sounded at the front door, amplified by the pounding rush of the rain. Asami winced, taking a moment to still her racing heart before checking the shop entrance. Could it be more of Governor Tadashi's debt collectors?

A figure holding a large emerald green umbrella waited at the front entrance. The bamboo umbrella blocked the visitor's features from view, though Asami could spot a matching tunic of the same rich emerald green. The color of the Tadashi Family.

正

Tadashi. Written in the variation of "correctness" and "righteous", the rigid discipline of discerning right from wrong.

Asami took a deep breath, mind swimming. The Tadashi Family were wealthy, comfortable, and crooked. Whoever had arrived at the door, Asami could not turn them away, for risk of more trouble or outrageous fines. She slid open the shoji door and gave a stiff bow.

"Good morning. What can I do for you?"

The umbrella tipped back to reveal a stern-looking woman, her complexion set with deep frown lines. Her dark hair was pulled back with a cloth in the style of an attendant.

The attendant mirrored Asami's bow, performative and tense. She spoke up over the pounding rain.

"My name is Kaya, an attendant of the Tadashi residence. I've come with an important notice and a summons from The Sages."

Asami's brows furrowed in confusion. The Sages had never given a summons indirectly through the governor or his family before, only through letters and notices in the mail. The two entities were meant to be separate, as local government and scholars of Tengu Hime.

"Why is the Tadashi Family giving summons on behalf of The Sages?"

"The Tadashi Family is interested in the well-being of Hisui Temple, given the severity of this rainstorm and the danger of flooding," Kaya replied. She continued without missing a beat, her head tilting in challenge. "Shall I note to Governor Tadashi that you questioned this reasoning?"

Heat flared Asami's cheeks. "No," she mumbled. She wished her mother could be here with her kind, wise words. She would know what to do, how to handle this situation.

Kaya nodded curtly, then produced a thick scroll sealed with wax. "You are to read this immediately and appear before The Sages tomorrow. I will come to collect you tomorrow morning."

Asami accepted the scroll pushed into her hands. It glittered with an emerald seal of a fox.

The rush of the rain roared in Asami's eardrums like a crashing tidal wave. Her stomach twisted at the speed by which everything seemed to be unfolding. There was no doubt The Sages wanted to hear a solution for quelling the rainstorm. What could Asami possibly tell The Sages tomorrow? What was she to say once they found out her power of Name Summoning was fruitless?

"Miss Asami? Do you understand?" Kaya asked. A muscle above her eyebrow twitched in annoyance. Asami fumbled with the scroll in her hand.

"Yes, I understand. I will be ready tomorrow morning."

Kaya excused herself with another curt bow before she took up the emerald umbrella and disappeared into the downpour like steel into a sheath. Asami closed the door and shut out the rain, still feeling the cold chill of the storm in her bones. Darkness flickered in the shadowed corners of the shop like unwanted guests. Asami lit a few spare candles to dispel a bit of the gloom.

She broke the seal, unfurled the scroll, and read.

By order of His Lord, Governor Tadashi, the Tengu Hime family calligraphy shop is to be reinstated immediately with Mizuki's daughter, Asami, serving as authorized Name Painter and enchanted protector of Hisui Temple. Asami is to appear before The Sages to address the ongoing rainstorm crisis and to implement a solution. Details of required fee payment of ten thousand yen for immediate flooding prevention of the dam and damage fines due to the storm have been enclosed.
This is your final and only notice on this matter.
Regards,
Consul Zuina
Daughter of His Lord, Governor Tadashi

The shadows around Asami rippled, and the candle flames flickered. Enclosed with the scroll was a thick, folded paper. Her eyes fell over the velvety black ink, the penmanship of a trained and aristocratic hand.

Tadashi Residence - personal rice crops destroyed - 97,350 yen
Tadashi Residence - back garden walls collapsed - 90,000 yen
Tadashi Residence - clothing and hair pieces ruined - 30,000 yen

Asami scoffed as she skimmed over the remaining lines. These were all damages to the Tadashi Family's personal property and nothing more. If the governor truly did care for Hisui Temple and its villagers, wouldn't there be more public damages listed? At least, she felt it should have included the villagers' personal damages. The rest of the ledger described the mandatory fee of ten thousand yen charged to each household, which would be used to provide sandbags to prevent further flood damage. Asami had never seen this kind of money, especially not before she was forced to take over the calligraphy shop in her mother's place.

Her stomach sank like a stone in water. The dam, the barrier upstream that collected runoff water from the mountains and conserved it for Hisui Temple, had been bone dry two years ago. Now, there was an impending flood. Asami was reeling from the exact inverse of what her mother had dealt with.

Panic hammered in time with Asami's heartbeat. If she couldn't find a way to break her mother's Name Summoning spell before the dam burst, Hisui Temple would be destroyed in the ensuing flood. Asami's hands would be drenched with the blood of her fellow villagers.

She hazarded a glance down at her ink-stained fingers, cracked with crimson. A bubble of anxiety expanded in Asami's chest, tight and full to bursting. What did she require so that the magic would bind to her name? Asami's credibility and reputation as Name Painter was already deep under water with this rainstorm. If the dam broke, there wouldn't even be a calligraphy shop left to save.

The characters of her name rippled across her mind.

朝美

Asami. Written in the variation of "beautiful morning": the promise of fresh beginnings.

Memories of sunlit shadows and the sweltering heat of drought flickered behind Asami's eyelids. If Asami could Name Summon, she knew she could dispel this storm.

Asami glanced at the torn emerald seal of the fox, the insignia of the Tadashi Family, and contemplated what tomorrow could bring. Kaya, the attendant, would come to collect her to meet with The Sages. Her mentors, whom she had not faced since her mother's death, since this rainstorm had broken over the temple, threatening to flood the entire village.

She bowed her head in front of the shrine portraits in shame, and the deafening heavy rain settled in a torrential waterfall.

Even if it meant facing the judgment and rebuke of her mentors, Asami had to face the ghosts of these inadequacies or risk washing away everything she had ever known.

* * *

Sunlight poured through the opened shop doors as the sounds of chirping birdsong and the rattling of passing oxcart wagons floated through the entryway. Asami and her mother sat in front of the household shrine with calligraphy brushes in hand, sheets of rice paper parchment waiting for fresh ink. Wisps of incense smoke drifted around them in a haze.

Asami's heart trembled with grief and anticipation as she glanced at her mother, her beauty as cold and serene as moonlight.

"Mother, why can't I Name Summon? What am I to do next?" Asami's questions hung in the warm air like the coasting seagulls of the northern ocean. Her mother turned, haloed by the sun, as beautiful as Tengu Hime herself. She ran a finger affectionately over Asami's cheek. Her touch was featherlike and chilling, a whisper from the realm beyond.

"As Name Painters, we must understand for ourselves how our names are a gift. Look within with help from The Sages, and you will find a way."

Before Asami could ask anything further, she was pulled from sleep by a sharp rapping, and the dream of the warm sunlit room melted away. Asami blinked awake as the knocking continued, resonating through the shop like the rumbling of thunder. Despite the churning darkness of the storm outside, the morning hour was still bleak and early.

Asami hastily fixed her appearance and pulled on an outer kimono robe, pulse hammering in her throat. The Sages often said that dreams were messages from the gods, and here she had had a second dream of her departed mother. Asami's heart felt heavy with foreboding, premonition.

Her ears still rang with her mother's words, her instruction to seek help from The Sages while Asami readied her calligraphy kit and slipped it into her robe pocket. Asami pulled open the door and was met with Kaya waiting in the rain, struggling to grip her umbrella with the force of the wind.

The walk to the temple was like wading through a hurricane. Storm water gushed down the main streets and alleyways in small rivers as rain whipped and sprayed in every direction. Gripping her own umbrella with bone-white knuckles, Asami gazed heavenward at the oppressing press of dark storm clouds as forks of lightning split the sky.

The main temple entrance was blocked by more fallen trees and debris, and the surrounding temple walls had crumbled from the force of the storm. This caused Kaya to escort Asami to an area of the temple she had not visited since childhood, to a connecting longhouse near the rock gardens. The teaching hall of The Sages.

Kaya led the way through wooden high-ceilinged hallways and shoji corridors. Statues of oni-faced deities glowered at them as they passed, like the disapproving faces of long forgotten ancestors. Asami hugged herself for warmth as memories of her calligraphy training flooded back to her: the muggy summers of early childhood; her mother by her side as she practiced the rigid strokes of calligraphy, of her name; the droning voice of Master Shigeru instructing the practice of drawing out its magic. Even back then, Asami's name had sputtered and died with the magic's light.

The longhouse strained and groaned around Kaya and Asami, like the belly of a great whale. They arrived at a large tatami room overlooking a rock garden courtyard, now flooded with rubble and the bends of a stream as the rain continued in a dull roar. Overhead, the dark mass of the storm lashed and roiled.

Three figures wearing scholar's caps sat at a raised wooden table at the center of the room. An old graying man with a pointed silver beard, a young woman with purple robes stitched with black moons, and a handsome young man with dark hair that shone almost violet in the lantern light.

Together, The Sages provided a balanced council of calligraphy and its harmonious, expressive artform. They were chosen by Tengu Hime to mentor the rise of the next Name Painter, and who had overseen a long maternal line of sorcerers in Asami's family. The lineages of maternal Name Painter sorcerers and Tengu Hime scholars mirrored each other in parallel like two shoots of the same leaf.

Kaya bowed low to the ground and heralded their arrival, then darted off into the safety of the siderooms. Asami struggled to swallow around her tongue, her mouth bone dry. Cold sweat beaded her armpits and she bent into a low, rigid bow.

"Good morning, Masters," Asami said in greeting. She stared at the tatami at her feet, how the straw pieces weaved and intertwined in strong strands.

The Sages acknowledged her presence with level, even stares. The woman with the purple robes set aside a scroll she had been poring over and regarded Asami with a pointed expression. She frowned over a pair of glaring black reading spectacles.

"Good morning, Asami. You must have received our

notice on how you are to be immediately called upon as Name Painter to address this ongoing rain crisis. How are you finding your Name Painter duties, since your mother passed?" Her billowing kimono sleeves were pulled back to reveal coils of ink markings on her inner forearms.

Master Shiori, adept at the discipline and control of the brush. Intimidating with just a few words.

Heat flashed through Asami's face as the emotion of the past two years swept over her in that moment. Grief, loss, heartbreak, inadequacy.

Asami drew in a breath and decided to let the truth slip for once. Given the circumstances of the storm and the summons, it wasn't as if The Sages or Hisui Temple did not already know. Though such a weighted question it was, the prospect of shortcoming and ineptitude.

"Challenging, Master Shiori," she replied. "My mother's gift has been incredibly missed and I understand I have big shoes to fill in her absence."

The young man at the table leaned forward with steepled fingers. "Our circumstances are quite unique, given the manner of your new appointment as Name Painter with Mizuki's passing." Master Kazuko was revered for his artful, precise calligraphy and keen eye for detail. His voice resonated in the manner of a practice orator, harmonized with the rush of rainfall. "Typically, a mentee is not deemed fit until they are given a final evaluation, as we had done with Mizuki."

The old man with the silver beard cleared his throat in irritation. "Then Asami is clearly unfit to preside over Tengu Hime's shop, or we must find a replacement! This storm has been damaging our village for weeks and a flood is imminent. We need a solution now!" Master Shigeru said, notorious in his rigid honor for custom and tradition.

Asami winced. Master Shigeru had a candid point. She

had no business keeping her family's calligraphy shop as Name Painter, if she couldn't keep the task of protecting the temple village.

Yet, a strange fierceness, almost a sudden combativeness and possessiveness wormed its way into Asami's heart at the thought of having it all taken from her. It was hers by birthright, hers to cultivate and cherish and bring to its fullest potential. It was hers because it was the last tether she had to her mother and she could not let go, for failure as a daughter.

"Master Shigeru, I wholeheartedly agree. That calligraphy shop and Mizuki's remaining talismans from the drought are too valuable in the hands of an amateur. Perhaps, then, it would be best in the hands of someone more capable."

Partly obscured by a paper screen partition, Asami was astonished to see a fourth figure amongst The Sages. With thinning dark hair pinned back into a noble topknot and wearing an oversized emerald green kimono, Governor Tadashi kneeled on a seat cushion at Master Shigeru's side. Asami's world tilted around her. To look the crooked man in the eye responsible for so much grief and debt after her mother's death, Asami felt sick with dread. Her clenched fists shook, her breath came ragged.

Why in the heavens was he sitting with The Sages as if he had any scholarly jurisdiction over calligraphy or Name Summoning?

Master Shiori quirked an eyebrow at Governor Tadashi's interjection. She leaned away from him with crossed arms, her body language suggesting a similar distaste.

"Hisui Temple appreciates your contributions in flooding prevention, Governor Tadashi, which is why you have been invited here for this summons. But you are no sorcerer, and neither are The Sages. We are only scholars. We cannot call upon magic as Tengu Hime and Asami's ancestral line of Name Painters can. What are you suggesting?"

Governor Tadashi smiled with blackened teeth, dyed with iron in the aristocratic fashion. Like his eyes, his lacquered smile glistened, ghoulish. Asami was reminded of an eel.

"Perhaps the calligraphy shop should be given over to the Tadashi Family to look after. It's clear to me that Name Painters may hold too much power and are a threat to local governance."

Asami felt her eyebrows lift in disbelief. To suggest a sudden claim in ownership so boldly was like a backhanded slap to the face, leaving her stunned and mute. Nothing of the sort had been disclosed in the summons letter. Could such a thing even be possible? Would The Sages allow such a nefarious shift between the generational Name Painter and mentor dynamic?

"And what of this rainstorm?" Master Shiori pressed, her arms still crossed tightly over her chest. Her expression was cold and unreadable.

"We do nothing. We let the dam break. If the villagers paid properly, my sandbags and flooding prevention should do the trick just fine." Governor Tadashi spread his arms wide. "I open my estate to the public. All are welcome to take shelter there until the storm passes."

Master Shigeru nodded, to which Asami felt another wave of cold sweat break over the back of her neck. "We will need to evacuate the village immediately. In addition to the flooding of the dam, the mountain conditions are worsening and we risk a landslide."

"*If* this storm does not pass, we may consider transferring ownership of the calligraphy shop," said Master Kazuko. "For now, the politics of this situation must wait. This problem can no longer be ignored."

"This problem has *already* been ignored for long enough." Master Shigeru muttered pointedly under his breath.

Asami's mind raced as the sharp edges of panic began to

take hold. Master Shiori was indecipherable, Master Kazuko was ambivalent, and Master Shigeru already seemed to have made up his mind about Asami on the matter. Asami knew she had to rid The Sages of Governor Tadashi's influence if she had any hope of keeping the calligraphy shop from his power-hungry clutches, and to save the temple village from disastrous flooding.

"I now request an audience for my final evaluation!" Asami blurted out.

The Sages looked at her in bewilderment. An uncomfortable silence filled the room, before it was pierced by a sharp, booming laughter. Governor Tadashi clutched his sides.

"What good will that do?" Governor Tadashi retorted. "You have already been deemed Name Painter, is that not correct?"

"As Master Kazuko pointed out earlier, given the circumstances, Asami has a right to have an evaluation with The Sages," Master Shiori interjected. "We have not done so since Mizuki passed."

A weak smile twinged the corners of Asami's mouth. This could be her chance.

Governor Tadashi's amusement quickly faded and he studied Asami with narrowed eyes. "Then which of The Sages do you request as your audience?"

Pulse pounding, Asami's gaze flickered between her three mentors. She had to choose carefully, as her private evaluation was her best chance at asking for help. She needed to choose a mentor who could understand her plight.

"Master Shiori."

Master Shiori gave a curt nod, acknowledging Governor Tadashi's glowering.

"I'm looking forward to hearing Asami's solution." Master Shiori said coolly.

Asami and The Sages exchanged another bow before she

was dismissed. Her footsteps thudded in time with her racing heartbeat as she trailed behind Master Shiori.

Master Shiori led the way to a side receiving room of the longhouse, which still overlooked the flooded courtyard and the distant mountain ranges. Asami wondered where Kaya could have gone and how many of Governor Tadahi's attendants waited on him inside the temple.

Taking a deep breath, Asami set out her calligraphy kit and prepared her tools. The red rubber stamp of the calligraphy shop sealant felt heavy in her hands. Master Shiori took a seat across the low table, her purple kimono robe rippling with the movement. This manner of Master Shiori monitoring her calligraphy work reminded Asami of her lessons as a young girl, when she could barely balance the brush upright and ink would stain her hands and clothes.

Asami fiddled with the handle of the calligraphy brush and its smooth red stone, her stomach twisting on itself like tangled seaweed.

"I have a solution, but I also present a problem," Asami said under her breath. "This rainstorm can be broken with my Name Summoning. I can see it in the essence of my name here."

Asami used her finger to trace the character strokes of her name as she spoke quickly. "*Morning light*. I believe I can disperse the rain clouds, if I can just Name Summon."

Master Shiori nodded in recognition at the characters. "Well, what is stopping you?"

Asami's skin felt like it was on fire. She swallowed the lump in her throat.

"My name is difficult to write out and even harder to concentrate on the magic while doing so. Sometimes, the ink blends together in a mess, or I write the strokes incorrectly. I ... I dislike my name. Because of that, I've never been able to properly Name Summon before."

Master Shiori stared at the blank parchment before them, as still as a statue. Her mouth was pursed so tightly that her lips disappeared into a thin white line.

"Show me."

Gripping her brush, Asami painted the angular strokes of her name with all its ugly, sharp corners. She felt the familiar warm sensation of light as it dappled through the page, but the light soon sputtered out as always.

"I see. That much is clear to me. To you, your name is a chore," said Master Shiori. "This art form has been lost on you. You do not feel it; you do not live it."

Asami's chest felt like it had caved in on itself. Her shoulders sagged, her gaze falling to the floor. This she knew to some extent, yet hearing it spoken from her mentor was disgracing. She thought of her mother and the smiling portraits waiting for her in the shrine back home. She thought of how she had let them all down.

Master Shiori raised Asami's chin with the crook of her finger. Her hands and joints felt calloused from a lifetime of study.

"But that does not mean you cannot learn," she continued. "Again, The Sages are not sorcerers, only scholars of the craft. At least, I can show you how to appreciate the artform. May I?"

Master Shiori held out her hand for the calligraphy brush. Asami relinquished it and watched as Master Shiori dutifully prepared the ink and a fresh piece of parchment, speaking as she painted the characters of Asami's name.

"Think of each stroke as building upon the other. What do they each contribute?"

It was breathtaking to watch the master at work as beauty and careful control seeped into the very essence of the ink. It was clear that Master Shiori commanded her own magic across the page.

Asami studied the strokes, the characters laid out before her eyes in a clarity she had never seen before.

朝美

She pointed to the familiar smooth strokes she recognized on the left. They flowed like water, like the pull of the ocean. She had seen this exact character two years ago in her mother's own name.

"The moon. I have my mother's moon within me."

Asami had always thought of herself as separate from her mother. Less magically adept, disjointed, her name an obstacle to overcome in the process. Her death had only solidified this separation. Yet, here was a little reminder of her mother's presence, nestled at the very center of her own name.

Asami's hands tingled with heat, a newfound energy slowly rising within her.

"Good," smiled Master Shiori. "We can go deeper. When you say your mother's moon, what does that mean to you?"

Asami's pulse quickened. She tasted hints of wind and rain on her tongue.

Nothing in her ability was missing. She had everything she could ever need.

"It means I carry part of her within me. It means I'm capable—that I can do it."

Another nod from Master Shiori, this one determined and steadfast. "Show me again. You *are* capable, Asami."

Heavy silence filled the room, save for the clash of the storm. The shoji doors rattled and the wooden structure of the temple crackled like old bones as Asami prepared another page. Then, a great crash resonated from the surrounding mountains and rumbled over the valley of the village.

Footsteps pounded in the hallway outside. The door

shoved open, and Master Kazuko stood panting, dark hair falling into his eyes.

"The dam is breaking! We must get to high ground."

His gaze slid to the blank page in front of Asami, her brush hand still poised. "Miss Asami, many people are depending on you," Master Kazuko said breathlessly. "Please, hurry."

It was the most desperate Asami had ever seen him, the fear in his eyes unmistakable. She set her shoulders, determined to not let the same fear overtake her, and turned her full attention back to the page before her.

It lay blank, spotless and intimidating.

As Name Painters, it is our duty to draw out the magic contained within, to protect Hisui Temple and its villagers.

Her mother's mantra, the old vow of Tengu Hime and Name Painters alike, came to Asami like a familiar melody.

She had to succeed.

Asami marched to the courtyard-facing doors and threw them wide open. Master Shiori and Master Kazuko both gasped as the storm blew into the room and papers flew about in a vortex of white. The room shook. Lightning crashed all around them.

Master Kazuko fell to his knees in fright. The churning energy of the storm engulfed Asami's senses completely, drowning her in the biting threads of a tempest magic. She slowly opened her mind to the connection, fueled by a new sense of fortitude.

With another deep breath, Asami snatched up a piece of parchment and let the flow of the wind and rain guide her wand hand. She cradled the character of the moon with her red inked brushstrokes, carrying each strike of her name with weight and purpose. Glowing light hummed from within the page, binding name and seal with magic.

Asami surrendered to it, embracing the magic's full potential for the first time. She saw countless threads of iridescent energy surrounding her in a shimmering heat wave, shadows and shades of spirits as apparitions manifested and dissipated around them. Ancestors from the shrine portraits.

A Name Painter's ultimate ability: the undoing of a name and its bearer.

As Asami reached for the red sealant, her heart clenched. She recalled her mother blessing visiting travelers and local families with charms and warding spells, chatting with customers about the mundane and simple. How Asami had observed it all, the generational gift from her family.

The storm raged on, throwing down sheets of rain as the trees arched and twisted in the wind. Asami mentally gathered the storm's remaining threads of Mizuki's magic, seeking the warm bits of energy she had grown up with throughout her girlhood, tucked away in the clouds like folded colorful paper. She collected them with a chilled sadness, taking note of how it felt like she was also losing something at the same time. At last, Asami stamped the sealant onto the page and severed the connection of Mizuki's old spell like the snipping of a cord.

Sunlight filtered through the storm in great, luminous sunbeams. A sunshower formed, and the beams burned brighter, radiant. Thunder and darkness dissipated with the parting clouds as the last final raindrops dribbled from the rooftops. A hushed silence fell over the temple grounds.

The drowned earth settled, the storm had broken at last.

* * *

*W*arm sunshine and soft birdsong ushered in a foreign sense of renewal to Hisui Temple. With Kaya's later scouting of the dam, she had reported that the dam wall had miraculously held, though a great lesion had now formed in the exterior. This had been the cause of the earlier commotion and distant crash.

Governor Tadashi's estate had not been so lucky with the storm's severity, as nearly half of the eastern wing had collapsed and flooded from a fallen ancient tree. With the estate openly exposed and the temple villagers already restless, the public had discovered proof of the governor's fraud; the promised sandbags had not been properly distributed, as they lay molded and unused in the cellars.

Over the next several days, Asami joined the villagers as they rallied outside the Tadashi Family estate in a passionate throng of young and old, demanding the collected flooding prevention funds be used to instead fix the dam wall's lesion. Asami and many others held up the ledgers given to them, calling for an end to the exploitation.

Governor Tadashi was to answer for his crimes and properly utilize his resources, or risk being run out of the temple village entirely.

A weighted but natural consequence in the aftermath of years of endured hardship, collecting like rainwater.

* * *

*A*sami sat in the calligraphy shop, her brush hand moving slow and composed. Instead of rice paper, however, her brush moved over a lacquered piece of wood as she deposited the strokes. The written characters connected in a blend of the old, familiar, and new.

Mizuki's Moon, the storesign read.

Tengu Hime's calligraphy shop, as it had simply come to be known, had lacked a name. With the new appointment of Asami as Name Painter of Hisui Temple, it seemed appropriate to finally give the shop one.

As she finished the final brushstroke, incense smoke

perfuming the air, Asami glanced outside as the sun crested over the mountaintops in a kaleidoscope of morning light. Several villagers waited outside the shop doors, eager to meet with Asami now that conditions were favorable to do so. A nervous anticipation seeped into her.

The path to recovery would be a long and winding one. Tensions had been unearthed and Asami would have to work hard to reestablish the trust Mizuki had built. But as she set aside the wooden sign to dry, Asami had a feeling her ancestors would appreciate the gesture, and smile favorably upon her.

* * *

Sara Kuzuoka is a Japanese writer of historical fantasy and fiction. Her work has also appeared in Goosewax Journal and Flash Fiction Friday. She is an alumna of the Critical Language Scholarship program and the Odyssey Online class workshops.

DRAGON'S BREATH

BY H. ROBERT BARLAND

"*D*ragon's breath."

The boy turned to Mersen, the oldest of the three trappers on the mountain path.

"That's what they call it," Mersen said and pointed a worn whetstone at the wisps of cloud that escaped the boy's mouth, "when your breath mists in the air like that."

The boy stared at the old man for a moment, then huffed on his fingers as he looked up to the snowline.

Mersen returned to whetting his blade, his bare, gnarled hands making long, confident strokes with the stone. Sometime in the past, the knife's point had snapped off, leaving a blunt-nosed blade the length of his thumb. He stopped and tested the edge across the back of his thumbnail. With a grunt, he pushed the knife home into its leather sheath then shoved it at the boy.

"Don't lose it." Mersen tucked his stone into a pouch then levered himself up with his staff. He joined the other two trappers as the boy tied the sheath to his belt.

"Dragon's breath," the boy repeated, watching the cloud drift away to disappear into the mountain air. "I hate it."

* * *

"He's a bit young to be apprenticed. What is he? Nine? Ten?"

"Fourteen. My sister-in-law's whelp."

Mersen looked across the market square at the boy who sat, head bowed. The boy's threadbare cloak outlined a bony frame. Mersen scratched at his beard.

"Scrawny," he said. "What are you offering me to take him?"

The boy's uncle stacked five grubby coins on the table in front of the old trapper. Mersen poked the stack so that they spilt across the table, then leaned back to massage his leg.

"It should be half that again," Mersen sniffed. "At least."

"I need rid of him."

"That's not my problem. I can't see what's in this for me."

The man looked at the trapper's grey temples. "It can't be easy on the mountain at your age ..." he said. Mersen stopped rubbing his leg. "Trudging around. In all that snow."

Mersen gave a quick shrug.

"Your brother has Donkey as his assistant. The boy would be smarter than him. He could be useful."

"Donkey can carry his own weight. More, even. He's as strong as—"

"A donkey, I get it."

"I was going to say ox."

The man leaned forward. "Garnish his wages until he's all paid up. Fill up that retirement pot." The chair creaked as he leaned back. "Unless you think you're going to finally land a dragon up there."

Mersen snorted. "There are no dragons on the mountain." He leaned on one elbow and tapped his temple. There was silence.

"And ... I'll buy three hare pelts," the boy's uncle added.

"Eight."

"Five. In their winter coats."

"Done."

They reached out to clasp hands, but Mersen pulled up short. He looked across the square to the boy as he sat, head still bowed.

"And if he proves useless?"

The boy's uncle glanced up at the distant mountain. "I understand it's very dangerous up there, on the mountain." He shrugged. "No one here bats an eye when someone doesn't come back."

* * *

The boy bound the ends of the string together. He held the trap trigger steady as he tipped a handful of leaves over the noose. Moving with exaggerated care, he released his hold on the trigger. It held. He looked up at Mersen who stared, expressionless, back at his apprentice. Mersen tapped the side of the trap with his staff. It sprang up, but the noose rose little more than a finger's breadth from the ground. He rapped the boy across the forearm with his staff.

"Idiot," he said.

Ammon, who had been watching, laughed. Donkey looked to Ammon, his broad, flat features uncomprehending, then finally joined in with a slow, drawling laugh.

"Hur-a-hur, hur-a-hur."

Mersen walked away, his staff crunching as it punched the thin ice atop the snow. He called back over his shoulder. "Do it again."

The boy rubbed at his arm, bent down, and began to shorten the cord.

* * *

He could hear a rasping in her shallow breaths, tiny puffs of cold in the chill of the cottage. The hearth was dark. Water dripped down the chimney onto the cracked stones.

She started coughing. They were weaker than just minutes ago. She looked across at him and tried to smile, but her eyes held trapped pain.

"You were," she said. Fatigue forced her speech into snippets. "Such a small boy. When you were born."

He began to speak, but she shook her head, every motion sluggish.

"So small. We thought. You might not live." She coughed and drew in a weak breath.

"Mother—"

"We gave you," she continued, her eyes far away. "A powerful name. A dragon's name. To give you strength". She paused again. One laboured breath. Two. "That name belongs to you. No one can take it."

The boy nodded. She looked at him, and when she spoke, her voice was barely more than a whisper.

"Don't forget your name."

He nodded again. Her mouth curved into a slight smile, and she held his eyes with hers. A long, curling cloud slipped from her mouth. It evaporated around him. He waited in silence before closing her eyes.

* * *

It was late afternoon, and the damp, white blanket that previously enshrouded the mountain had cleared, affording the boy a view of the valley. The township below was dark now that it had slipped into the mountain's shadow. He took a step closer to the edge of the snow covered precipice, eyes raised to stare into the distance. Nestled among the far hills, bathed in the fast-fading light of the sun, would be the village where he was born. He took a deep breath.

"My name is—"

The snow lurched and slipped away. The boy was carried over the edge. His hands tore at the lip, grasping for purchase. His fingers caught a shallow crack and wedged themselves. Pain lanced through his fingers, the jagged rock gouging at his palm. With his chest pressed against the face of the cliff, he clung to the edge. The dark red stone was slick, like clotted blood. Snow continued to cascade over him. He stared as it dispersed like sifted flour. The boy's eyes hardened, and he looked back up the cliff face. With a grunt, he pulled himself upward, pain accentuating each movement. Slowly, he moved his upper body up and over the lip until he had leverage, then rolled over to safety. He lay there panting, breath misting in the air. When the boy regained his composure, he sat up and looked out over the edge. The far hills of his home had slipped into shadow. He lurched to his feet and stumbled back towards the camp.

Mersen stood under the boughs of a tree. He twisted his staff in the snow as he watched the boy trudge out of sight.

"Idiot."

* * *

The boy stepped away from the deadfall and looked back over his shoulder. Mersen nodded at him.

"You're learning."

The boy felt a small flush of heat. He turned back to the trap and pulled up the weight. He leaned awkwardly under it to tie it off.

"Keep your head out from under the weight when you tie it off," the old man said, "idiot."

The boy finished tying off the cord.

"I have a name," he mumbled. Then he took a deep breath, bent his chilled hands into fists, and spun around. "It's —" he began, but Mersen had already gone.

* * *

"Now, like last time, cut that second thread."

The boy reached to his belt. His hand froze. He bit his bottom lip before looking up at Mersen. Mersen looked at the boy and then into the mouth of the empty scabbard. He released the trap and shoved the boy over in the snow. The boy scrambled back, feet scrabbling for purchase. Mersen stepped to him, bent and grabbed him by the jacket.

"You will go." Mersen thrust the boy backwards again. "And you will find it." He stood upright, placed his staff into the boy's chest, and twisted. "That knife belongs to me."

The boy grimaced and nodded.

Mersen leaned him. Flecks of spittle struck him in the face as the trapper spoke.

"So. Do. You."

* * *

The boy stepped into the clearing, his torn and aching hand tucked under his arm. Donkey sat cross-legged on the ground, grinning. Mersen sat nearby, tapping his staff into the snow. The boy turned his body sideways to display the sheath, knife nestled within. Mersen didn't look but thrust a slender wedge of hard cheese and a fist-sized chunk of dark bread at him. The boy took them and sank to his knees by the campfire.

The fire hissed as its flames were extinguished. Wisps of steam wafted from under the dumped snow. Ammon stood behind the boy, brushing flakes from his gloves, his wide mouth twisted into a crooked grin.

"Time to go. You'll eat as we go," he said.

The boy looked to Mersen, who sat twisting his staff in the snow.

"Hur-a-hur, hur-a-hur," drawled Donkey.

* * *

"Empty again," Mersen growled. "That's the ninth in a row."

"Tenth, if you count that triggered one," Ammon said.

Mersen glared at his brother. Ammon stepped back and raised his palms in a conciliatory gesture. The boy flinched and tensed, but Mersen had already turned away, mumbling under his breath, too frustrated to vent on the boy anymore. Ammon had no such qualms. The boy bent to retrieve the trap. Ammon cuffed him across the back of the head. The boy stumbled and half jumped over the trap. Donkey pushed out his foot, tripping him up. He landed face down in the snow. A hidden rock punched at his cheek, and pain blossomed across his face.

"Hur-a-hur, hur-a-hur."

"Get up, idiot."

Mersen had returned. He threw a small leather bucket at the boy. "We're taking a break. Go and get some water from the river."

The boy clambered to his feet to face Donkey, only to find him already turned away, staring at the others. His expression was desperate, a need to fit in. The boy understood. There was no true ill will here; he was affirming his place in the pecking order. With a sigh, the boy collected the bucket and lurched down the steep slope.

Mersen's voice called out to him.

"Check the bear trap near the river. By the old dead pine."

There were a few seconds of silence before the boy heard Mersen's voice again. "Don't step in it."

"Hur-a-hur."

* * *

The boy held a handful of snow against his cheek. Cold numbed his pain even as it bit through the tattered remains of his glove. He ran his eyes along the river. An ancient pine had toppled into the river. Its roots had erupted from the ground and now clawed at the mountain's slope. Its passing had left an earthen void that now held a dusting of snow, and the damp smell of fresh earth snuck past the cloying scent of pine. Ice had begun to form where denuded branches and trunk touched the surface of the river.

The boy approached the toppled tree, wary of falling foul of Mersen's trap. He skirted the fallen giant, trying to find the end of the chain. He froze when he heard the sound. It was the snort of something breathing. A desperate, wet snort that overlaid a whine deep and plaintive. He stretched his neck and squinted at the darkness within the fallen tree. There was a glint of rust-tinged black. The bear trap's anchor chain was pulled taught and led into the river.

A broken branch lifted from under the water. A glacial rise then a wet slap as it fell back onto the river's surface. Tattered leather was strung between it and attached to it.

It was not a branch at all; it was a wing. There was another bubbling snort, and breath misted up from the far side of the tree. The boy scrambled down and peered over the fallen trunk. Two scaled nostrils reached from under the water. A blast of air and blood bubbled up to spray the already reddened trap that bit down on the scaled snout. Slitted amber eyes, partially hidden behind the blackened steel of the trap, stared up at him from under the surface. Flaring nostrils slipped beneath the surface, but the eyes continued to hold onto the boy as they drifted down.

He plunged into the river. Numbing cold forced a cry from his lips, and the flesh of his hands screamed. Reaching past the trap, he pulled. Ice crawled inside his thin shoes to clutch at his feet. Losing his footing on the riverbed, he slipped backward and slammed against the bank. The boy scrambled over the trunk and dropped back into the water. Moving back to the creature, he wrapped his arms around it and dove under the tree. His bruised face protested as it rubbed against the creature's scales. His jacket snagged on shattered trunk, holding him under the surface. Planting his feet, he wrenched upwards. Stitching gave way as he pushed up from under the tree.

Breaking through to the surface, he sucked in searing gulps of frigid air. He pulled the creature onto the bank where it sank down to the ground, limp. Collapsing beside it, his fingers curled into a mass of searing pain. Slipping them into his mouth, he shivered. The creature lay on the snow. The size of a small dog, its only movement was the slow rise and fall of its chest. Brown and grey scales ran along its slender neck and covered its long body. A tan membrane stretched between its forefingers. They were tipped with curved talons the length of his thumb. A sinuous tail lay limp.

The boy looked back to its head to find an amber eye staring at him, its gaze unfathomable. There was not the panic the boy had seen in other creatures' eyes when caught. He looked at the trap. Its steel jaws hadn't bitten as deep as he imagined they should, but they held fast the creature's reptilian snout. He pulled his fingers from his mouth, embarrassed at the image he presented. Reaching out his pained hand, he grasped the jaws of the trap.

"Idiot!"

Mersen's voice made him jump. He snatched his hands away from the trap. Mersen and his brother pushed their way past a snow-laden pine.

"Why are you wet? Did you fall ..." Mersen's voice trailed away. The pair pulled up short.

Ammon was the first to recover. "Is that ...?"

"Yes," Mersen breathed.

"A dragon?"

"Yes."

"Then we're—"

"Rich?" Mersen prompted. He turned back to inspect the trapped beast. He smiled, but there was no humour in it. "Yes. Yes, we are."

* * *

The boy squatted by the fire, his jacket propped on a stick to dry. His teeth had stopped chattering.

"Come away from it," Merson demanded.

The dragon's wings were bound to its body with rope, and the whole creature was tied to two poles. The bear trap was gone, replaced by broad leather straps around the creature's snout, which Ammon gave a quick tug. He nodded to himself then re-joined the group.

"How much will we get? Do you think?"

"Lots."

Ammon snorted. He looked at Mersen and waved his hands upwards, encouraging him to elaborate. His eyes danced with avarice.

"Enough for us to retire comfortably. Buy yourself a tavern, if you wanted.'

Ammon grinned and skipped around, kicking snow into the air. Donkey clapped his hands together in a steady rhythm. Ammon turned his manic actions into a dance.

Donkey stopped his clapping and pointed, mouth agape, to where the dragon had been bound. The straps and rope were still there, but the dragon had vanished.

"Where'd it go?" Ammon wailed. Panic tinged his voice.

"Idiot," Mersen scoffed. "Look again."

Ammon stared. The bindings gave the illusion away. He

walked up and tugged on the leather. The dragon hadn't moved. Its scales had changed to the colour of fresh snow, a perfect match.

"This is why we haven't seen one before," Mersen said.

"Or it's new to the mountain," Ammon said.

"Doesn't matter,' his brother replied. He turned to the boy. "You did well."

Ammon frowned. "It was the trap that caught it," he said.

"The thing was exhausted and could barely move. Much longer and it would've drowned."

Ammon conceded a nod. "You could buy yourself out of your apprenticeship with your share," he said to the boy as he held out his fingers to the fire. "If you wanted."

"Shut up, Ammon." Mersen's voice was a low growl.

The boy stopped rubbing his hands. What would he do if he was released from his apprenticeship? Where could he go? He looked down the mountainside. A mist obscured the town below.

The boy looked across at the bound creature. An amber eye, clear and bright, was fixed on him. He felt something pull at his chest, and he wrenched his gaze away. His cheeks had started to burn in the freezing air. When he turned back, the dragon's eyes had closed.

Ammon picked up a branch from the pile of firewood and leaned on it like a crutch. He tapped his upper lip as he watched Donkey strip the skin from a hare.

"Mersen?"

"Yes."

"When we go back, everyone is going to see this thing."

"No doubt."

"They'll expect to see the bounty spread evenly." Ammon took a step towards his brother. It brought him directly behind Donkey. "Amongst the four of us."

"That's the law."

"What if there wasn't four of us?"

Mersen was quiet for a moment. He stopped twisting his staff. "I see what you are saying."

The boys's eyes widened in shock as Ammon took the log in two hands and swung it flat.

"No!" His cry was too late. Donkey toppled sideways into the snow. The boy started to stand.

"Nothing personal, kid," he heard Mersen say from behind before a flash of pain sent his entire world into darkness.

* * *

His ears rang and cold burned his bruised cheek. Opening his eyes brought more pain, stabbing at him as the light pierced his skull. The dragon was blurred in his sight. Was it watching him again?

Voices drifted through his foggy thoughts.

"... so, we're saying they fell in and were washed downstream, right? Mersen?"

"Yeah. Good thinking to use a log rather than a knife. Would've been suspicious if they came across the bodies and found knife wounds."

"I ... ah, just whacked him." Ammon's voice was sheepish.

"Idiot," Mersen sounded tired.

The boy heard a grunt and splash. His vision cleared a little. The dragon strained against the leather straps that muzzled it, muscles tensed under the scales. The boy heard the crunch of feet on snow. He inched his knife from its scabbard. The smooth, wooden handle felt comforting. It felt better to have a weapon, even if it was small.

"He's awake!" Ammon's voice called.

"Don't care. Throw him in."

The boy rose and brandished the tiny knife before him.

He cast his gaze to the side. He could see Mersen's staff standing upright in a drift of snow, too far to reach. His vision swam, and nausea flared within him.

Mersen walked up and tapped his thick trapper's coat.

"That little thing won't cut through these."

Ammon joined his brother and looked down his nose at the boy. The boy twisted his head. A body floated face down in the freezing water. Donkey.

Mersen plucked his staff from the snow and lashed out. The boy flinched, but the blow landed on his shoulder with numbing force, the knife tumbling from his hand. He lurched toward it, but another blow fell across his back. He stumbled and rolled in the snow. Finding his knife nearby, he grasped it and rose to face the trapper again. His breath exploded out of him in a cloud as Mersen's staff drove into his stomach. Each shallow breath was a struggle. His strength had left him, and he sank to the ground.

Mersen squatted in front of him. "A nice try, but you couldn't win here."

"Idiot," Ammon laughed.

The boy looked across at the dragon. Its flanks moved, but it made no other movement, eyes held focused on him again.

"I'm sorry," he said to it.

"Apologising won't help you," Ammon said as he stepped up to the boy, log in hand.-"Idiot."

"I have a name."

Ammon shrugged.

"I don't care." He raised the log above his head.

The boy dove sideways, colliding with the dragon. A glancing blow from the log caught him across the shoulder. It overshot, struck the ground, and Ammon lost his grip on it. He grabbed at the boy with bare hands. The boy twisted in his grip, lashing out with panicked slashes of the knife.

Ammon waved the boy's wrist aside with ease, the knife instead slicing across the dragon's muzzle. With a laugh, Ammon struck the boy across the face, and the knife flew off into the snow. Ammon struck him again and dragged him to the water's edge. Eyeing the water, the boy twisted sideways, the desperate squirm of the trapped. There was a shout, a brief struggle, and they both fell into the icy stream.

The boy's breath burst from him as Ammon held him down. He tried to pull the trapper's hands away, but exhaustion drained him. It was too much. He'd done all he could. Darkness shrouded his vision.

As the darkness was overtaking him, orange light burst across his eyes, and Ammon's steel grip was gone. The boy pushed upwards. He broke the surface and pulled himself, dripping, onto the bank to flop face down on the snow. When he managed to turn over and regain his focus, he saw two amber eyes staring at him, set above a bloody maw. The boy studied the dragon, eyes wary, but it remained crouched and still.

The boy stumbled back to the site to find Mersen lying on his side, unmoving. Blood seeped from his torn throat. Severed leather straps from the dragon's snout lay next to the body. Torn fragments of rope were scattered about. Teeth chattering, the boy pulled Mersen's furs from his corpse. He stripped away his sodden woollens. Cinching in the waist with some scraps of rope, he walked over to the river's edge. Donkey had disappeared, carried away by the current, and the boy felt a pinch of sorrow at his passing. Ammon's body swayed in the current, caught in the same tree where the boy had found the dragon. His charred, eyeless face stared upward. The boy kicked the corpse out into the flow and turned back to the dragon.

"Maybe I could get used to dragon's breath after all."

He bent down and collected Mersen's staff. The boy

started on his way as the dragon spread its wings and leapt into the air. Two sharp downstrokes brought the dragon to him. It grasped the furs of the coat and draped itself catlike around his neck. Its scales flickered and darkened until they matched the furs of the coat. New scales had formed on the dragon's snout where the trap had bitten, pure white against the surrounding grey scales. The dragon sniffed his hand. Its tongue slid out to lap against his palm. Stinging pain shot through his hand, and he whipped it away. The pain flared then faded as it if it had never been. He looked down to see the skin had knitted together with a sharp, white scar.

The boy looked down onto the village, tiny and distant. He could see the small puffs of his breath lit by the slanted rays of the morning sun. The dragon snaked its head around to look him in the eyes. He drifted into their alien depths and —rather than heard—felt a word. A name.

He nodded to the beast then turned from the village and started walking. As he spoke, his breath again misted in the air, curling away behind him.

"That's my name, too."

* * *

H. Robert Barland is a teacher, historical re-enactor and black belt martial artist. A former motorcyclist, climber, film extra, and resident of the UK. He has now returned to Newcastle, Australia where he lives with his wife and two boys.

BLOOD AND STONE

BY MIKA GRIMMER

"You will come when you are called," a familiar, husky voice commanded me from beneath the shadows of a hooded cloak. Blood dripped from her closed fist onto the base of the altar stone.

An offering of her blood to renew the pact between us.

"I always do," I said, appearing in the boughs above her.

It hadn't always been this way. I had been free once. But when we were little more than children, she spoke the words of binding and tied red ribbons around my forearms as she fed me on her own blood willingly. Since then, I have been hers to summon as she wills.

Her hood fell around her slender shoulders when she looked up. Her hair flashed silver in the dappled sunlight, though she stood unbent by the years. Each strand of silver was a reminder that I was failing my side of our bargain. I had slowed her aging, yes, but I was not able to stop it no matter what new magic we devised together. When I'd made the pact with my priestess, I hadn't understood how swiftly the years would turn that young maiden into a woman on the cusp of cronehood.

I lowered myself from the trees to kneel at her feet. Even kneeling, I stood nearly as tall as her. She held out her bleeding hand to me, and I felt the wound close beneath my tongue as I savored the blood she offered me. The familiar mélange of iron and salt lingered on my lips. The years had deepened the flavor.

"Are you done?" she asked.

"Yes," I purred. In the past, we'd both taken pleasure in our ritual, but tonight her voice rang with impatience.

"Good," she said, then stepped away from me.

I cocked my head and looked down at her face, but only the indifferent mask of a priestess gazed back up at me.

"Have I offended you?" I asked.

"Your failures offend me," she said.

Her words cut me deeper than she could have known. I looked down at the red ribbons looped around my forearms by a girl who'd loved me once. I couldn't see that girl in the woman who stood before me, but I couldn't help but love her. I would have torn down the sky to give her what she most desired.

"If I had more time, I could find the right magic to give you what you wish," I said.

"Soon it will be too late," she said, starting to pace in the glade, her long robes trailing behind her in the grass. "The new moon is tonight, and the current of magic I will be calling upon runs strongest in the absence of the moon's interference."

"But, I am of the moon." How could she have forgotten that the moon is my mother, and it is from her grace that I have any magic at all? "I cannot act tonight."

She stopped and looked up at me, then said, "If you do not act tonight, I will not have the strength to summon you again, and you shall nevermore taste my blood."

I bowed my head. I could let this woman go, it was true,

but if there was a chance to bring back the girl she once was, I would risk anything to do it. "Tell me what you would have me do." I tried not to think about the vows to my mother that I would break tonight as I listened to my priestess's plans to regain her youth.

* * *

Clouds covered the moonless sky. Not even the stars bore witness, and for that, I was grateful. Tendrils of fog curled from the lakeshore to the east of the cloister. The scent of ozone filled my nostrils as I approached.

I moved like a shadow through the village and then slipped into the building where the young women slept. Within, I found a young woman, a girl really, who was younger than my priestess ever was while I knew her. By the light of a guttering candle at her bedside, I could see her long chestnut hair and slightly too thin lips. This girl was more than a mere sacrifice—she was the daughter of my priestess.

Could a mother sacrifice her own daughter in search of the power that she sought? Maybe humans think little of their offspring. My mother has more children than she can count, and on all nights but those of the new moon, she shows her love with the protection and gift of magic that she bestows on each of us with her silver light.

When I picked up the girl, she rolled toward my chest, gently clutching the folds of my robes in her small fist like a babe. Try as I might to ignore it, the blood flowing in her veins sang to me. It smelled so much like her mother's did the first time that she summoned me from the stones. But this girl was not my priestess, and she would never offer her blood to me of her own volition. After tonight, she would have no blood to give. My heart sunk at the thought of the waste, but I did as I was bid and crept through the shadows back into the shelter of the forest, cradling the girl in my arms.

I set the sleeping girl on a slab of cold stone and placed my hands on the smooth rock to warm it.

"What are you doing?" my priestess said from behind me.

I turned to see the half sardonic smile on her face by the light of a torch. "Warming her, as I used to do for you," I said, reminding my priestess of the nights when she slept in the forest with me.

"You are a demon. Have you gone soft with age?" she asked.

"I am young yet for my kind."

Her eyes blazed with sudden anger, but her attention shifted as the girl stirred.

"Ceinwen?" The girl's voice was full of sleep. "What are we doing here?"

"You stupid girl! I told you never to call me that." My priestess turned to the girl and bent to whisper a stream of angry words that I could not make out. It didn't matter. What she said was of little concern to me. What mattered was the gift of knowledge that the girl had unwittingly given to me.

So, Ceinwen was my priestess's name. Never in all our years together did we exchange our true names. We'd kept those words of power to ourselves, though more than once she had tried to winkle mine from me, and now I knew hers. I was drunk on the power of knowing my priestess's true name.

"It's time, demon," Ceinwen said.

My priestess bound the girl to the stone. I bowed my head and waited. Everything went still all around us, and the night air quivered with anticipation of building magic. My priestess stood over the girl, facing the depths of the forest. The ceremonial blade flashed in her hand, drawing a crimson line across her daughter's palm. Blood dripped onto the stone. I tasted the sweet vibrancy of it. Any blood that fell on those stones was mine by right, and I savored each drop.

I watched as the magic around my priestess grew, and the deathly silence of the forest thundered in my ears. A forest should never be truly silent. Whatever she was summoning, it was something against all the laws of nature.

"Ceinwen, stop," I said, invoking her name for the first time. I reached out and pulled her away from the girl. I was surprised by how small her body felt in my arms. She weighed little more than the girl.

"What are you doing?" she demanded, fighting my embrace.

"This magic is folly; you mustn't invoke it. It's not worth the cost," I said, calling upon her reason.

"The cost? What do I care for a child of ritual consummation given away at birth to become yet another useless novice?" Her voice was full of venom, eyes wide and polluted with madness.

"You would destroy much more than her life," I said. "The magic that you planned to summon goes against nature. Against me. You would break the bond that has connected us for so many years."

"What do I care?" Her words cut deeper than ever before. "You never intended to uphold your side of our bargain," she spat at me.

"I did everything I could, you know I did," I said.

"I rue the day that I ever bound you to my service." She spoke so softly it was little more than a whisper. "I squandered my youth on your unfulfilled promises."

I looked down at the woman I held in my grasp, but no matter how hard I tried, I could no longer find any trace of the girl whom I'd loved and who had once claimed to love me. It was then I knew that I never wanted to taste her blood again. She truly was no longer the girl I had bonded myself to so many years ago, and there was nothing I could do to bring her back to me.

I closed my eyes to block out this dreadful night. My chest ached with the loss. I wanted to plead to my mother for help, but I knew she would not heed my words after acting on the new moon. Instead, I called upon any magic that would come to me.

The woman shrieked curses into the sky. Her words were nothing more than a vain attempt to hurt me. She had chosen her fate long ago.

"Be still, Ceinwen," I said, invoking her name for a second time.

In the next instant, I felt her flesh and bones harden beneath my fingers and then, at last, grow cold.

I opened my eyes and looked down on the one whom I had called 'my priestess' for so long. She was gone. A pillar of cold stone stood in her place. My hands dropped to my sides, and when they did, the red ribbons Ceinwen had bestowed on me as a sign of our bonding slipped from around my forearms in a heap to the forest floor.

I turned away from the pillar and saw the girl still tied to the stone slab, trembling with fear and cold. But there was something else I saw, too: a chance to start anew. But this time it would be different.

"I will not harm you," I said in my most gentle voice, and when I leaned down to cut her bonds, she did not flinch away from me.

"Th-thank you," she said, rubbing her wrists where the ropes had chafed them.

"What is your name?"

"Rhian," she said.

She should have known better than to give me her true

name, but then again, she should have known better than to say my old priestess' name too.

She held her arms close to her, the blood from her palm leaching into her white shift, dying it red.

"I could heal your wound," I said, gesturing toward her hand.

"You can?" she asked.

I nodded.

She hesitated for a moment, then held out her hand to me. I cradled it in my own, and slowly, ever so slowly, I closed the wound with a lick of my tongue. Her blood was even more satisfying than when I'd tasted it through the stones. Everything was when freely given.

She looked up at me, wide-eyed and full of wonder. She looked so much like her mother had. And, despite myself, my chest ached again.

"Stay awhile," I offered. "I will keep you safe and warm."

Slowly she nodded her acquiescence.

A smile touched my lips as I wrapped my arms around her and drew warmth into the stones beneath her. When at last she slept, the foul magic her mother attempted to bring into the world receded, and the song of the creatures of the forest returned.

For three nights, she stayed with me, and I showed her the secrets of the forest until a waxing crescent hung in the night sky as sharp as a knife.

"Rhian, my child," I said, picking up the red ribbons that had for so long encircled my arms from the forest floor. I cut two segments of the ribbon and wrapped them gently around the girl's forearms.

"I am of the moon," I told her. "And by the moon, I bind you."

* * *

Mika Grimmer is a queer and neurodivergent author of fantasy short stories and novels of various flavors. She graduated from the University of Washington with a bachelor's degree in interdisciplinary studies with a concentration in culture, literature, and the arts in 2008. She is also a member of the twice-postponed 2020 Taos Toolbox cohort that finally took place in the summer of 2022. Mika lives with her husband in Seattle, Washington, and when she isn't writing, she is likely throwing pottery, knitting, or participating amateur sumo.

THE SERPENT QUEEN

BY FREYA BELL

*V*iolet wiped sea spray from her face without looking away from the sea serpent undulating under the prow of her ship. The fearsome beast was twice the length of her vessel, blue scales reflecting shards of weak sunlight back into her eyes. Fog roiled around the serpent, making it difficult to track, and she snarled.

"More sails!" Violet hollered, and Sally hesitated only a moment before repeating the call. The broad woman turned to the three sailors scrambling among the sails.

"More sails, ye water-loving snails. More speed!" Sally's voice roared over the flapping of the sailcloth and waves.

"Captain, there's no sail left!" said Newman from the rigging.

Violet snarled again and looked back over her shoulder. Sure enough, every scrap of cloth on the ship was strung up, the off-white fabric a bellyful of wind.

"The cargo," Violet shouted at Sally. "Throw it overboard."

Sally's lips tightened, and she shook her head. "You can't."

Violet scowled. "Am I captain or not?"

Sally looked away. "I can't watch you throw away your money like that! Your father—"

"Is dead, and now you are *my* second. Not his. Are you not?"

Sally flinched. "The serpent isn't worth it."

Violet flung an arm out and pointed at the serpent. "You heard what Captain Amore said: There's a bounty of a thousand crowns on this beast's head. Not to mention the fame it would bring."

"Damn the fame. Some of us have families. We need the money."

"I'll see you paid, Sally. I promise. But we need this serpent. *I* need this serpent."

Sally sighed and wiped a hand over her face. "This better work."

Violet brightened and turned back to the serpent. "It will. Trust me."

Behind her came the splashes of bales of cloth meeting the ocean, and she repressed a flinch lest Sally see it. But it worked, the distance between her and the serpent shortening. She pushed herself off the railing.

"Harpooners at the ready! Miss Netley, bring us alongside the beast!"

The nose of the ship swung to the left, and Violet hurried portside, where Irwin and Denny were loading a harpoon into a cannon. Denny carefully poured the gunpowder under Irwin's watchful eye, ignoring Violet's approach.

"Irwin," said Violet. "Aim for the eye. It's twice as big as a dinner plate—you shouldn't miss."

Irwin's salt-roughened face cracked into a smile. "Don't worry captain, me and Denny got this covered."

Violet nodded and watched Irwin line up the shot. The serpent was just below the surface, its silver eyes staring wide as it forged through the waves. Her hand tightened on the hilt of her sword, and her breath caught in her throat.

Denny lit a match and, at Irwin's nod, set it to the wick. The fuse lit, shooting white sparks, and a moment later the cannon boomed.

With reflexes faster than a cat's, the serpent twisted in the water, the barbed hook of the harpoon setting into the meat of its neck.

A piercing cry made Violet clap her hands to her ears, the mournful tone tugging at her heart. Beautiful as it was, it was hard not to sympathize. But no. This beast had sunk more than a dozen ships in the Strait of Anteros. It had to die.

The serpent hauled to the right and the ship went with it, listing hard to the side. The bolts holding the harpoon to the deck groaned, and Irwin threw his weight onto it. The serpent put on a burst of speed, and Violet slammed into the railing, breath leaving her in a rush.

Newman shouted from the rigging, pointing through the clearing fog. Waves foamed up on a rapidly approaching shoreline, little more than a sliver of sand in the mist.

"Land!" Violet croaked, and Miss Netley hauled on the ship's wheel, trying to pull the beast away from the sand, but it made no difference. The serpent shimmied onto the sand, pulling the ship along with it.

The ship crashed into the atoll, boards splintering as they ran aground. Violet flew over the railing at the impact and landed in the water just before the serpent. It coiled in on itself and, with its flexible neck, reached around and bit at the harpoon in vain. Its teeth were unable to find purchase on the wood and steel.

The serpent swung its great head around, salt water and spit dripping from its clear fangs, and screeched at her. Violet clapped her hands over her ears and scrambled to her feet.

The cry faded over the waves, leaving Violet and the beast to stare at each other.

Violet drew her sword from its sheath and pointed the tip at the serpent's nose.

"I have you now, you evil thing. Prepare to die."

"Die?" said the serpent, her voice sibilant. "What did I do to deserve such a fate?"

Violet jumped and dropped her sword in the surf. "You can talk?"

The serpent gazed down her snout at Violet. "Of course I can talk. I'm a dragon. Now, leave before I summon a storm and drown you all."

Violet looked over her shoulder at her grounded ship. The front was caved in and was taking in water at an appalling rate, and the mast leaned at an awkward angle. She turned back to face the sea dragon.

"Thanks to you, we won't be going anywhere. You wrecked my ship!"

"Me? You are the one who gave chase and *shot* me," the serpent said, baring her teeth.

"You're a sea serpent! Or a dragon—whatever. You've been sinking ships! Killing you will cement my name in history!" Violet dipped to grab her sword, but a rogue wave washed over the stern, causing her to stumble. She scrambled to her feet and scowled.

"Only the ones that got too close to my island. It's only fair."

Violet crossed her arms. "If you can talk, why didn't you try reasoning with them?"

The serpent gave her a withering look. "You humans have a tendency to shoot first. I hardly had the chance."

"I've got my eye on her, Captain," shouted Miss Netley from the ship's listing deck. The weapons master had a musket to her shoulder, and her teeth were bared.

"See what I mean?" said the serpent.

Violet reluctantly nodded. She raised an arm and lowered it.

"Stand down, Miss Netley. I've got this under control."

"Do you?" The serpent wove her head back and forth, the chain on the harpoon jingling. "Even with this harpoon in my neck, I can end you. Why, with my magic ..."

Violet's scowl redoubled. "You're bluffing. If you could summon a storm, you would have done so already."

A hint of panic seeped into the serpent's eyes. "I summoned the fog."

"A fat lot of good it did you. Once you pull that harpoon out, you'll bleed to death. As far as I see it, we're both dead."

The serpent hissed, the blue scales of her body rasping together as she shifted.

"Watch your tongue, human. You are speaking to a daughter of the king of dragons."

Violet fished her sword out of the surf and wiped it on her sleeve before sheathing it.

"Apologies for not being impressed. I, myself, am the daughter of the pirate king, but you don't see me expectin' everyone to bow and scrape."

The serpent looked frustrated. "Are you going to kill me or not?"

Violet hesitated. "I've never actually killed in cold blood before."

The serpent gathered her height and loomed over Violet. Violet stiffened her spine and glared.

"Allow me to propose this," said the serpent, lowering her head onto her scales. "Let me live, bandage my wounds, and I will give you the name you seek."

Violet shook her head. "What can you give me that would get me off this slip of sand? Look at my ship! I can bandage you, but unless you're sitting on a ship, I'm pretty sure my crew and I are dead."

"Not necessarily." She turned her head and the fog behind her boiled and swirled. Bright beams of sunlight pierced the cloud, and the fog parted, revealing a mountain island covered in an ancient forest.

When the serpent turned back, she looked smug. "On my island I have many treasures. I grant you permission to take trees from my island to repair your ship, fruit and water for yourself and your crew, and you may choose one treasure to take as proof of my 'death.' Then you will have the fame you crave."

Violet chewed on her bottom lip. "You'll have to stop attacking ships. Find a new home, maybe." After a moment's hesitation, the serpent nodded carefully. "Alright," Violet said, thrusting out her hand on reflex. The serpent stared at her, and she withdrew it. "My name's Violet. What do I call you?"

"You may call me serpent. My name is not for one such as you." She paused, and when Violet didn't react, she frowned. "As I said, I am the daughter of the dragon king."

Violet snorted. "Well, I've never heard of you. So you can't be one of the famous ones."

Sally clapped a hand on Violet's shoulder, and Violet jumped.

"Everything alright?" asked Sally.

Violet clutched at her chest. "How many times must I *tell you*—"

"Yes, captain, of course captain. Now, will you please explain why you are standing here chatting when we should be killing?"

Violet drew herself to her full height, which was barely enough to come to Sally's collarbone. "I negotiated a deal." Behind her, the serpent rolled her eyes. "The serpent requires medical attention. Fetch the supplies." Violet leaned around

Sally and shouted up to the rest of the crew lining the deck, muskets and swords in hand.

"Stow your weapons. Irwin, Denny, go gather firewood and start a nice campfire here on the beach. Newman, help Sally remove the harpoon from the beast, and do as she says to help patch her up. Miss Netley, you and I are going to pull supplies out of the hold as best we can and haul them up the beach. Understood?"

"Understood, Captain!" a chorus of voices replied.

An hour later, an exhausted sea serpent was curled up beside a roaring fire, her neck heavily bandaged. A markshift camp had been set up above the tideline, and Violet sat under a sheet of sailcloth beside Miss Netley, sorting out the supplies recovered from the ship.

"Alright, so if we supplement with fishing and foraging, I say we have about a month's worth of supplies. Serpent says there's fresh water, but I still want to scout the island in the morning for ourselves," said Violet, winding a piece of rope.

"I'll get the rain catchers set up; those clouds are looking mighty wet," said Miss Netley. The navigator jutted her chin to the sky. "Makes for a pretty sunset, though."

Violet followed the direction of Miss Netley's gaze. Billowing clouds to the west were painted vivid pink, their underbellies staining to deep purple. The wind stirred their scrap of sailcloth, and Violet frowned.

"Sally," she shouted towards the beached ship. "Rain's moving in. Bring more sailcloth!"

The crew spent the night huddled under sailcloth strung between the palms, feeding driftwood to a small fire. Morning was a long time coming, the weak beams of sunlight peeking over the edge of the world to assault Violet's eyelids.

The pirate captain woke suddenly and groaned, her back complaining. She pushed herself off the crate she had fallen asleep against and looked around.

Her crew slept soundly in the predawn light, their sea-roughened faces at peace. Not wanting to wake them, she picked her way over them and emerged out onto the beach.

The serpent still slept as well, bandaged neck resting on a coil of rope. Violet eyed her, but the beast was oblivious to the world, and she heaved a sigh of relief.

Treasure.

The word seeped up from her subconscious, tickled by the sight of the sea serpent. The serpent had promised one treasure. It had to be somewhere on the island. Her gaze went to the treeline, where a thick jungle climbed the sides of a hill. No time like the present to look.

Leaving her crew to sleep, Violet packed a waterskin and some hardtack into a sack and tied it to her belt before adjusting her sword on her hip. With some luck, she could find the treasure and be back in time to get started on repairing the ship.

The ship. Violet walked through the surf to where the shattered hull rested on the sand. They'd need a tall, straight tree for a new mast, and at least a half dozen trees to make into planks. Not to mention the scaffolding needed to hoist the ship into position so they could replace the boards.

What a nightmare. But there was no choice. The sea serpent's wrath protecting this island meant few sailed this way anymore, afraid of being sunk. There was a king's ransom on her head, not to mention the fame.

Violet sighed and began the march up the beach to the forest. The fame would be a wooden victory, a falsehood. Just because she was too big of a softy to kill in cold blood. Some pirate she was. At least the reward money from the serpent's bounty would be there to catch her tears.

The serpent promised them enough treasure to set them up for life. With the money she could buy a bigger, better ship with a bigger crew. And then she'd really be able to make a name for herself.

She daydreamed about the look on the other captains' faces as she'd sail up on a galleon with a hold full of treasure. The barmaids would fall over her, and she'd have her pick of the ladies.

So occupied was she that the climb up the hill was an afterthought, lungs heaving as she imagined what she'd call herself. The Redhaired Devil had a nice ring.

Sunlight pierced the canopy, and the path opened up before her. Violet caught herself on a tree, foot hovering over open air. The hill disappeared, and below her was an eroded sea cave, the rocks slowly being eaten away by beating waves.

Violet flung herself backwards with a gasp, landing on her behind and scrambling away from the edge. Heart pounding, she slowly moved onto her stomach and crawled toward the edge of the precipice, looking over it.

She gulped. It was a long way down. Waves pounded through a narrow channel carved into the grey rock and disappeared into darkness. But just enough sunlight penetrated the depths below her for her to see the glint of gold.

Among the rocks at the entrance to the cave were coins, just strewn about without a care. It was enough to make up her mind. She had to get down there. The serpent wasn't lying: she did have treasure on this island.

Violet surveyed the hill. If she were careful, she would be able to shimmy down the rocks and reach the cave entrance. She'd need rope, though. Reluctantly, she pulled back from the edge and turned back towards camp.

* * *

Sally ran up as soon as Violet emerged from the trees.

"Vi-Captain! Where have you been?"

Violet winked. "Just scouting the island." She looked down the beach, where the serpent watched her. "I didn't find much of interest. Just trees, trees, trees."

The serpent lay her head back on the rope, and Violet heaved a sigh of relief. Sally gave her an odd look, and Violet tapped on the side of her nose, grinning. She strolled towards the serpent.

"Well, my friend, I think it's about time we talk about treasure."

The serpent stirred. "Now? But your ship is still damaged. You cannot eat gold."

"Yes, but I'd rather secure my payment before you heal— no offense."

"No offense? You accuse me of backing out of our agreement."

Violet held up her hands consolingly. "I'm sure you'll hold true. Chalk it up to human impatience if you like. Now, the treasure?"

The serpent sighed and uncoiled her length, heading up the beach in the opposite direction Violet had come from.

Violet motioned for Sally to come with her, and they followed the serpent into the trees.

The serpent led them a short way, to a clearing with a pile of rocks in the center. She knocked them away with her nose, revealing a battered chest with a flat lid.

"Here we are," the serpent said, coiling in on herself. "My treasure. Since I am feeling generous, and acknowledge the medical aid, I have chosen to give you the entire chest."

Violet flung the chest open. Inside was a small pile of gold, silver, and precious stones, along with a handful of jewelry. It wasn't even enough to half fill the chest. She settled back on her heels.

"This is it?"

The serpent gave an indignant snort. "Pardon me? I'll bet you've never seen such wealth in your life!"

Violet gave the serpent a withering glare. "I am the daughter of the pirate king. I drank from golden bowls and slept on the finest silks. Calling this treasure is an insult."

"Insult!" The serpent tried to rear up, but flinched and settled back on the forest floor. "You insult me by insulting my hoard."

"Hoard!" Violet barked a laugh. "Sally, come on. Let's leave the little worm to her coins."

The serpent hissed, but Violet ignored her and strode back toward camp. By the time she reached the outskirts of the forest, Sally caught up with her.

"What gives, Captain? It's not much, but it would more than replace what we threw overboard. We may not live like kings, but——"

"Oh, we aren't done here," Violet said with a wink. "She claims to be the daughter of the king of the ocean. There's no way that's all the treasure she has. Think of all the ships she's sank! There's a reason there's a bounty on her head."

Miss Netley saluted as Violet stormed into camp.

"How'd it go, Captain?"

Violet wrinkled her nose. "I've seen more jewels on a lady of the night. The serpent's holding out on us."

Sally gave Violet a considering look. "You think so?"

"Call it a hunch. Sally, find me a length of rope and a torch. There's a cave I want to explore."

"I'll come with you," said the taller woman.

"No, thank you, Sally. I need you here to distract the serpent when she comes back. I don't know how long I'll be gone."

Sally handed a coil of rope to Violet, and she strung it over a shoulder. Miss Netley passed over a torch, and Violet nodded.

"Continue repairs on the ship. I'll be back as soon as I can."

* * *

One sweaty hour later, Violet stood at the entrance to the cave. The waves created a rhythm she could feel through her feet, but the dangers of tides and slippery rocks were at the back of her mind with the scent of gold in her nose.

A trail of scattered coins led further into the massive cave, and she picked them up as she went deeper, until her pockets rang with the sweet clink of metal on metal. The sun only pierced the darkness for so long, and it took time for her eyes to adjust to the murk.

She picked her way carefully along a path that took her alongside a deep channel of water. This wasn't a large island, and based on her calculations, the cave had to have hollowed most of it out, leaving a shell of rock.

It was difficult not to imagine the massive weight above her, just waiting to come crashing down. But the gold kept her spirit high, and she continued to follow her breadcrumb trail of coins into the darkness.

When it became too dark to see, she lit her torch. The light transformed the cave. Stalactites dripped overhead, and stalagmites rose to meet them, glistening in the orange light of her fire. It was beautiful, in an eerie way, like a gleaming gold-toothed maw about to close around her. But Violet had treasure to find, and standing around wasn't doing her any good.

The deeper she went, the cooler it got, but the passage

didn't narrow. It grew wider, the ceiling of the cave taller than the tallest mast. There was light ahead, and when she turned the corner, she stopped in her tracks.

Before her was a treasure chamber beyond imagination. Gold and silver coins spilled from crates, forming gleaming rivers that snaked through the cave. Precious gems of every colour and size were strewn across the floor, their facets catching the torch light and sending sparkles dancing across the walls. Ornate goblets, intricately carved figurines, and ancient artifacts were displayed on natural stone shelves, each item seeming to carry its own story.

She picked her way through piles of gold and silver, her boots crunching on uncut gems, her mind whirling. What did one take from a dragon's hoard?

There was an ornate sword, a jewel encrusted crown, a silver chalice, even a pile of golden chains and bracelets.

But the centerpiece of this wondrous collection was a ship moored at an ancient dock, its grandeur and opulence unmatched. Its hull was painted a deep, rich black, adorned with gold trim that caught the light and seemed to set the ship ablaze. The sails were made of the finest silk, embroidered with intricate designs that told tales of far-off lands and daring adventures.

Violet's gaze was drawn to an old wooden dock that extended from the cavern's edge, the worn planks creaking softly in the waves. The ship was tethered to the dock by ropes as ancient as time itself, the knots expertly tied as if they had been waiting for her arrival. It exuded an air of regal authority, a king among vessels, ruling over this hidden realm of treasure and secrets.

She sat with a thump, torch falling from her hand. It sputtered on the damp stone but didn't go out. So much treasure. More gold than she had seen in her lifetime. And the ship.

That ship was hers.

She knew it from the bottom of her soul. Her luck had finally turned; she was rich.

No, the sea serpent was rich. This all belonged to the creature, and Violet had permission to take just one treasure. The ship was a treasure, right?

Violet approached the ancient, wooden dock with caution, testing each block before putting her weight on it. But it was well constructed and offered up only a soft creak to compete with the gentle waves lapping against its supports.

The ship loomed in her view, a rope ladder hanging down the lacquered side. She pulled herself up, the ship so steady that she barely felt the pulse of the waves.

She stepped onto the deck and looked around, the hairs on the back of her neck rising. There was something strange about this place.

As a sailor, ships were her life. She had been aboard ships from the dingiest merchant vessels to the grandest of the royal navy. Granted, the latter wasn't as a willing passenger, though it had set the standard by which all other ships were measured. But this ship was different.

The deck was flawless, not a board out of place, no sign of wear or weathering. No rope was frayed, no metal loose, no wood rotting.

A chill crept up her spine and she drew her sword. There was something on this ship, she was sure of it.

Violet stepped forward and paused. There was something under the silence, a song or music. She followed the gang-plank into the ship. The sound grew louder the closer she got to the captain's quarters.

The door was shut tight, the dark wood stained and polished. It looked new, but the door was locked. A quick search didn't reveal a keyhole. She tried to slide her sword between the door and the jam, but there was no gap.

With a scowl, Violet backed up and threw her shoulder against the door. She bounced off, landing on her rear, pain blossoming in it and her shoulder.

She hissed, rubbing the abused limb, and stared at the door. Something was behind that door, and she was going to get in. Violet stood and kicked the door, leaving a scuff on the perfect wood. She snarled and kicked again, the pain in her toes radiating up her leg. She backed up again and ran at the door, throwing her whole weight into the blow.

It opened easily, letting her fly into the cabin. The air left her lungs in a rush as she slammed into the carpeted floor, her sword skittering across the boards.

Her breath came in gasps as she looked around the room. It was an opulent suite, the floor covered in plush red carpet, the walls lined with bookshelves, a four poster bed, a desk, and a couch arranged in a sitting area.

But that wasn't what drew her eye. In the bed was a skeleton, dressed in the rags of a captain, with a glowing orb in a bony hand. The faint music came from the orb, and Violet approached it cautiously.

She snatched the orb from the skeletal grip, and the music stopped, a single word filling her mind.

The knowledge of what she had found made her gasp. Violet tucked the orb into her pocket and hurried out of the cabin. She needed to get back to her crew, now.

* * *

Sally trotted up to her as soon as Violet breached the trees.

"She's been asking where you are," said the second mate in a low voice, falling into step beside Violet.

The serpent was coiled up on the beach, watching Newman and Irwin building a scaffold to pull the ship up onto for repairs. Violet eyed her ship dismissively. It was a piece of junk compared to what she had found.

"Have you come back to claim your treasure?" asked the serpent as Violet approached. The battered wooden chest lay in the sand near her coiled body.

"You might say that," Violet said, hand straying towards her coat pocket. "You aren't a very good liar, you know."

The serpent glared at her. "What on earth are you talking about?"

"I went for a little walk, you see. Your offer of treasure was generous, of course, but I knew you were hiding something. And I found it." She paused for dramatic effect and to savour the moment. "I found your hoard. Your *real* hoard."

Hissing, the serpent tried to rise to a threatening posture, but her neck injury and blood loss kept her low. "We made a deal. One treasure and supplies for you, your crew, and your ship in exchange for my life. Are you breaking your word, human?"

Violet would have been offended, but she was still giddy with her prize. She pulled the orb from her pocket, and the serpent reared up, fangs bared for a moment though it obviously pained her.

"Return that immediately!"

Violet smiled and held the orb aloft.

"Silence, Nimaea. And lie down before you open your wound again."

The serpent obeyed, eyes going wide.

Violet was trembling just a little. She'd been right. "This is the real reason you didn't want to give me your name. Isn't it?"

Nimaea gave a single, sharp nod.

"And now that I know it, you are bound to obey me, is that not correct?"

Another nod.

"Good. You are my prisoner, and will be until I release you. You will not harm me, nor my crew, nor the ship. You will no longer attack other ships, unless on my command. Do you understand?"

"Yes, mistress," said Nimaea, her voice furious.

Violet tucked the orb back into her pocket.

"You are mine." Violet grinned and motioned for Sally and Miss Netlsey to collect the chest. "No point in wasting this. Come, we've got work to do."

"You can't do this," hissed Nimaea, and Violet crossed her arms.

"Not my fault you didn't secure your treasure very well. Don't you royal dragons normally have undersea caves for this sort of thing?"

Nimaea's scales rattled and she looked away. "I ... no longer have access to the royal caves."

The sadness in Nimaea's voice made Violet pause. Several things came together in her mind: Nimaea's predation of the shipping routes, her isolation on this island, her inability to claim her birthright as a royal dragon.

"You're an outcast, aren't you?" said Violet in a quiet voice.

Nimaea hung her head. "It was a mistake. A young, foolish mistake any dragon could make, but father— It doesn't matter. It's in the past."

Violet chewed on her bottom lip. She knew what it felt like to be an outcast. As the only daughter of the last pirate king, she was picked on and ridiculed. No one thought she could live up to her father's legend. But perhaps there was another way. The orb was cool in her hand as she palmed it in her pocket.

"How do you feel about another deal?"

Nimaea's head jerked up, her eyes narrowed. "What did you have in mind?"

Violet drew the orb from her pocket, and Nimaea's eyes burned as she followed it.

"I'm giving you a chance, serpent. I can understand trying to trick us with your treasure. It's what any pirate would do. So ... maybe you would like to be one?"

Nimaea looked at her blankly.

"Join the crew," Violet said, tossing the orb to her other hand. "Become one of us. Prove your trustworthiness."

"Captain, really!" said Sally, and Violet held up a restraining hand.

"I propose this: Become a member of my crew, and once I trust you, I'll give you your name back. Until then, you work like any of us."

Nimaea shook her head. "What would I do? I am a serpent."

Violet's grin revealed a gold tooth. "I can think of a dozen good uses for your ability to raise a fog. What do you say?"

Nimaea met her eyes for a long moment before looking back to the orb. She took a deep breath.

"Alright. I'll join your crew."

* * *

*V*iolet led her crew into the cave, Nimaea following in the water. Her chest nearly burst as the ship came into view again. It was perfect, and it was hers.

The next three days were spent hauling the supplies from her ruined ship to the hold of her new ship. Miss Netley carefully painted over the old name, and once the treasure was on board, Violet prepared a bottle of wine.

She gathered everyone on the old dock and held the wine bottle aloft by its neck.

"Thank you for all of your hard work, everyone. Thanks to Nimaea's treasure, we are now each as wealthy as kings.

You are welcome to leave and purchase your own ships, to become captains in your own right. Or you are welcome to stay on board with me, as part of the wealthiest pirate crew to ever sail the seas."

Denny and Irwin cheered, joined by Miss Netley. "We're with you!"

Violet turned to Sally. "Sally? I completely understand if you want to leave, as I'm nothing like my father."

Sally sniffled. "I know, kid. That's why I like you. I'm just so proud of you."

Violet turned sharply, lest Sally's tears infect her as well, and raised the wine bottle.

"I hereby name our ship the Serpent Queen!" She smashed the wine bottle against the hull, and her crew cheered.

Violet joined in the cheer. Nimaea slipped into the sea as Violet scrambled onboard The Serpent Queen. Denny cast them off, and Irwin scrambled into the sails. Miss Netley took her place at the helm, and Sally joined her at the bow.

"We're ready, Captain!" said Sally in her booming voice.

Violet drew her sword. "Cast off! The Serpent Queen sails for the high seas!"

The ship emerged from the cave, sails billowing, and Nimaea trailed in her wake.

* * *

Freya Bell is a Canadian speculative fiction and romance author, hailing from British Columbia. She has a dog, Thorn, and a cat, Rosie, who do their best to interrupt her writing whenever possible. Writing is her world, and she hopes to one day make a living from it.

HER NAME UPON THEIR LIPS

BY KATHRYN REILLY

The battered knight stood resigned to his fate: helmet crushed, sword bent beyond use, and armor rent by talons, signifying the battle he'd waged and lost. He'd landed several well-placed blows, blood matting the fur across the creature's abdomen, turning white fur pink, and several large scales from its arms now lay across the uneven stone floor. The scent of copper saturated the air, and blood pooled in his boots as he swayed, his last thoughts on his failure and how now, he'd never marry the princess. As the creature's final fury rained down upon him, a cloven hoof breaking his femur, he wondered if she would consume the armor or remove his shell as he did when he ate the crustaceans fished from the rivers. He looked straight into sorrowful eyes, tri-colored and gold crackled like the small frogs that sung the summers down, and saw his sunset within them. The knight released a shuddering breath, and it stepped away; he realized the creature had only attacked after he'd advanced. He whispered, "My apologies, I did not know," and died.

* * *

hen the latest knight did not return, Princess Saige sighed in relief. Of course she was saddened by his likely demise, but she wholly resented her father, the King, using her as a bargaining chip. Several years ago, he'd sent heralds to the five closest kingdoms, ordering pages to post notices on nearly every tree and light post in the kingdom declaring her hand in marriage to the man that slayed the beast. He'd had the palace mages enchant the papers so they sung sweetly of her virtues in her very own voice. Men were enchanted, some literally, to accept the quest, and she resented the whole affair greatly. Three years later and dozens dead, she remained unwed. She had rather liked the last knight; older than the rest, he'd engaged her in conversation and seemed genuinely interested in her thoughts and interests. Yet he too perished. She hoped, for his sake, that his death was quick and painless. But after three relent-less years of the beast defending itself, she imagined it might have been quite the opposite. Closing her eyes, she imagined bones littering its lair, blood-splattered armor askew.

Walking aimlessly through the gardens, she pondered her fate. In the beginning, three of the kingdom's most experi-enced mages descended upon the beast, learning to their peril it seemed impervious to fire or ice or any magic, really. The lone survivor of the trio had noted as much as he limped home, stinking of death, and declared the beast to be unslayable in his last, wheezing breath. Thus, the king began sending knights to the beast's cave, one after another failing to kill it—not that any of them knew what to expect, as no one in the kingdom had ever seen it in the first place. The common people declared it a dragon, others a minotaur, others a remnant or some wild amalgamation of evil.

Guilt settled lightly upon the princess's soul. While she had not offered her hand in marriage, being offered as the prize encouraged many to risk their lives. For who would not wish to eventually be king, surrounded by servants, whims and desires granted, wielding great power? Still, none of those men thought about the daily minutiae, settling commoners' disputes, worrying about food stores or neighboring kingdom's invasions. Even as other kings declared friendship, greed rode every man's mind, whispering the importance of more: more land, more gold, more power, more fear, more adoration. Standing before the reflection pool, gaze traveling between floating flowers releasing the scent of sweet rains, she resolved that enough was enough.

"This problem is mine alone to solve," she declared quietly to no one save the world itself and, turning, returned to the castle to saddle her least favorite horse.

* * *

She arrived at the cave, wishing the beast lived a bit closer to the kingdom instead of on its borders. Dust-covered and travel-sore, she dismounted and led her horse into the mountain's crevice. Uncorking tart yable wine, she sated her thirst, allowing its warmth to ease into tired muscles. Her plan was simple: she would treat the beast as an equal—everything else had failed.

"Hello?" she called. The horse shifted side to side, snorting its disapproval.

Not detritus, the princess thought. *That smell in the gardens as the plants break down helped with the gardeners' hands. This smells more of animal, of the butcher's alley where the discards reside until farmers collect them for slop.* Walking farther in the cave, the darkness encroached, and she squinted to make use of the remaining light. Navigating slowly into the darkness, her foot knocked into something that rattled. Instinctively, she bent to ascertain the object, and her hand closed upon something hard, coated in a gelatinous mess. Feeling her way about the cave's litter, she realized it was a rather large set of ribs just as a rumble echoed in the cave.

"Hello?" she called again, firming her voice, harnessing the authority her birthright bestowed upon her. A terrible scraping sound reverberated upon the stone walls, growing ever louder as the creature approached. *Scales*, the princess thought. *The beast must have many scales.*

Before her rose a creature she would never be able to describe. A terrible beauty radiated from it, and the princess immediately recognized a sadness she herself shared, one borne of life devoid of choice.

The creature stood silently watching, its patches of scales all along both arms seemingly shimmering, forcing the cave's darkness to recede. Several areas shone more brightly, and Saige realized some scales were missing. *Battle scars*, her mind whispered. Suddenly, she felt warm and couldn't decide if it was the berry wine or the light, warm like the sun. Though the light wasn't unpleasant, it did come with shadowy figures cast by rocks, stalagmites, and stalactites, as well as bits of the creature itself that seemed to grow taller and move of their own accord. She watched as the creature nodded to the shadows, and the shadows nodded back. But, always one to follow decorum no matter the circumstances, the princess curtsied deeply.

"I am Princess Saige, and I come to bargain." A silence stretched between the creature and the princess. Nevertheless, she would wait, fearless, for a reply. Moments ticked by and the princess itched to move, to shift her weight, to brush her hair back, but she stood resolute. She caught herself wishing she still wore her warm traveling cloak to stay the cave's cooler air, but it lay within her saddlepack and maintaining eye contact took priority right now. Suddenly, movement from behind the creature drew her attention to the spot just left of its tail. Slowly, a haret inched out, nose twitching, scenting. It hopped between the creature's feet and stopped, comfortable and unafraid, and that told the princess all she needed to know. Small creatures possessed an excellent sense of self-preservation, and this haret obviously felt no threat from the beast.

"I have heard such words before: before a sword was drawn, before a spell was cast, before my executioners gasped their last breath."

"Truly, regal creature, I come to bargain for both our sakes."

"To bargain or slay?"

"To bargain upon my word as a future queen."

"But you have no position yet?" the beast asked, reaching a claw down to scratch the haret under its small chin until a happy purring reverberated across the stone room. "Who will honor any bargain struck today? Your king? His council? The knights and wizards that trespass here? Will they agree to terms struck here?"

"I come to represent the interests of my people, and to stop the bloodshed between us."

"Princess, I have only defended myself against those who have come here from your father's kingdom. Does he pledge to cease sending men to slay me?"

This was, of course, tricky to answer. It was against the law to speak for the king unless he explicitly gave one permission to speak for him, and he certainly had not given his daughter, who did not sit upon the council or hold position as emissary, such permission. *Best to side-step this bit of quandary,* she thought. Taking a breath, she asked, "Do you have a name?"

"No."

Princess Saige raised her eyebrow. "You do not have a name or you will not share your name?"

"I have no name." The beast's inner light dimmed, darkening the cave, its shame hanging softly between them, sadness descending. Stretching upward, the haret snuggled the beast's leg and chittered comfortingly.

"But why?"

"To name something is to love it. I have not a name because I am not loved. The gods banished me here after my birth, unnamed. Here I remain."

Princess Saige did not know what to say to that, and so she wisely said nothing at all. The beast, quite comfortable with silence, simply stared at the princess. After several moments, the princess asked, "Why not name yourself?"

"It's not the same," the creature replied. "Names are a gift."

The princess thought of how her mother had chosen her name before she died, and she agreed; it was the only thing her mother had given to her: her name was precious.

"Would you like to eat my horse?"

"Your horse?" The great beast cocked its head, considering Saige for the first time. "But don't you value your horse?"

"He is my least favorite horse, and eating a meal together is a good way to begin any bargain—don't you agree? Typically I prefer smaller fare, more tender and with sauce preferably made from the golden larkberry, but the kingdom's cooks prepare horse at times and it can be a fine dish." The princess turned her back and began to gather some of the smaller stones strewn about the cave to create a circle to contain a cooking fire.

"You're not afraid of me," the beast spoke quietly, realizing that perhaps for the very first time, a creature that could talk and wield some power in the world, did not feel fear in its presence. It took a step towards Saige, finally intrigued with this girl who had arrived to bargain. Eventually, they worked together to move some of the larger stones into the circle. Saige marveled at the creature's form —a true amalgamation, a celebration, of woodland creatures.

"No, I'm not." Sage replied, now arranging kindling within the stone circle.

"And how will you return?"

"Will I return?"

The creature shrugged. "I suppose that depends upon you."

"Honestly, sometimes I do get in my own way, but I'd like to consider you a friend. Let's make that a tomorrow problem to solve," the princess said. "Right now, I'm a bit hungry. Thank you for helping me."

"Thank you for letting me assist. I do enjoy meat. Shall I dispatch the horse?" the creature asked, motioning to the equine with its sharp talons. The bright feathers along its nape seemed to rise in anticipation as the unsuspecting horse continued grazing on sweet grass just beyond the cave's boundaries.

"No thank you. As it is my horse, its death is my responsibility," the princess solemnly replied. "One should only take life with respect and reverence for such an act's purpose."

The princess approached her horse and, petting his neck, thanked him for his service and recalled several of their best rides. Then, drawing a short sword, she dispatched him efficiently and nearly without pain.

* * *

Stomachs full, the princess and the beast sat together.

"Shall we begin the bargain?" Princess Saige asked.

"I will listen."

"Feeding yourself from our shepherds' flocks must cease. And no eating people. We—"

"I don't eat people. Not enough meat to make it worthwhile. That's merely human fabrication."

"The knights?"

"I bury their bodies within the forest. I simply defended myself. My life may be lonely, but it is mine, and I defend it."

Princess Saige stared, too long to be polite, before beginning again.

"What if I promise to provide you with your preferred foodstuffs? And company so you will never be lonely. A garden filled with sweet fruits. My friendship. And a name."

"A name? But you are not a god."

"But royalty can bestow gifts: lands, castles, and most importantly titles, which are names—important names. And a name is a gift. But I must convince the kingdom I slayed the beast within these stone walls. I have a plan for after, a rather good one, but I must convince them you are dead. I need a head. A beastly head."

The creature stretched bat-like wings, nearly touching both sides of the cave, and lumbered towards the horse carcass, cloven hoofs echoing loudly with each clomp. With two talon swipes, the head severed from the limp neck. As if it weighed nothing, the creature deposited it upon the fire where the flank meat still slowly cooked. Smoke rose as the fur and meat burned off, until the bone shone. The creature removed it, holding it between talons larger than the princess's head, and hissed an incantation that Princess Saige wished she could hear but couldn't. Before her eyes the skull elongated, a multitude of horns protruding. The jaw became a maw with rows upon rows of sharpened teeth. Finally, fur and feathers sprouted everywhere, and viscera dangled from the stout neck.

"That is quite well done and doesn't resemble you in the slightest," Princess Saige complimented.

"Well, I believe that your kingdom will embrace this to be my likeness. Is it not fearsome, worthy of those the kingdom sent?"

"Truly, it is. The spiraling horns and many teeth will surely explain why so many knights failed to return to the kingdom. These are true creations, yes? They are not illusions?"

"They are true; you can touch them if you'd like."

"Yes, I will." Saige reached out her hands and ran them over the obsidian spiraled horns, smooth but etched with fine lines, similar to the patterns upon dragonfly wings. Opening the maw a bit wider, she touched the teeth, which drew blood effortlessly. Its coopery tang scented the air, and the creature's snout twitched.

"Very well done indeed! Your transformative magic is quite impressive. Creating the horse's head into this nightmare demonstrates great skill."

"Being god-born has some advantages here in the human realm, though I would much rather create things of beauty."

"Such as?" Saige inquired.

"Perhaps mountains shaped as clouds with chambers for many woodland creatures within. Sculpted rocks delicately portraying ant lions and butterflies and praying mantises, all creatures the world often overlooks, sprinkled throughout the countryside. I could weave tree branches into beautiful patterns, creating dappled light and playgrounds for blue jays and cardinals and wrens, squirrels and chipmunks. I can sing flowers and vines into being." The beast smiled.

"Parts of our kingdom are destroyed by war—burned to the ground, ravaged, strewn with bones. Could you bring the forests and meadows back?"

"I could. And streams as well."

Saige smiled. "Creation is so much better than destruction. I hope I can show you our entire realm one day. Could you perhaps transform me a horse to return home upon?"

"Apologies, Princess, but I cannot create heartbeats."

Standing before the talented beast, Princess Saige motioned towards the monstrous head bloodying the cave's floor. "I will need a litter to drag this head. I will take my leave in the morning and begin the long journey home."

"A sound plan then. I invite you to rest within the cave. If you would follow me, then." Turning, the beast lead the princess further into the cave. Relief sculptures decorated the smooth walls, capturing the most beautiful creatures, both real and imagined. Down, down they walked until they entered a large room with an underground brook babbling across the far wall and the softest, nearly purple moss along the floor. With a talon flick, soft light burned, illuminating the underground chamber.

Saige paused; the cave was actually quite nice. It would do. "Purple moss?"

The creature smiled, sharp, pearlescent teeth gleaming. "Yes! I enjoy adding just a bit of color to my creations."

For a moment, they both stood in silence, smiling.

"Thank you for not bringing violence into my home," the creature said.

"You are most welcome. If only the world outside could find common ground as we have."

"The gods' realm is no better, Saige," the beast sighed. "They cast me out for my differences, never seeing my strengths."

"I'm glad I came, great beast. After I set my plan in motion, I will return to uphold our bargain within a fort-night. You have my word."

"I hope so, Princess. I would very much like a friend."

"Would you mind assisting me in felling young saplings in

the morning? Your talons will make quick work of slicing them so that I might make the litter more quickly."

"I will assist. May we converse while we work? I enjoy speaking with you and I have many things to say." The beast stretched its wings before lying upon the moss and readying for sleep.

"Of course! I do enjoy conversing with you. Can we speak of the gods' realm tomorrow?

"I am willing to share a bit about their world, but I would like to speak of oceans—have you seen one?"

"I have! Amazing creatures live within them." Saige yawned. "Until tomorrow then."

"Until tomorrow."

* * *

After a night of good dreams, Saige woke to a slightly snoring hare whose breath lightly moved her hair on every exhale. Sitting up, she stretched and looking over at the beast and smiled, seeing a variety of woodland creatures snuggling with the beast whom the gods had cast out. A chorus of tweets and hisses and clicks and the lightest of snores accompanied the beast's impressive rumbles.

Rising, Saige walked out of the inner chamber and stoked the coals, readying for the day. Before long, all the small creatures scampered past her, scurrying into the forest to greet the day. The beast lumbered last, stretching as it moved. After a breakfast of slow-roasted equine, Saige stood and straightened her quite rumpled clothing.

"To the forest to fell the saplings, then?" she asked.

"I am happy to help." The beast paused briefly. "Do share, please, about the oceans."

"Yes! Of course! We often visit the vast body of water in the hottest months. It stretches to the horizon, blues of all hues, hosting life swimming and swirling beneath it. Many creatures have scales, like yours, but small and in all rainbows. Some can be eaten, some are deadly. Grasses undulate beneath the waters, and creatures with homes upon their backs crawl across the sandy floor. We should go, you and I, when I become Queen.

"I would like that, Saige, very much."

And so the two left the cave, human and creature, to work together.

* * *

Princess Saige approached her father's kingdom covered in filth and a good measure of blood. The journey home had taken eleven days on foot, and she'd had to catch and skin several rabbits along the way. With forethought, she'd taken their blood and soaked it into her skin, her clothes, and her hair to create the appearance of a fearsome battle. Standing before the iron gates, she demanded entry, declaring herself since her appearance was not very princess-like.

Through the uneven cobblestone streets she struggled, dragging the monstrous head behind her, past inns and smithies, past specialty stalls scenting the air with spices and leathers and fowls sans heads. The kingdom's people followed her, flowing from their shops and homes, joining together as streams form rivers. Her father, both furious and relieved, stood beside the king's chair upon the podium in the square's center. Tired, she knelt before him, waiting, her kingdom's people watching in shock.

"Rise daughter, and explain yourself."

"Father, I have slayed the beast, and bring this proof of my words. I ask that I be allowed the same prize offered to the knights who quested before me."

The King stilled. No girl in the history of the kingdom, or indeed any kingdom, had ever chosen her husband; this was a task fathers or brothers or uncles arranged. "You wish to select whom you will marry?"

"Yes. I have slain the beast and burned its body. I have returned victorious, saving the kingdom. I ask no other reward than that which your highness already promised to the conqueror of this great task."

"Very well," the king granted. "What you ask shall be given. Whose hand do you request in marriage?"

"My own. I will marry myself."

For the first time ever, no words came to the king. The crowd mirrored their king's silence, broken only by the chirps of tree-bound birds and squabbles of mongrels over forgotten lunches on benches and street stones. The princess continued.

"I will cherish and honor myself. I will lead the kingdom when it is my time. I will become Queen Saige, first of her name, and I will rule cleverly and courageously. I have proven that a princess can succeed where mages and knights fail. I have demonstrated my courage in confronting the kingdom's beast and, upon my ascension, I will continue to protect the realm."

A single feminine cheer rose from the crowd, and a chorus of daughters' and mothers' and wives' and aunts' celebratory voices rose until it became a roar with fathers and husbands and sons joining in until the king had no choice but to change his Kingdom's trajectory forever.

* * *

True to her word, Princess Saige arrived at the creature's cave within the fortnight. She brought with her a small band of brave, trustworthy women to meet the creature and keep it company, for Princess Saige planned on visiting monthly, but good friends existed as one's cornerstone of happiness. She had selected intelligent, adventurous women for the task, though they were also all orphans, either from war or disease or simply bad luck. With open minds, they could quell their own loneliness and the creature's. The princess confided in them she had discovered a magical being, likely a gift from the gods, that could change the kingdom's fortunes forever. What's more, the creature bore a bit of every woodland creature in tribute to the gods' creations: scales and a tail, fur and feathers, talons and skin, and—above all—wisdom. Everything, after all, is a matter of perspective, so the princess established a positive one. Of course, the promise of small cottages to be built forthwith where they could live independently, without need of marriage, sweetened their acceptance. Dismounting from her favorite horse, she helped the women unload an orchard's worth of fruit trees and bushes: apples and pears and berries and her very favorite, yables, which left one's lips purple and tongue tingling. She left the women to plant the orchards and entered the cave.

"Hello!" she called out once again.

"Return greetings to you," the creature called, leaving the darkness and moving towards the mouth of the cave. This close to the light, the creature's blue and green scales shimmered and even its white fur seemed to shine. Its three smallest shoulder horns slightly swayed as insects' antenna do in gentle breezes. Its six-taloned hands stilled at its sides, and cloven feet stood obscured by a long tail curled around them.

"True to my word, I have returned. I bring an orchard worthy of a kingdom's gardens for your sweetest tooth. I have brought a large number of both sheep and cows to roam about, multiply, and sate your hungers. Trusted women will stay here. Perhaps they will become future friends; you may discuss everything with them except our bargain. No one living knows what the beast in the cave looked like, as no mage or knight lived to tell any tales. Therefore, upon my return, I will say I discovered you in the forest, a creature sent to guard the kingdom, surrounded by beautiful light, and asked you to live within our realm to watch our lands far and wide. No violence will ever seek you out again. And, of course, I will visit you every month."

"And a name?" the creature asked.

Princess Saige strode confidently forward, withdrawing her sword. With a clear, commanding voice, she spoke:

"I, Princess Saige, future Queen, first ruler of her name, bestow upon thee the name Amata, Protector of the Realm and Regent of all Wild Lands. Amata means beloved, and you will be beloved by our people, beloved by the creatures, beloved by the very land itself. Will you rise, Amata, and serve the kingdom, friend to the future Queen?"

"I will."

The princess gently touched each shoulder and stepping back, smiled. "We will create a new realm together, Amata, where no one is ever cast aside or out."

With a dazzlingly toothy grin, Amata followed Princess Saige into the sun's light, leaving the cave's darkness behind forever.

* * *

The king ruled well for several more years, but eventually his health began to fail, and the kingdom crowned Queen Saige. Knowing how most people pushed against change, she introduced her ideas to the kingdom slowly, beginning by appointing three women to the traditionally male council. Over her lifetime, she provided a voice to all her subjects, and her realm flourished. Eventually, the fate of all mortals befell her, and Amata unleashed her magic to create a beautiful mausoleum in tribute to a true and loyal leader.

Carved into the outside of her tomb, it reads, "Here lies Queen Saige, first of her name; her name will be on her people's lips eternally." Birdfolk reverently hymn throughout the day and night, offering sweetest songs honoring the eternally resting Queen.

To this day, centuries after her passing, descendants of her kingdom's people invoke Queen Saige's name reverently. When those who sit within her grove, softest purple moss beneath them, will the world to quiet, the wind arrives with Saige's name. It is a name spoken through the centuries, strung together as a song. It is a blessing the wind bestows—a memory of each life she bettered. Amata lives still, guarding the kingdom, beloved by all who live there, and often tends the flowers growing ever-green beside her friend's grave.

* * *

By day, Kathryn helps students investigate words' power; by night, she resurrects goddesses and ghosts, spinning new speculative tales that sometimes share the truth. Enjoy poetry in Shadow Atlas, A Flight of Dragons, Last Girls Club, Paris Morning and fiction in Seaside Gothic, Diet Milk, Blink Ink, and Fish Gather to Listen. Her rescue mutts hear all the stories first and encourage readers to follow at @Katecanwrite or visit katecanwrite.com.

SOUL MUSIC

BY MJ PIELOOR

*E*llen ran an idle finger across the curve of the sphere, humming softly to herself. Despite her attention, the mottled grey surface remained dark, reflecting only the yellow light in her room.

'You're not much fun,' she said, pouting. She leaned back into her pillows and prodded the small sphere with her foot. She'd tried everything, but it still refused to sing.

She was sure it had been a good swap. But what if the stupid thing never sang for *her* and all she had was Jack's stupid itch in her chest?

She clicked her tongue and slid the crackly yellow pages from Grandpa Harry's book with the palm of her hand until she found Jack. She read through the poem again slowly, trying to ignore the drawing of the boy's eyes burning out from the page at her. There were only two lines, and neither mentioned the itch or how to make the sphere sing. The second line had long, loopy words that made no sound when she said them. Silent words for 'fixing', Grandpa Harry had once said.

He only used that word when the men in dark clothes

who didn't smile came to the house for his help. Sometimes he'd take the book with him, but not always. When he left the book behind, Ellen would sneak it from the cupboard and squeeze herself under the kitchen bench away from Mother Ta's anxious eyes. She'd pour over the pages tainted with the tang of stale tobacco from Grandpa Harry's pipe. Each poem and picture whispered the names of ancient things and dark paths trod in the red mud of the valley. Some pages had always been crossed through in blotchy red ink; already fixed. Others had Grandpa Harry's curly writing in the margin.

If he was successful, Grandpa Harry would pour them mugs of chocolate when he returned. Sometimes he'd cross through a poem with a careful hand. He'd laughed deeply when she'd suggested they call it the fixing book. 'Better the naming book' he'd whispered, his eyes sparkling. 'The fix is always in the name.' Ellen had liked that. It had been a good name for a book without a title.

'Books aren't toys,' said Mother Ta wearily from the doorway.

Ellen kicked her bedcovers over the sphere and made a show of ignoring the old woman by flipping quickly through the book. It wouldn't do to share the swap; Mother Ta would just worry.

The old woman trundled into the room and neatly plucked the book out of Ellen's hands. 'Mother Rala says you were in the park again.' She rested her elbows neatly onto her chest and raised an eyebrow. 'By the pond.'

Ellen did her best to feign interest in the peeling ceiling.

Mother Ta huffed and flipped the light with a chubby hand. 'Don't go to the park again!'

Ellen stuck out her tongue at Mother Ta's back, then slid grumpily under her covers with a pout. Did the old woman know about Jack and the swap? Those silly girls had obviously seen her down by the pond. But they mustn't have seen Jack.

Otherwise, they would have told Mother Rala about him. She turned the covers over until the sphere rolled into her hand. She didn't want to upset Mother Ta, but she had to get the book and go back to the park; it was only fair. Jack's sphere wouldn't sing, and she hated the itch. It had been a bad swap. Of course, she'd be fair, but if Jack wouldn't swap back, well, then there was always the poem with Jack's name. That would fix him.

* * *

In the morning, Ellen woke before Mother Ta and slinked into the kitchen to search for the book, the grey sphere hidden in her pocket. The book wasn't hard to find. Mother Ta wasn't as good at hiding things as Grandpa Harry had been. The old woman had stuck it haphazardly on the top shelf of the old cupboard by the kitchen door. Ellen had to drag a protesting stool to reach. Satisfied she hadn't woken the old woman, Ellen pressed the book hard against her chest and slipped silently from the house. She passed quickly under the towering trees silhouetted in the morning mist and along the empty road that wound around the park.

Trying to ignore the itch, she skipped into the park humming the first verse of 'Cut-me-Jack', her braided hair tapping her shoulders. She'd memorised the poem, including the words that made no sound. She ran over their odd lettering in her head, trying to think out the long swirling vowels as Grandpa Harry had taught her. Even in her head they seemed to make no sound. That worried her. How could she recall words that she couldn't hear? She'd have to keep the book close in case she needed it.

The pond welcomed her. Its familiar surface was broken only by reflections and the dark leaves of half-submerged plants that tumbled among the black rocks. It had been hard to find the first time: secreted away behind the memorial, shaded by a cranky willow, and hidden by tall, whispery rushes that sang in the gentle, cold breezes from the high country. No one could have visited it—not since forever.

Ellen carefully balanced the book on a large rock by the bank, then tucked her blue dress tight against her legs and sat quietly by the edge to wait for the eyes. Slowly, she slid a small, grey pebble along the pond's edge with her toes, balancing it on a crack between two stones. She let it fall with a satisfying *plop* and watched her reflection dance. Without taking her eyes from the water, she lined up a second pebble, humming through the poem and enjoying the tickle on her lips.

'You know I'm not scared?' She said quietly to the water. 'Not since yesterday.' She leaned back and rubbed her chest, her face a knot of concentration. Had it only been yesterday she'd first seen Jack's eyes? It felt like the memory was murky, as if she'd been in the dark. She recalled the smell of mud and the two sparkling orbs, watching her from the water. They'd shared names and discussed the swap. Then the sphere, and finally the itch: like a tiny hole that started to burn white hot, deep within her. But it wasn't hers; it was Jack's itch.

Laughter drifted nearby, and Ellen squinted through the reeds into the bright morning light spotting a group of familiar figures scattered over the red play equipment.

'It's those girls again,' she whispered to the silent water.

They hadn't noticed her this time, keeping to the far end of the park.

'Tattle tails,' she muttered, turning back to the water, willing the eyes to appear. But what if he didn't come today? She sighed, letting her fingers trail along the pond's cool surface.

As if in response, an orange glow flickered below, reflecting dimly on the rocks.

'Oh! There you are.' She smiled into the water, relieved. 'I nearly couldn't come, you know. Mother Ta was furious.' She looked questioningly at the eyes, but they continued to burn softly. 'You weren't in any of *my* books,' she explained, frowning. 'There weren't even any pictures.'

Cool hands prickled her skin, and she smiled at the faint memory of flowing water and scattered sunlight. Then Jack was sitting crookedly beside her, his grey, scaly skin shiny with pond water, offering a wide, toothy smile from his black mouth. He seemed more solid today. He also didn't smell as rotten; instead, the air around him reminded her of thunderstorms and burnt toast. Ellen wondered if she'd smell that way if she stayed under the water long enough.

'I'm hard to find, I am,' gurgled Jack, smacking his lips.

Ellen nodded and glanced over at the book waiting patiently in the shade. First, she'd be fair. Grandpa Harry would expect that. You don't need to fix someone if they play fair. She grabbed the grey sphere from her pocket, holding it out to Jack. 'It's broken!'

Jack flinched. 'You're not supposed to keep it there,' he said, eyeing the grey surface warily.

'It doesn't sing, and I don't want it anymore.'

Jack clicked his tongue and made an elaborate show of twirling his speckled arms in the air. As if from nowhere, he produced a pale pink sphere. It was slightly larger than the one she held and had smoother skin. It was instantly familiar.

Jack tilted his head and grinned at the pink sphere. 'Good souls are for singing.' Mouthing silent words with his rubbery, black lips, he raised his other hand above it and trailed long, reedy fingers across the surface. The sphere pulsed in response, producing a faint piping melody that filled the air above the pond.

The music wasn't like yesterday. It grew out from the itch inside her, each painful note tugging and squeezing Ellen's body, filling her shoulders and gnawing into her belly like hunger, until there was only the itch and she was lost, drowning in sadness.

Jack didn't seem to notice; his attention was focused on the sphere, his face twisting and shifting with glee to the rising and falling music. Finally, he dropped his hand, and the last note faded up into the trees and sunlight.

Ellen exhaled slowly in the silence. Before long, the itch flooded back into her. 'Don't want your itch, either!' she said through gritted teeth.

Jack disappeared the sphere and shook his head, sending brown water droplets onto the grey stones. 'No itch for Jack. That's your itch, that is.'

Ellen frowned. He was making her angry now. She stood promptly and leaned forward to wag her finger, hoping she looked as angry as Mother Ta did when someone broke something 'Well, I don't want it now. And I don't want this, either.' She thrust out the grey sphere again. 'You can have them both back.'

Jack leapt to his feet and hissed. 'No un-swaps. That's yours now. You gotta keep it proper.'

'But it doesn't sing, and I didn't want an itch.'

He gurgled with laughter. 'Swap wasn't for itch. Itch is what's left, stupid.'

'Left ...?'

'After swaps,' said Jack, dancing away effortlessly across the slippery stones. He paused a few metres away and produced the pink sphere from its nowhere place. He shook it gently in her direction.

'Your soul for mine. Remember, Ellen?'

Something about the way he said her name made her skin crawl. She stared at the grey sphere in her hand. Had she agreed to this swap?

'No itch if you keep it right,' continued Jack, holding Ellen's pink soul close to his wet chest.

Yesterday still seemed so far away. But if Jack was right, he must have tricked her. And that wasn't playing fair. She glared at him. 'Well, I want it back.'

'No un-swaps. I won't have it back.' Jack's face twisted into a sneer. 'You can't make me.'

Ellen took a step backward toward Grandpa Harry's book, using her heel to carefully feel her way through the twisting stones. She'd have to try the poem after all. 'I ... I can make you un-swap, Cut-Me-Jack.'

Jack's eyes widened and flared dangerously.

Her foot bumped gently against the spine of the book. If she could distract him, she could read the poem and make him take it back. It had to work—after all, it was Grandpa Harry's book. And Jack needed to be fixed. But she would need to be sneaky.

'All right,' she sighed dramatically and pocketed Jack's soul in mock defeat.

Jack narrowed his eyes but didn't move.

She dropped onto her haunches, spreading her dress across the book to hide it. 'A swap is a swap. But I want to hear it again.' She pointed at the pink sphere in Jack's hand. 'My soul?' She smiled her best smile.

Slowly, Jack relaxed into his crooked stoop. With his eyes focused on Ellen, he raised his free hand above her soul and stretched his fingers.

Ellen casually dropped her hands to her lap and made a show of straightening out her dress.

Jack watched her carefully as he moved her soul close to his wet mouth and parted his lips. He gurgled softly at the shiny surface, and the music started.

Before she could lose herself in the sadness, Ellen swept

back her dress and spun the book open, frantically flipping the pages, trying to recall the silent words. The page with Jack's eyes flashed past, and she hastily retrieved Jack's soul from her pocket, shouting aloud the first line: 'Call me Cut-me-Jack ...' The silent words followed, her mouth gaping like a fish.

But it appeared to have no effect, and Jack had cleared the space between them. With a snarl, he kicked the book from under her. It toppled into the pond with a splash. He gripped her wrist with his free hand, the cold wet skin sending an army of pins and needles spreading up her arm.

Ellen lashed out with the grey soul wrapped tightly in her fist. It connected with Jack's arm. He screamed and flailed as if burnt. Her soul flew from his hand and fell onto the stones with a sickening crack. The itch exploded within her, filling her body with its empty hunger.

Jack screamed and half lifted, half dragged Ellen backward as he staggered and splashed into the icy water, his face twisted in anger.

'Call me Cut-me-Jack ...' yelled Ellen. She could see the other words in her mind, but still Jack held tight. Around them, the pond widened, spreading out into a lake, the rocks sinking into an impossibly distant shore.

Panic gripped her as Jack dragged her down. Foul water and bitter weed surged into her mouth as she tried again to mouth the silent words. The pressure in her chest tightened. Only the itch kept her from disappearing into the darkness: it flowed hot and scratchy under her skin, keeping her attention and strengthening her resolve. She'd show Jack—make him eat his rotten soul if it was the last thing she did. Tightening her fist around the grey sphere, she pulled on the arm that gripped her in the gloom and kicked out toward the glow of his eyes. She connected with his cold, thrashing body, and the water swirled around them angrily. She yelled the first line into the water. The words were distorted in bubbles and vibrated in her ears and chest. Jack's eyes flared up in front of her, blazing and crackling. She closed her eyes, concentrated on her memory of the second line, and screamed them into the frenzied water with the last of her air. The words sounded in the mud and bubbles, brought to life by the water.

They were silenced by Jack's scream: a single note of despair that vibrated in the water around her.

Then Ellen was free, floating alone in the darkness.

She threw back her head and spluttered up from the surface, gasping. The water around her foamed and swirled green and brown as the mud and weed spiralled back into the dark.

There was no sign of Jack, or the glow of his eyes. Only the silent black stones that circled the pond. And the itch. There was still the itch.

Ellen balanced herself on the soft, cool mud that oozed up between her fingers and across her knees. She stood slowly, breathing deeply, trying to keep the burning that flowed on the inside of her skin under control. What had the words sounded like? No matter how hard she tried, she couldn't recall their sound. But Jack had heard them. Had heard his true name in the silent words the water had turned to music.

'Fixed,' she shouted at the surface of the pond, kicking a splash into the air.

Wiping sticky black silt from her hand on her dripping dress, she spied the familiar pink sphere bobbing gently by the bank. Flapping awkwardly out and over the wet stones, she lifted her soul gently from the brown water. A long crack snaked its way across the smooth surface. She frowned and tutted loudly. 'How are we going to fix that, hmm?'

She held her soul close, and a faint piping filled the air. Warmth tingled up her arms, banishing the itch to a dull ache. She laughed. It was enough.

Looking around, she realized that she'd lost the book. Mother Ta would be furious about that, but Grandpa Harry would be proud: she'd made Jack take it back. Carefully, she slipped her soul into a sodden pocket and stepped lightly back onto the edge of the pond. Without looking back, she skipped over the rocks and out of the park, humming tunelessly to herself.

* * *

Mike loves the challenge of writing short stories and has published a handful of dark fiction shorts. He particularly enjoys alternate history speculative fiction. He lives in Australia, grows orchids and loves all things dark and fantastic.

MY FAERY NAME

BY C.P. MILLER

When I was born, my parents named me Eibhlín, which means "shining light." With this name they had hoped to counter any ill fate being born under the dark of a faery moon might bring into my life. I'm not sure if it worked quite how they'd hoped, but I am at peace with my fate whether I die tomorrow or fight for a century.

Growing up, I loved the stories my grandmother would tell by the fire before bed. Stories of Queen Mab and her mischievous court's antics with drunks and non-believers made for tales that were equal parts frightening and funny. She taught me to show respect for the merrow folk, who are half fish and half human, for they might share a secret with a worthy child but would ruthlessly drown anyone who was rude. I learned leprechauns were not to be underestimated because of their size, for magic cares not about physical stature. My dreams were full of Inifri Duir, the oakmen, who live in the tallest and most ancient trees, of which so few are left, and whose stories taught me much about the importance of protecting the land and all who dwell in it.

Of course, tales of the Tuatha Dé Danann, the beautiful and bold children of the Goddess Danu, were always welcome. From them I learned lessons of wisdom and heroism. But one cannot learn to be brave without also learning of fear. Sometimes the scary stories were my favorites. The Pooka's pranks which could turn deadly, the bloodthirsty redcaps who dyed their hats with the blood of arrogant fools, and the headless Dullahan on its black horse. Darkest and bloodiest were legends of war against the Fomorians, those monstrous and beautiful folk who fought so often with the Tuatha Dé Danann in the ancient times, but also sometimes married. A testament to peace's power to rise from even the bloodiest and most ancient feuds.

I learned much from all of these stories my grandmother told me, and more from the people who filled them. But you are not here to listen to a young warrior sing the praises of the Folk, and I thank you for your patience. You are here for my story, whether it is the first time you're hearing it or the hundredth, and so I shall give it to you.

When I was twelve years old, a girl on the cusp of becoming a woman, I snuck out of my village. It was not as difficult back then as it is today. The Royal Investigative Order of Thaumaturgical Knights had no iron automatons tirelessly patrolling the towns and cities. The church's unsleeping eyes were mortal back then, not the holy sigils so many have paid to have put on their own homes out of fear and paranoia. My greatest obstacle was old Father Aiden, and he was only a serious threat to an unwatched keg of mead.

I snuck past drowsing dogs and silent nightbirds, hoping to catch a glimpse of the fae dancing on their grassy hill to celebrate the first full moon of spring. The sun had set already when I climbed into a shadowed perch high in a maple tree, and I settled in to wait. Upon seeing the first tiny pixies riding little white moths, I clutched reflexively to the amulet my father had given me. A family heirloom woven twigs my grandmother said would provide protection from the less friendly sorts of wild folk. She wasn't entirely wrong.

Before I saw the giants, I felt them. The branch I was balanced on vibrated with their heavy footsteps, and I grabbed it tight with both hands to steady myself. Neighboring trees creaked and groaned, some of their limbs snapping and tumbling to the ground as a trio of two men and a woman strode through the wood then climbed the hill in a few steps. At the top they stood beneath the ancient oak and greeted the Inifri Duir who lived within. The giants were twice the height of a tall man, and their heads nearly brushed the enormous oak's lowest branches. They had to duck slightly or risk damaging the tree and insulting the tree's guardian.

All around me, more and more fae gathered. They darted through the tall grasses and bobbing spring flowers that skirted the hill from its oaken crown all the way down to the edge of the wood. Spring's sweet scent drifted on a gentle breeze that carried sounds of their mirth. Goblins that bore a striking resemblance to cats and dogs and foxes ran and jumped, the bells on their hats and shoes making a merry tune. My toes twitched, and my feet itched to join their dance. Swallowing my rising fear, I tightened my grip on my branch until the urge eased.

All at once, the gathering crowd of Other Folk grew silent and still. A troop of a dozen Fomorians had arrived. I strained to see them, those legendary foes and infrequent lovers of the Tuatha Dé Danann. Some had only a single yellow or blood-red eye, others had three or more, and the same was true of their limbs. One had no legs at all, but two arms and a lower half like a serpent. And a handful among them looked almost human, but eerie in their beauty in a way that raised bumps on my arms and sent a cold prickle down my spine.

I held my breath as more and more creatures gathered and the tense silence grew heavier. This was supposed to be a celebration, but the redcaps were eyeing the pixies hungrily, some of the goblin cats had begun to scuffle with goblin dogs, and the Fomorians were eyeing everyone as if waiting for the real fighting to begin, but reluctant to initiate it.

Then, from the top of the hill, nestled in among the great and gnarled roots, a door opened and bright blue light spilled out across the gathering. I clutched again at my amulet of twigs and feared it might fail to hide me from whoever would step out of that shining portal. I squinted, trying in vain to see the shadowy backlit figure stepping out to preside over the gathering. The Father of Oaks? The Mother of Rivers? Or one of their children? King Oberon, or perhaps one of the great faery queens?

I gripped the rough bark of the branch beneath me tightly and inched a little further out. The light softened to a faint glow as the door slowly closed, and a subdued cry of welcome went up from about half the assembled folks. When they had quieted again, she spoke, and her voice made my heart ache and my eyes water. Her voice was velvet soft, yet it carried clearly. My stomach tied itself in knots as I shut my eyes to focus on her words of welcome.

"Well met and be welcome, allies new and old. Tonight we gather in peace and set aside our differences to band together against greater foes. Tonight we drink and feast and dance until dawn heralds a new day. A day when we are all one people, comrades in a shared fight for survival against our shared enemies. Drink and dance!"

At this, the crowd's reply was truly uproarious. There was cackling and cawing, braying and howling, and singing so beautiful it made tears spill from my eyes. Somewhere, someone began to strum a harp, and soon other instruments joined. The

Fomorians beat great drums with their monstrous hands and sang in deep smooth voices that matched their rhythms. The merrow folk gathered on the riverbank that touched the eastern side of the hill; I could just barely see them through the trees. They began to play flutes and whistles made from bone and reed.

From right under me the Pooka began to play a fiddle, late to the party, he walked blithely past my hiding spot in a mostly human form with only his hooved feet, curling black ram horns, and a short tufty tail sticking out of his trousers to betray him for what he truly was. I dared not even breathe as he passed me by. Then he was gone, stepping out into the mad crowd of forms beyond the treeline.

I let my breath out slow and tightened my grip on the branch once more. My feet ached to dance. I could feel the urge to climb down and join the dancers forming lines and circles, and I prayed silently to Sentua, goddess of the moon and all true lights, to spare me from that fate. I thought I would dance myself to death and die with a smile if I didn't resist the music's lure.

Suddenly, a silence fell over the crowd. They were as still as if they had all been turned to stone. Once more the queen's voice, low and rich with power, echoed over the hill. This time though, its haunting beauty was tainted by a tone of quiet fury. "Human, come out from your hiding place and state your purpose for trespassing on our celebrations."

I squinted once more, but could barely make out her figure. It was such a large hill, and she was still at the top under the ancient tree. As I heard her words, an icy chill washed over me and my lips began to tremble. Too scared to think, I swallowed and waited, wishing I could quiet my heart as easily as I could hold my breath. Could she hear my heart pounding from the Pooka startling me? Or had a shift in the wind carried my scent? Did the amulet hide my scent? My sounds? My grandmother had never really specified how it hid me, only that it would.

Some of the goblins had moved, putting their noses up to sniff at the night air. I prayed hard to any god or goddess listening as the seconds dragged by. The crowd began to grow restless, shifting on feet or hooves or tails or things I scarcely had words for. Some began to prowl through the treeline, searching the ground. Others flew, on wings of their own or on winged mounts, searching steadily higher.

"Our patience is finite, mortal. I will not ask again. Step forward and give us an account of yourself, or we will allow nature to take its course," her tone darkened as she banished any lingering uncertainty with her next words, "and we will continue our celebration after you are dead and devoured."

My first thought was to run, to climb down and flee as fast as my legs could carry me. But, I didn't move. I knew I could never escape so many. And I remembered then my grandmother's words, "It will hide you from *folk of ill intent*, but if you have done wrong, only courage and honesty can save you."

The queen was demanding I explain myself, and she had every right to do so. I was trespassing. I knew then what I had to do.

Against my instincts to stay silent and run, my voice rose in a quaver. "W-wait! I'm coming down! Please! Just wait a moment! I can explain!" Would my explanation satisfy them, though? I had no idea as I scrambled quickly to the ground. My feet had barely touched the soft earth when a goblin with a badger's snout leapt at me from a bush. I dodged the crea-ture, and it landed with a growl.

A redcap put a hand on the badger goblin's shoulder as the Pooka stepped between us and stared down at me. His fiddle was gone, and he studied me intently for a few moments before his bright blue eyes settled on the amulet at my throat.

He gave a slightly goaty laugh and clapped a hand on my shoulder. Without a word, he began steering me out of the wood and toward the oak-crowned hill. I didn't know it then, but it was Pooka who had laid the charm of protection on the amulet my grandmother had passed down to me.

The crowd parted before us, creating a narrow path. Claws, paws, and hands tugged at my skinny arm, my rough clothes. I caught murmurings of hunger and hatred and shifted a little closer to the Pooka as I tried to evade the unfriendly grasps. One of the Fomorians stepped out to block our way. He was a tall warrior with an axe on either hip and two dark yellow eyes set in a craggy face. Two of his arms were crossed over his broad chest and the second pair rested lightly on his weapons.

I clenched my hands into fists at my side and met his gaze, waiting for him to move or kill me on the spot. The quiet pressed in around me, suffocating and deafening. A slow grin formed on his thin lips and he took up a position on my other side. I could barely move, I was shaking so badly, but somehow I kept walking.

Years later, I learned that my terrified stillness had looked to Lord Kreth like courage. He had thought me bold for meeting his gaze, but I had been too scared to look away. He saw my clenched fists, and thought I was prepared to strike. I was just trying not to shake.

I learned that day that courage is being terrified, but still walking forward.

Together, we three climbed the hill, and along the way I found myself somehow taking the lead as the Pooka and Lord Kreth fell back to allow me my audience with the queen. Dizzy and weak-kneed, I faced her a moment before dropping to one knee and bowing my head. She was exquisite. Freckles were sprinkled across moonlit skin that seemed to glow softly of its own accord. Her black hair was shot through with silver and scarlet, and it flowed over the ground to mingle with the roots of the oak as if they were part of each other. Her gown was midnight black and studded with glittering gems that mimicked the starry sky above.

It was cooler on the hill top, and I blamed my fearful shivering on a sudden chill in the breeze as I tried to speak. "Your majesty. I..." What to say in that moment? I had been so distracted by my escort and the grasping crowd, I hadn't come up with anything. I thought of the stories my grandmother had told me of heroes visiting great human courts as well as fae and Fomorian.

I cleared my throat and started again. "Your majesty honors me with, uhm, with the opportunity to speak."

"Stand and meet my gaze."

I swallowed and obeyed. Her eyes were a deep summer-sky blue and flecked with stars. Red lips and bone-white skin tightened the fear in my soul. I felt miniscule next to her, a mayfly in the presence of a bonfire.

"Why are you here, human child?"

"I'm not a child." I bit my tongue and quickly added a contrite, "your majesty. I'm almost an adult..."

She waited, and with only a look, she silenced a cry from below to have me roasted and served at the feast.

"I came to see if the stories my grandmother told me were true or if Father Aiden was right and that the church had driven all of the other folk away."

"The *church*?" The queen's beautiful voice was rife with contempt and and inky blackness swallowed up the stars in her eyes. "They have certainly tried, but we are part of the land, and we will not be driven from it." She paused a moment, then asked a second question. "Why do you wear that amulet?"

I touched the bundle of knotted twigs worn smooth by generations of nervous fingers. "For protection. My grandmother said it would protect me from *folk of ill intent*." I tried to imitate my grandmother's knowing tone, but fear made my voice weak. The queen's silence pulled more words from me as I struggled to satisfy her curiosity. "I wanted to protect myself. Just in case..." I glanced nervously over my shoulder at the four-armed warrior.

A dark chuckle escaped the queen before she composed her features once more into a stern expression. "Cold iron is a more typical choice for your kind and more effective protection in most cases." Her red lips frowned ever so slightly, and I began to grow a little flustered.

"I didn't want to hurt anyone." I glanced around and pointed to a tiny fae with moth-like wings. "The little ones, Grandma told me, they can get hurt just by being near iron. So, I didn't bring a knife or even a nail."

There was a twitch at her lips that made me think she was trying very hard not to smile, but when she spoke her voice was winter-cold. "Why come here at all if you feared for your own safety?"

"I know I could have stayed home instead. That would have been safest, but I..." I faltered, unsure of what the truth was and absolutely unwilling to lie. The fae folk do not treat liars kindly, so I told her the truth while I tried to find an honest answer. "Majesty, I have spent my whole life in my village, serving the wealthy city folk who come laugh at me and my people. They call us stupid because we respect our ancestors' traditions. We keep the old ways and give offerings to the old gods. My family does, at least. But large trade guilds have gutted the market square with cheap foreign goods. The Royal Society of Agriculture buys up the farmland and poisons the local waters and, and..." Angry tears blurred my eyes, and I wiped them away again and again. "My town is dying, and my father wants us to move to the city so he can find work, but I don't want to leave, your majesty. This land is my *home*!"

My heart was aching as I poured my pain out in words. I stood there, blinking back my slowing tears, feeling the flush in my cheeks, and the tremble in my lips and fists. I was shaking all over as I clenched myself against my frustration and fear and hated my powerlessness. Finally, I choked out a few more words. "I came tonight to see if the old stories are true, because I can't stop everything that's happening, and I hate it."

The queen smiled. Her eyes which had been dark as moonless midnight had grown studded with stars once more. Slowly they returned to summer-sky blue. "I am satisfied with your answers young human." When she spoke again, it was to everyone. "Tonight, many former enemies have come together, their weapons left sheathed. Each and every one of you was invited by me personally. And each of you has kin invited to similar celebrations throughout our land, too long held in the hands of our enemies. This," she hesitated for half a breath and shot me a quick smile, "young woman is here to celebrate with us. She is our guest and accorded all such privileges."

I glanced around the hill, my gaze lingering in particular on the yellow-eyed Fomorian and the Pooka, and then I turned and looked up at her. In a low whisper I asked, "Is it safe for me now? I mean, now that I'm a guest? I don't want to die dancing..."

She laughed a small bell-like sound that startled me despite it's joyfulness. "Be at ease, my dear. You have amused me with your fear and charmed me with your passion. I give you my blessing for this night and welcome you to join as my guest." She held a pale hand out to me with long black lacquered nails that gleamed like still water. Tentatively, my own fingers trembling, I accepted her hand and she pulled me to my feet. "Go and dance. You may eat and drink without fear, and no one will harm you. Not tonight, at least." She chuckled, a little more deeply this time, and gestured to the gathering. As one, all of the musicians began to play anew.

I had always imagined that it would feel like a strange prickle if I was granted a blessing by one of the good folk. Something small, but undeniable. However, I didn't feel any different, as the tense silence swiftly gave way to noisy revelry. I was still anxious and my palms were sweaty, but the music was so much louder here on the hill than it had been from my hiding place in the maple tree, and it soon moved me with a will of its own.

I began to dance.

I danced first with a goblin who had a cat's head and a goat's legs. She was barely as tall as my hip, but able to jump twice her height. With Pooka, my feet settled into a jig inspired by his fiddle, and my fear began to melt away. I leapt and spun and found myself slipping on wet river-rocks on the banks where the merrow folk played and sang. They helped me to my feet and I danced among them as well even dipping my feet in the icy river water to join them in their splashing.

I even danced with the yellow-eyed four-armed Fomorian. His sharp teeth filled a mouth that was too wide for his head, and his smile stretched from one dangling, flopping ear to the other. He was hideously frightful, but an excellent dancer, *and* more importantly, he didn't eat me.

As pre-dawn crept over the treetops, I was surrounded by a whirlwind of pixies and other wee folk. Some flew on moths, beetles, and butterflies, others on birds and bats, and a few had wings of their own. More rode on squirrels, wild cats and dogs, and even the animals were dancing, jumping, darting in circles, or rising up on their hind legs for a few steps.

The queen's handmaidens moved gracefully among the

dancers with great golden goblets and silver pitchers full of sweet strong drink. Some carried platters covered in all manner of foods from berries and bugs to cakes and fresh baked buns stuffed with meat. The smells were tantalizing, and the dancing made me thirsty, but I resisted out of lingering fear despite the queen's assurances. I danced all night without a drop to drink or a bite to eat, and that is the only thing I regret about that night for our allies are fine cooks and brewers.

When at last the sun peeked over the woods and struck the top of the faery oak, the music stopped. I stumbled along in silence until I too came to a dizzy stop and dropped to the dewy grass. For a moment, I was captivated by the softly gleaming little droplets. How had they formed with everyone dancing and celebrating all over the place all night? I glanced behind me and saw a trail of footprints that marked my passage, but all the rest of the hill seemed untouched. Everyone was swiftly retreating into the wood or river, diving into holes in the earth or vanishing among the branches of the trees.

I sat and caught my breath and wondered how even the giants hadn't managed to trample the grasses. I clearly remembered them knocking a few branches down in their passage through the wood. Before I could ponder the mystery further, the queen's voice spilled out over the departing crowd. I marveled anew at how she could speak so softly from so far away, yet I could hear her as clearly as if she were standing next to me.

"Today begins a new way for us all. Tonight will convene our war council. I look forward to fighting beside you all and to welcoming you all again next year to celebrate and renew our allegiance to one another."

My head was spinning anew. War? What war? If all the fae were at peace, who were they planning to fight? The questions hadn't quite managed to form in the night when the queen had spoken of enemies and allies. I'd assumed some tribal skirmish between fae, but that couldn't be right. She'd said everyone had kin who had been invited to similar celebrations. The only race missing from this party, excluding myself, and so presumably from the other gatherings, was humans...

My stomach knotted at the thought of war, but on the tails of that fear was a desperate longing to return next year. This celebration had been unlike any other I had ever known before that night. Surely, I thought, they wouldn't go to war with all humanity. We weren't all the same.

My feet carried me forward against the dwindling crowd, and I sprinted up the side of the tall hill. My throat was dry, my lungs burning, and my legs aching when I finally reached her majesty. She seemed to have been waiting for me. "Majesty, your majesty, can I... can I return next year? Will you invite me?" I breathlessly pleaded with her and sank to my knees to await her answer.

She smiled down at me, beautiful but with a mischievous little smile. "No." My heart ached and I choked my protest back as the tears began to well up in my eyes. "Your people are not a formal part of this truce."

I swallowed against the dryness of my throat and licked my lips. "Majesty... are you going to war with humans? With all humans?" Something flashed in her eyes, and for a moment I feared she might kill me with a delicate but deadly swipe of her black nails.

"It was humans who began this war many centuries ago when they chose to break their pacts and invade our lands."

I dropped my gaze and shifted uncomfortably on my knees.

She continued, "We did not start this war, but we will

finish it or fight until our last breaths. Everything depends on our success."

"We're not all bad," I whispered and raised my gaze to plead with her. "Most in my village keep the old ways. We haven't betrayed anything."

"Your people stand by and allow others to destroy. You are, by your own words, not a child and certainly not ignorant of the harms and wrongs being done around you, but do you seek to stop them?"

"I... I don't know how."

"No? Has your grandmother told you no stories of tyrants and rebellion?"

I frowned at her and bit my tongue to avoid saying something I might regret. I thought hard and fast. "Life is not as simple as stories. My grandfather tried to rebel. His rebellion attacked churches and government buildings and royalists. A lot of innocent people got hurt. A lot of children got hurt." Her eyes had gone starless and midnight-black again, but she listened patiently. "My father taught me the rebels were fighting the wrong way for the right thing. He died fighting the rebels. Fighting doesn't fix things in the real world."

"Perhaps not, but our children too are dying. Our people grow sick and weak. If we do not fight, we will die, and we are not willing to die for the greed of humans."

"Some humans."

She met my gaze for a long and anxious moment as dawn spilled slowly over us. "Some humans." Her agreement loosened a knot in my belly. "If you learn of other means to end the poisoning and pillaging of the land, it would be my pleasure and my honor to grant you safe passage to speak before the other kings and queens. My heart tells me you are right to turn away from war, but I cannot stand by and do nothing any longer. I must make war to protect my people. We have no other options at present."

I had no answer for that.

"Perhaps," she spoke softly, her handmaids gathering around us, "it is time for a new covenant between our peoples. Will you make a new vow with me, and accept a faery name? If you do so, you will always be welcome in my court so long as you abide by our laws and customs." She gave me a very solemn look. "Of course, I can offer no guarantee of other courts."

I nodded. "What vow would you ask of me?" Sweat pricked at my palms and the soles of my bare feet.

"You are far too cute when you're frightened, my dear." She gave that bell-like laugh again, mirth softening her solemn air. "Give me your word you will take care of this land for the rest of your life, that you will not abuse your power over it, and that you will guard against other humans who would exploit the land without thought for tomorrow's generations. In return, I and all of my court will aid you in any way we see fit."

"I won't hurt people."

She smiled patiently. "You may guard against other humans in any way you see fit. Violence is our answer at present, but it need not be yours. Will you give me your word that you will do these things?"

I licked my lips and nodded after a moment. "Yes. I will give you my word." I didn't ask her what would happen if I broke my word. Everyone knows the Wylde Hunt kills oathbreakers and drags their souls to a place of suffering. And I had no intention of breaking my oath.

"Very well. I accept your vow, and I will give you a name in return. You must never share this name with anyone or it will give them power to command you. Do you understand?" I nodded as solemnly as I could manage. "Kneel." Bowing my head, I settled onto my knees. "I name you ＿＿＿."

And so I was the first in centuries to form a new pact

with one of the queens of the Tuatha Dé Danann. Since then, many of you have taken similar vows and been given similar names. It is not an easy path we choose to follow, but I believe it is the right one, and I will treasure my faery name forever, and I will take its secret to my grave.

* * *

C. P. Miller has been writing stories since she was a child. She has three cats, a husband, and too many books (or not enough books in her opinion).

THE MERCHANT OF NAMES

BY D.T. POWELL

His name was close. Its faint, familiar warmth clung to his fingers and crept up his hand as he neared it.

The crowd pressed and jostled, and busy market clamor made him wish to leave, but he wouldn't go without his name.

The Wonder Exchange boasted magics from this world and many others. Ahead, mirrors of all shapes adorned a wooden vendor stall. He knew better than to look into any of them. Across the aisle, a man peddled fruit that changed appearance—and presumably flavor—at its holder's whim. The vibrant blue apple the merchant held shifted to a deep fuchsia melon. Tempting. But there was no knowing what effects could result from a single bite, and he'd rather avoid any more ill-fated encounters of the magical kind.

He passed creatures, machines, clothes, and other marvels he couldn't identify as heat inched past the middle of his open palm. When the sensation reached his wrist, he muscled through the wall of marketgoers until he reached a vendor stall strikingly devoid of merchandise. The stall's only occupant was a merchant wearing deep blue. The man's long beard brushed his robe collar, and a single golden stripe ran down one wide sleeve.

The merchant eyed him with curiosity as he approached.

It wasn't his habit to avoid the point, but The Wonder Exchange was no place to garner hostility, and opening with an accusation might earn him an armed escort to the exit—or a lifetime ban. He swallowed his indignation before speaking.

"I'm looking for a name."

"For a friend? A loved one?" The vendor folded wrinkled hands atop the stall's narrow counter.

He shook his head. "For me."

"Hmm. You don't seem the nameless sort. Is this a second name, perhaps? Looking to add some variety to those roadside introductions?" A spark of mirth lit the merchant's eyes.

Heat gripped his arm, betraying the nearness of his missing name. He wanted—needed it back.

"No. I just need a name." Irritation flared, and he failed to bridle it. "Preferably the same one I had three days ago."

The vendor seemed perplexed. "Dealing in stolen names is illegal, good sir. I do not buy or sell them. Now, rejected, forgotten names, or ones that no longer fit their wearer I have in abundance. Please, have a look. My wares are of the highest quality." The man motioned him around the counter.

Inside the stall, the merchant unlocked a thick, wooden trunk. Inside, a crystal sphere housed more than fifty specks of light, each one a slightly different color. If he listened hard enough, faint whispers leaked through the glass. Some names were somber and rang with deep, rich tones. Others were bright, cheerful notes of brilliance and clarity. Still more were sensible and strong, practical names. He always marveled how so many people could inhabit the world without any two possessing the same name at once.

His hand drifted toward the sphere and the name he

needed to retrieve, but the merchant shooed his hand from the glass.

"Do not touch the merchandise."

His name hovered near the top of the sphere, a healthy red speck exuding strength. He could take it by force, make this man return it. Already, his hand strayed to the hilt of his dirk. He wouldn't hurt the merchant, but a healthy dose of intimidation would do the job. If the man alerted security, making it out of the Exchange without losing his name a second time might be challenging, but at least he'd have tried to reclaim what was his.

"I see you are troubled." The merchant pocketed the key, but he didn't close the trunk as expected. "You lost your name three days ago?"

"I didn't lose it. Someone took it while I slept. When I woke, it was gone."

"I see." The merchant gestured to the sphere. "Which one do you believe is yours?"

He indicated the red spark.

"Oh. I am sorry, sir, but that name already belongs to someone."

"What?!" His exclamation drew attention from several passersby, but the merchant waved everyone away with a smile and perfunctory greetings.

This had to be a mistake. The name sparkling inside that sphere had been his for thirty-seven years. Losing it would be losing part of who he was. He couldn't live without a name, couldn't easily conduct business, or get regular work. He couldn't even have a proper conversation.

"I'm truly sorry. It seems you have a legitimate connection to this name, but there is nothing I can do to reassign it." The merchant produced a signed contract. Beside the signatory's name was a dab of scarlet blood. "This binds me, you understand. You may petition the owner, but I do not believe she's willing to part with her name." He put the contract away and shut the trunk. "I wish you good fortune in your future endeavors, sir, but I must ask you leave me to my business now."

A blood contract was unbreakable. He'd have to do as the merchant suggested and plead with the woman who'd bought his name. If she conceded, he'd have his name back by the end of the day. The prospect eased the fear simmering in his gut as he found a place out of the name merchant's line of sight and waited.

* * *

After nearly four hours of crouching behind an unoccupied stall, his legs ached, and he'd adjusted position countless times to stave off stiffness and the pain associated with being only a few years shy of forty.

He searched his pack for something to eat, but just as he ripped off a bite of dried meat, two people neared the name merchant's stall. The crowd had thinned enough to allow the stuttered lilt of weeping to reach his hiding place.

Of the two customers, one was a young man, perhaps half his age, well-built, strong, probably fast. The person accompanying the twenty-something was an old woman. Her snowy hair was a shoulder-length mass of curls, and her wrinkled eyes were red-rimmed and lost. She looked to the young man in bewilderment. He put a comforting arm around her shoulders and whispered something that blunted her distress but didn't cure it.

As the pair approached the name merchant's counter, the old woman's eyes lit, and her pace rose until the young man had to hold her arm to keep her from running. When they reached the stall, the merchant immediately ushered them behind the counter.

To hear the conversation, he stole across the aisle and around the back of the stall. A knot in the wall allowed him full view of the exchange.

"I—I can have it?" The old woman's voice was paper-thin and crumbling, and only a tiny speck of hope kept it from disintegrating.

"Yes, Grandmother," said the young man. "You signed the contract yesterday. Remember?" He guided the woman to the now-open trunk.

"Oh... Yes. Yes, I signed a paper." She stared at the name-filled sphere in wonder, and tears sparkled on her cheeks as the merchant sang over the names, trapping the red speck in a bubble and easing it through the sphere's crystal wall. "It's beautiful. And warm," the woman whispered as the transparent bubble settled into her hand. "And so strong!" She held the bubble near her heart. The longer it was in her possession, the less clouded her expression, and in her first moment of clarity, she threw a wrinkled arm around her grandson and kissed his forehead. "Thank you, my sweet boy." A sob of joy shook her as she faced the merchant and held out the bubble containing the purchased name. "I'm ready."

With practiced precision, the merchant uttered an ancient song over the name. The rush of music whisked the name from the bubble and planted it in the woman's hand.

The name seeped into her skin, turning it a lovely red gold as it eased up her arm. Even through her dress's dark sleeve, the name glowed, and when it reached her heart, she clasped both hands over it. A look of peace spread across her face, and she hummed with the merchant's song.

When the music ceased, the woman staggered forward a step.

Her grandson reached for her.

"No." The merchant stopped the young man. "Touch her

now, and the transfer may not hold. Wait until she speaks the name."

The old woman took a labored breath before standing straight. Sweat beaded on her forehead as the intense glow over her heart shifted from red gold to brilliant white.

She said her new name, softly at first, then with confidence.

Her voice held the same strength and will *he'd* possessed so long. His father told him his name once belonged to a great warrior, a hero of legend, and he should carry it with honor. The moment this woman said his name, the warmth that drew him here dissipated, replaced by a sense of loss. But it wasn't the desperate confusion that had gripped the old woman moments ago. It was a quieter, lighter grief—one that touched his soul with sorrow but somehow also promised hope.

The old woman grasped the merchant's hands, and her smile shone with wonder.

"Thank you! Thank you!"

"You are most welcome." The merchant bowed his head to her. "May you wear this name well."

The old woman hugged her grandson with more vigor than before, and her joy-filled laugh drew others to the stall.

"I have a new name!" she declared to anyone in earshot. When she left with her grandson several minutes later, the merchant watched them go. Only when they were safely swallowed by the crowd did his attention return to the crystal sphere of names.

"You can come out now," the merchant said as he crossed his legs and took a seat on the slatted wood floor.

"You knew I was here." He slipped from behind the stall.

"If you'll pardon my saying so, you breathe loudly." The merchant motioned for him to sit. "I expected you to leap out of hiding and protest. If that truly was your name, why didn't you try to retrieve it?"

The look of utter despair on the old woman's face when she'd arrived at the stall came back to him.

"She needed it more than I did."

"Admirable," said the merchant. "But many would argue you should have attempted to reclaim the name, regardless."

He leaned forward, elbows propped atop his knees. Losing his name hadn't crippled him as he'd feared. If anything, the void left behind was exhilarating.

"I'm not confident that name still represents who I am."

"Ah," the merchant said with a smile, "now we've reached the truth. You've given up who you used to be and let your old name pass to someone who will love and treasure it. To surrender something so dear—and to a stranger no less—is a deed worthy of reward." The merchant gestured to the sphere of names, but a glint of mischief lingered in his eyes. "Choose whichever of these you like."

A vibrant blue speck hovered in the middle of the sphere.

"That one belonged to the king of a faraway land. Some say he could command the sea."

A glowing orange spark flitted in energetic circles.

"And that was a warrior-chief's name."

A green speck floated near the sphere's base.

"Oh, that is a good one too. It belonged to a great master of music. Legends say her name could strike fear into servants of evil."

He sat straight. "Those are all fine choices, and I wish you good fortune in selling them to worthy holders, but... I won't be needing them."

"Really? And why's that?" Knowing laced the merchant's tone as he closed and locked his trunk.

"I need a new name, but it can't be one someone else has had. It has to be a new one—something that won't slip away as I sleep—something that fits so well I can't ever take it off. I need a name I can wear."

"Ah. You've quite the task ahead of you. To find a new name is a journey all its own. It is difficult—impossible some might say—and it could take years, decades even. Are you willing to invest your life in this endeavor?"

"Yes." To speak that single word thrilled him.

"Then may your steps be blessed." The merchant bowed his head.

"Thank you." He stood and left the stall. As he wove through the thinning crowd, he glanced over his shoulder.

The name merchant raised a hand in farewell.

He waved back and headed for The Wonder Exchange's nearest exit.

When he stepped into gathering twilight, he shouldered his travel bag and set out.

* * *

D. T. has loved stories since before she can remember, and it was love for one of those many stories that prompted her to start writing. She's worked in the fanfiction community since 2013 and continues to contribute to it regularly. While she pursues publication for her novel-length and short-form original fiction, she spends time reading, playing pickleball, and the occasional video game. Her work has been published by Writer's Digest, Clean Fiction Magazine, and Cadence Writing.

UNIVERSAL KEY

BY CAS C. MORGAN

If a key can unlock any door with a matching lock, then so the power of a name also turns the tumblers to certain mystical secrets: opening paths to distant lands, adventures that transcend time, knowledge in its purest form. Perhaps it is within each of us to understand our identity, our place in the universe which is coded into a simple string of letters: our names.

- The Nameless Gate

* * *

An explosion of thunder transported Mirasol from dream-world to reality, and she sat up in bed with a gasp. The same dream again. One in which she was a baby, held warm and close in her mother's arms. A lullaby and a gentle sway. How she wished she could hold onto that feeling.

"Oh, Mom," she murmured into the darkness. "What happened to you? Where are you? Where's Dad?"

No doubt the morning's dream was brought on by the ten-year anniversary of their disappearance. And, as per the will, she was to receive her inheritance this year now that she turned twenty-one.

She rose from the bed and drifted towards her desk, switching it on.

"Good morning, Mir-a-sol," the voice of her parents sang. The built-in tabletop screen displayed the research paper she'd been working on for college, with options to re-watch some of her professor's lectures. But today wasn't about schoolwork.

Mirasol pressed a button, and the screen became a map of the world. Tiny hearts were scattered across the map, and some could be found on every continent. She tapped one of them, an old favorite.

A video hologram popped up. One of the rare times the family had been at home together, instead of excavating an archaeological site. Even Van, her parents' longtime friend, was there, wearing a party hat, plate of cake in his hand.

"Mir-a-sol," her parents sang. "Can you find your birthday present? Here's a clue. It has many keys but can't open any doors."

"Oh ho ho, that's a tough one, isn't it?" Van asked.

The little girl in the video wearing the birthday crown thought for a moment.

"A piano!" she cried as adult Mirasol murmured the answer alongside her. The little girl ran to the piano stool and tried to lift the lid, but it was locked. Mom held up the key to the stool.

"Mir-a-sol!" she sang again, with a glance toward the piano.

Her child-self turned around and considered the instrument.

"Mir-a-sol," Mom repeated and played the notes to match. She beamed and passed her the key.

The piano stool obscured the view, but Mirasol remembered the gift. A picture book about secret magic portals called *The Nameless Gate*. Mirasol chuckled, remembering how many times she had squeezed between Mom and Dad on a cot while at a dig site, opening the book and turning through its pages together.

When the memory-video was over, Mirasol sat for a moment, a sob threatening to overwhelm her and pinpricks at the back of her eyes. She remained still, picturing a red balloon full of air. Exhaling a slow controlled breath, the imaginary balloon deflated. With it went the sadness, she told herself. The questions she could not answer, all the things she could not control. The lump in her throat subsided, as did the pressure behind her eyes. A new breath was drawn, swelling within her lungs, and she straightened her posture. Much better.

Refreshed, she made her way to the small apartment bathroom, where she ran a quick hair brush through her curly red hair.

"Thanks for this, Dad," she teased, comparing a lock to the photo of her parents taped to the mirror frame. For just a moment, her reflection slipped. She twisted it back into a half smile. "Well, Mom and Dad," she said out loud, ignoring the catch in her throat. "What surprises do you have in store for me today?"

Now, for her favorite distraction: fashion. She'd programmed her closet last night with today's weather forecast, her destination, and marking the day as a special occasion. Mirasol pushed the display button. With a spotlight and a playful musical sequence, the closet revealed black denim jeans, a tank top, and a pair of slip-on shoes.

"Hmm ... too simple," she declared, pushing a red button. The jeans and top combo vanished, replaced with a glittering purple dress that mimicked a night sky, paired with knee-high black boots. "Oh, so pretty! Well done! But still ..." she giggled. "What else do you have?" The dress vanished and a new option shimmered into view.

If the previous outfit showed the night, this one brought on the sunrise. Hues of orange, red, and yellow danced in Mirasol's eyes. A beret hovered above a flowing top that connected to a skirt with knee-high socks and high tops for footwear. The colors were akin to a sunrise streaming down, and the outfit elicited a smile from Mirasol.

Another flash brought all three choices to the front as a voice sounded, "Which would you like to wear, Mirasol?"

I need to shine. Today more than ever.

A smirk crossed her lips, followed by a raised eyebrow. "Let's brighten up a gloomy day with the sunrise and a cute beret."

Her chosen outfit enlarged as the voice replied, "Very good choice."

"Why thank you," she replied with another giggle.

The outfit image rippled as the clothes came through the image. Mirasol turned around, backing into the outfit that melded onto her. She spun around as the mirror appeared just in time to reflect a smiling, confident Mirasol.

Posing a few times, Mirasol winked at herself. "Perfect."

Outfit, hair, and makeup complete, she exited her apartment and stepped outside.

The awning above detected her presence and extended to shield her from the rain. In the street, among the flow of traffic, a dark sedan pulled over to the curb and stopped alongside her. The backseat window slid down.

"How does he always know?" she asked with a rueful smile. She opened the door and climbed in.

The car was empty, but the AI Self-Drive pulled away from her apartment and smoothly merged into traffic. As the drove through the city, Mirasol gazed up at the towering skyscrapers. Despite the rainstorm, they were aglow with peaceful projections of the clear sky above the clouds, where the moons and stars still reigned.

Mirasol had tried not to think about this day, as every reminder only exacerbated her impatience. Today, on the tenth anniversary of her parents' disappearance, their estate would officially fall to her. Van had told her that sometimes people recorded messages for their loved ones that became unsealed when the estate ownership was transferred. Had her parents done that? Would she see some fresh footage or hear their voices one last time? She hoped so, of course, but a part of her dreaded the billow of grief. Best not to think about it.

"We have arrived at the destination," the AI announced. "Would you like an umbrella or shall I bring you to the stairs?"

She was so lost in thought, the AI had to beep and repeat itself. Mirasol cleared her throat. "Please bring me to the stairs." *I don't want to wait any longer for this moment.*

The AI beeped twice and drove up to the entranceway stairs. The awning extended as Mirasol's door opened. She climbed the stairs to the building's door, which opened automatically.

Van's office never changed much, and she relished the nostalgia. The decor was an archaeological mix of old-world and new-world technology, with artificial lamps dotting the hallways. She paused to admire a photo on the wall of her parents and Van from a symposium where they were honored for their work in developing safety equipment and protocols at precarious sites. Officially, Van was included in the ceremony for preparing and filing the patents, but Mirasol remembered long evenings with him at their dining room table or in her mother's study, consulting over the blueprints, physics, and mechanics of the design. He was just as much a part of it as they were. These patents supplemented the meagre income brought in from research grants and finders fees. Their net worth was among the largest in their line of work. Is that what was in store today? A payout? Access to a trust fund? She touched a fingertip to the photo. If only she could reject the money in exchange for their lives.

Before she knew it, she was standing in front of Van's door. Butterflies dive-bombed her gut, making her body tremble with anxiety. Why she suddenly felt so nervous, she didn't know. This was Van. His business card may describe him as a shark, but he'd been nothing but a teddy bear to her.

The door slid open, and Mirasol tucked the thoughts away, her face lighting up with a smile. Van sat at his desk, already motioning impatiently for her to come in.

"Mirasol! My favorite client!" His words made her giggle. He probably said this to everyone. "Beautiful dress, by the way. You always brighten up the room, don't you?"

As he spoke, he withdrew from a desk drawer a sealed envelope. He sliced the packet with an old letter opener and a scowl of concentration. From within, he fished out a wafer thin silver disc and set it on the desk. Mirasol's heart thumped. Technology like this was old-fashioned, out of date by a generation. It was also exactly what her parents would have used.

"I don't know what's on here," Van said. "Do you want to hear it alone first?"

"No," she answered quickly. "Stay. Please."

Van glided his finger around the disk. A faint glow emanated from it as a video of her parents started to play above the envelope. Her fingers intertwined, clutching tightly. She struggled to maintain composure as she stared intently at the images of Mom and Dad.

"Hello sweetheart!" They stood in a cavernous natural stone archway, covered in strange symbols. The video and audio quality wavered—sometimes crystal clear, sometimes scratchy and glitchy. Her parents' hands stretched out, as if they could reach through time and space. "Mirasol, honey, your Mom and I have uncovered something. Bigger and more important than anything we've ever seen before." Dad glanced over his shoulder at the archway. "If we're right about this ... it could change everything."

Mom spoke up. "If you're watching this, Mirasol, it means we were separated too soon." Mom paused then slowly began to sob at the possibility of her own words. As Mirasol watched, sitting in Van's office ten years later, she echoed it.

"We're going to try to open a door," Dad said. The wind picked up around them, lifting his curly hair. He shouted to be heard. "But we can't risk the whole world knowing about this yet. That's why we're entrusting this to you alone. We've left some clues with Van. Use them to find this place. To come here. To find—" The message garbled, and she couldn't make out what Dad said next. When the video quality stabilized, her mother was looking at the camera intently.

"We gave you the key, Mirasol. We gave it to you a long time ago." Mom smiled, but there was sadness in it. "Even before you were born."

With that, there was a surge of bright light and a rumbling sound—rocks or thunder, Mirasol couldn't tell. The video flickered to show the archway, this time without her parents, and then it went dark.

Mirasol's hand hovered over the disc as it flickered out, wishing she could clutch the miniature figures of her mom and dad. Finally, she met Van's eyes. He looked as stunned as she felt.

"I'm guessing you didn't know about any of that?" she asked.

He shook his head slowly. "No. No, I did not. Uh, as to the clues they referenced ... There's some other files here for you. Let's see what these are." He spread papers and photos out on the desk. "Firstly, we need to find the location of that last site."

Mirasol stood and bent over the desk for a better look. She found a scrap of notepaper in her mother's handwriting and read from it:

"There is a lock for every key, and no matter what material they're cut from, the lock will always open for the right fit."

"Your parents sure had a flair for making things interesting. What the heck is that supposed to mean?"

Together, they sifted through the pile, examining each paper, photo, and possible clue in turn. Anything that could be a reference to a key or a lock.

Mirasol pushed aside a legal document and found below it a glossy photograph. Her gaze lingered on the image of a mountainous landscape. Absently, she zig-zagged a finger over the mountain peaks. Why did this look so familiar? She flipped the photo over. Nothing written on the back. Not a postcard, then. She examined the front side again. A beautiful wild scene of dramatic icy peaks, enrobed by the clouds. Off to the left was a smaller mountain huddled against a larger one, a kitten and its mother. That's what kept nagging at her: She'd seen this formation before, but where?

Van's watch beeped. "Sir," his receptionist spoke through the device. "Your next appointment is here."

"I'm sorry, sweetie, I've got to take this. Here, why don't you take this stuff home for now, and we'll set up a time to go over it together?"

"Pro bono, right?" she teased, sweeping up the documents and sliding them into the envelope.

"Of course," he laughed.

Their tone was light, but as soon as she was out of his office and the door shut behind his next set of clients, Mirasol lowered herself into one of the lobby chairs. Seeing that video, hearing their voices was intense. Since their disappearance, the same questions had run circles in her mind. What happened? Where were they? She'd always believed awful accidents had occurred—a climbing accident, maybe, or a cave-in. But this message. It was like they almost expected not to return. What kind of experiment had they been doing? And what could have been so important that they would abandon her?

Van's secretary smiled politely, and Mirasol returned the expression automatically. The balloon. She needed the balloon. Deep breath, hold, exhale, deep breath, hold, exhale. There.

The AI Self Drive returned her home. She carried the envelope to her desk and began sorting through the contents, grateful not to have Van peeking at her with worry. She set the disc to replay on a loop. The voices of her parents begged her to find them as she pulled out the photo again. Tapping on the hearts on the desk brought up video memories, the audio clashing with the new message. She scoured the backgrounds of the videos and called up information and images about each place, comparing it all to the mysterious mountain photo.

No matches.

Why did this photo look so familiar?

Well, she thought, *it's nowhere that I've been. So where haven't you been?*

She returned her attention to the map display. This time she had to look beyond the hearts. Where weren't there memories? Moreover, where were there mountain ranges, without video memories?

She scoured the data until she finally hit upon a clue. The map reported a mountain range called *Ax Fichadonuras.* AKA "The Locks." The name alone twisted her gut, but there were no photos of it. "Virtually uninhabited", the map said. "Undeveloped."

So why do I recognize these mountains? She squinted at it again. *Why do I see a kitten and its mother?* The peaks looked like cat ears. It was the first thing she'd noticed. And she could almost see cuddly expressions drawn onto each mountain. Drawn. *Drawn—that's it!*

She swept the documents off the desk, setting them hastily on the bed. The desk lid opened up, revealing a shallow space for just a few treasures. From within, she withdrew her childhood copy of The Nameless Gate.

* * *

"It makes sense, doesn't it?" she said to Van over the phone, when he returned her call that evening. "With the clue and the shape and the name." She tapped a finger on the map. "It's not easy to get there, though. No airport. Lots of red tape to get permission."

For a long moment, Van was uncharacteristically quiet. "Your parents were great people," he finally said. "My best friends, the both of them. No matter how much time we spent apart, whenever we were together again, it was like nothing had changed. I've always wanted to know what happened at that final dig. I know you do too." When he spoke again, the warmth was back in his tone. "That money and the connections they always teased me for chasing are finally going to pay off. I'm going to make some calls. You pack a bag. I'll pick you up in a couple of hours. With any luck, we'll be flying out tonight."

"Tonight? But—" Finals were coming up. Skipping classes now would surely torch the whole semester. Should she wait? It was the sensible thing. Then again, could she really sit through another algebra class with these questions looming over her? Now that she might actually have a lead? Her deliberation only lasted a few seconds. "It won't take me long to pack."

* * *

It's amazing how easy things get done when the right name is used, Mirasol thought, admiring the luxurious cabin of Van's private plane. He'd been on the phone nonstop with clients, government officials, and his secretary, since she'd climbed into his car. Even now, sitting on the other side of the cabin, he was still at it.

Turning towards the window, she watched the world fall away. *A Nameless Gate. Did they really find one?* From her bag, she withdrew the book from her bag and flipped through the pages.

At certain locations across the globe, it read, *portals exist that open to other dimensions. At various sites across continents, cultures, and time, objects have been found that resemble keys with a dark unidentifiable stone embedded into the handles. However, no "locks" have ever been found to fit these mysterious keys.*

Had her parents done it? Found a Nameless Gate and gone through it?

The plane landed at an airstrip, then they had to transfer to a helicopter that carried them up into the mountains, to the highest point it could safely land. At this altitude, the wind sliced against her cheeks, and she shivered into her warm mountaineer's coat.

One of Van's many calls was arranging for guides. They were greeted at the landing pad by two strange men, whose skin Mirasol swore was actually glowing. It had to be a trick of the mountain light, but they seemed practically luminescent. They were dressed, impractically Mirasol thought, in long dark robes threaded with gold. At first she thought the color was black, but when one of them moved and caught the thin sunlight, she realized it was a deep, rich, violet. Though the wind whipped her hair and made her eyes water, the robes of these strange men hardly moved.

Van bowed as he spoke. "Good evening gentlemen," he said as smoothly as if they'd just arrived at his home for a dinner party. "May I present Mirasol Zaltana, daughter of Lyric and Eagle Zaltana."

Mirasol wasn't sure what to think of the glance the men exchanged between themselves and the way their attention seemed so focused on her.

Van nudged her elbow. "Curtsy," he muttered from the side of his mouth. Mirasol blinked at him, uncomprehending. "*Curtsy*," he said with more emphasis and a pointed look towards the waiting men. *Oh right, silly me,* she thought. *Just a normal, every day curtsy.*

Mirasol did her best affectation, accompanying it with her practiced warm smile. The two men exchanged glances and bowed back.

"We are overjoyed to receive you both," one said, though their expressions remained solemn. "It is an honor to have the daughter of Lyric and Eagle here. They told us when they first arrived that one day you would visit here."

"They did?"

The men nodded, offering neither further elaboration nor a suggestion to move indoors. After a short silence, Mirasol fished the photographs from her zippered pocket and offered it out.

"Do you recognize this spot? Do you know where this photo would have been taken?"

They took the photo and examined it for a moment, whispering to each other before turning their attention back to Mirasol.

"We do know where this is. It is due west from here,

about a ten- to thirty-minute hike. Of course, this is the last place your parents were seen alive. We hope that won't be too troubling for you. Would you like us to guide you?"

"We would appreciate that very much, thank you," Van answered.

Mirasol had tuned out everything after they had told her this was the last place her parents were seen alive. The moment got the best of her. She turned her head so Van wouldn't see the tears welling up. The imaginary balloon was puffing too fast, and she couldn't get control of it. It had been such a strange day. A normal person would have been curled up on the couch with a box of tissues on the anniversary of their parents' disappearance. Here she was in a foreign country, about to hike up a mountain with two strangers and her lawyer.

The men turned to lead the way. She should follow them, she knew. It was why she came here, after all. This was what she wanted. Answers. But the ache in her throat and her stifled chest held her back.

Van squeezed her shoulder. "Mirasol? Are you sure that you are still up for this? We can take a beat to breathe, if you need it."

"I'm alright," she answered quickly without turning around to face him. All her breath came out in a rush. She straightened and tugged her winter hat low over her ears. "I have to do this."

There wasn't much conversation on the hike, aside from the two guides urging them along and telling them where to step on the narrow pathways. Straying could mean sliding down a deep ravine from which there was no recovery.

Mirasol's excitement rose as the jagged peaks of the mountain range started to resemble the photograph. They scrambled up a steep uneven pile of rocks and emerged at the top of a sheer cliff. Even six feet back from the edge, the height was dizzying. The mountains cradled the valley in a deep bowl. Above, the sky was an unbroken dome.

"No further," a guide said to Van. He pointed alongside the cliff to a spot fifty feet away where a long ice-covered outcropping bridged the two valley floors. "She must go alone."

Mirasol's mouth dried up.

Van spoke up, verbalizing her thoughts. "Oh, hell no! She's not walking across that death trap! And definitely not alone! We had an agreement! You two were supposed to take us to the spot!"

"This is the spot," Mirasol answered. Her voice sounded soft and dazed, even to herself. There, on the far side of that narrow, railing-less bridge, was the kitty-cat mountain nestling against its mother.

"We can only go this far," one guide told Van.

The other said to Mirasol, "What you seek is across the bridge."

'Mirasol," Van said. There was a warning tone in his voice as though he already knew what she planned to do. "I know we've come a long way, but you don't have to do this. Not alone. We'll go back to the 'copter and hire different guides. I'll pay them more if that's what it takes. I can't lose you too, sweetheart."

Mirasol pulled her gaze from the bridge and looked into Van's face, all riddled with worry. Mom and Dad had asked her to come here. To find them, they said. They didn't say not to cross the bridge. If this was how they had gotten across, then she would have to as well. That thought put her in motion. "I have to."

Van swallowed. "That fire in your eyes reminds me so much of your mother. I see both of them in you. I miss them too, but you don't have to do this."

A smile crept across her face, accompanied by a few tears

that she wiped away quickly. She needed to stay strong—to concentrate on the task ahead. When it was all over, she could let emotion overwhelm her. She deflated and re-inflated the imaginary balloon.

"I'm going ahead," she announced, adjusting her pack.

They devised a plan to use the radio to stay in contact and set a meeting place for the following morning. "I'm not going anywhere, though, until I see you on the other side of this bridge." Van said, pacing back and forth.

Mirasol went to the narrow ledge that served as bridge and set one foot on it. The frosty layer of ice prevented her from seeing its base. The view of tall pines, hundreds of feet below, made her heart pound. She felt lightheaded. A gust of wind pushed her sideways, and she wrestled for balance.

One foot in front of the other. There wasn't even enough room for her feet to be side by side. *Careful. Don't rush it.* She forced herself to move, arms outstretched for balance. The wind filled her ears. Only the screech of the birds beneath her feet pierced the sound.

Finally, she lurched onto the opposite cliffside. She waved to Van but couldn't make out his figure in the distance. *I can't believe I just did that!*

When she turned around again, it was like seeing a postcard come to life. Mirasol stared with wonder. This might have been the same sight her parents viewed all those years ago. Small buildings carved out of the mountain formed a village. Her first impulse was to charge towards it, but she knew better. Dad had maintained a reputation for safety his whole career. Many of her parents' friends had told her stories of being frustrated with the slow pace due to safety precautions he imposed and strictly enforced, only to be grateful for them later when something unexpected happened.

The first building was her parents' headquarters, complete

with tools, workstations, and their personal effects. Every-thing was coated in dust. She brushed her fingertips against every surface, trying to bring the past to life.

A curtain covered what appeared to be an entranceway into a private room. Beyond that was a double sized cot. On a bedside table, Mirasol inspected some small items: a jewelry box revealed a small bag with the words "Our Key to Happiness" stitched into it.

Mirasol opened the bag and withdrew an elongated object. A dark stone was embedded in one end. She stared in disbelief. *A key to a Nameless Gate?* As strange as the day had been, this took it to a new level.

She left the dormitory yurt and went back outside, exploring the village, trying to imagine how the ancient inhabitants lived. An icicle lodged in the mountain wall showed where, in the warmer seasons, a waterfall trickled into a sloping pool made of smooth round rocks. At the bottom of the basin a single dark stone protruded up. It glittered the way the one in the key did. *Well, now I have to check it out.* Doing a sideways shuffle into this pool was nothing after the terror of the ice bridge. Splotches of thin ice cracked under her boots. When she reached the bottom, she crouched beside a pedestal that bore the sparkling stone. It was about two feet tall and, from her examination of the base, seemed to be on some kind of hinge. A lever. *If I pull on this rock, is this whole pool going to crumble beneath me like some kind of trap?*

Mirasol stepped back from the hinged pedestal and braced herself. Gingerly, she gave it a kick. Nothing. She swallowed, exhaled, and shook out her hands in an attempt to psych herself up. Then, she gave the lever a slow solid press of her boot.

The ground quaked. Beneath her feet, the stones rattled and clacked. A hundred birds took flight, cawing and squawking into the sky. A boom sounded, cracking like thunder but louder and closer than any thunder she'd heard. *Rockslide!* She dropped her water bottle and charged up the sides of the pool, slipping on the clear ice and banging her kneecap hard against the stones.

The mountain trembled.

Mirasol clambered to her feet. In the mountain wall, a panel slid aside. She gaped at the sheer size. At least twelve feet wide and maybe twice that in height. Darkness loomed within the hidden chamber. *I'd be an idiot to go in there, right? What if it closes once I'm inside and I'm trapped?*

Cautiously, she approached. Though a dozen dangers flicked through her mind, her feet continued on. As her eyes adjusted to the interior gloom, her breath caught. Just beyond the door were the archways, just like the video in Van's office.

And, just as in the video, she found as she stepped inside, the chamber was a dead end. Using the mysterious key, Mirasol tapped the interior walls, listening for hollow places, searching for another button or lever to activate the gate. Even after sunset, Mirasol braved the dark and used her flashlight to continue scouring the walls.

Finally, she rested her head against the pebbly stone. *Mom, Dad, what am I missing? Please. I just need one more clue. I can do this, but I need your help.*

She replayed the memories of the puzzle games they'd played, all the riddles. "We gave you the key," her mom had said. "We gave it to you before you were even born."

A gift that's given before you're born. She stood up straight. *A name?* There wasn't a doubt in her mind. "Mirasol?" she said aloud, tentatively. Nothing. She tried again, louder, more confident. "Mirasol." The silence of a tomb.

Then, feeling almost silly, she tried again. "Mir-a-sol!" she sang out, bright and clear. "I am Mir-a-sol!" Her voice echoed through the high arches. *Mir-a-sol.* The name bombarded her from all sides, swirling around her like an invisible ribbon.

The wall at the back of the hidden room flickered. When she'd seen the video in Van's office, she'd assumed it was lightning and the high winds from a storm. But this illumination lit from behind or even within the rock. A rectangular shape, seven feet tall with sharp angles jutting out in all directions, came into focus. Her fingers shook as she tapped the key against it.

Warmth emanated from the rock, massaging the cold out of her bones, the soreness of her muscles, all the fatigue. Deep breaths came easily now, without needing to visualize the balloon. There was a catch in the air, a scent and texture like salt. It reminded her of a sauna; relaxation seeped in despite the circumstances.

And then there were the voices she'd believed for so long that she'd never hear again.

"Mir-a-sol."

She gasped to see her mother materialize. Dressed in robes similar to the mountain guides, her long hair in an elegant braid, she exuded calm and wisdom. Dad was dressed the same, though his hair was wilder, pinned back from his face with gold and silver clasps. He held out his arms, inviting her to embrace him.

"We knew you would come. Finally, we can be together again."

"Mom? Dad? Is it really you? What is this place? Where have you been?"

"We discovered," Dad began, "and you did too, one of the Nameless Gates. The book was right. They're portals to other dimensions: time, space, planes. A gate that can take you anywhere. But we were too eager. It's so much more advanced than we expected."

Mom spoke up. "The gate shut behind us. It was always a

risk, so we prepared a message to reach you when you were old enough."

"Your mother and I became lost," Dad continued. "Unable to control where it took us. We've gained some mastery now and have learned much, but it took your reopening this gate to rebuild the pathway. Now that we've returned and gotten the coordinates, so to speak, we should all be able to come and go at will."

Mom shared one of those heartbreakingly warm smiles. "Your bright spirit, your courage, and determination were all represented not just by the letters of your name but by the way you say it." She chuckled. "Or sing it, in your case. You rescued us. And now there's so much lost time to make up for."

Dad beckoned. "Will you come with us? Let us show you how it works?"

"I want to," Mirasol said. "I do. But Van ... he's waiting for me. Across the bridge. I can't just disappear on him too."

"Van?" Mom and Dad looked at each other in shock. "He's here too? He came all the way up the mountain?"

"Van made my whole trip possible. It was thanks to him that I'm here at all. He wants answers too."

"Well, we need to see him immediately." Dad chuckled. "And we can't go walking over that bridge at this time of night. How about a demonstration? Cross the threshold, Mirasol, and we'll show you."

Mirasol hesitated. What if this was all a hallucination? Or a dream? A trick? What if they were wrong and she never returned after all?

But no matter the risk, she couldn't turn back now—no more than she could have at the ice-covered bridge. Just like then, just like her parents had done, she had to uncover the truth. If she turned back now, she'd go crazy, always wondering what would have happened. So, she crossed the threshold.

Immediately, her parents enveloped her in a giddy, awkward group hug. They certainly felt real, the press of their bodies crinkling her coat, their laughter, the texture of their strange clothes. Dad broke away first, his eyes glistening with tears. He went to a metallic wall lit with characters in an alphabet she didn't recognize. Mom continued to hold her in a tight embrace, swaying and murmuring her name. Dad pressed some keys, and the chamber flooded with light. She blinked against it and felt a purring vibration for only a few seconds.

A cold breeze tickled her neck. Mirasol pulled back from Mom and turned around. Through the arches, the scene had changed. Instead of the hidden chamber, she viewed an open ledge with a helicopter waiting on the ground. Neon colored tents were set up around the copter, an obvious base camp.

Her heart softened to see Van, scowling and pacing among the tents, arms crossed over his chest. She knew exactly what he was going through.

"Van!" she cried out. "Look who I found!"

Her friend whipped around. He gaped when his eyes lifted to take in the people behind her. His jaw moved, but no words came out.

"So, you have returned." The two guides appeared beside Van, seeming pleased but somehow unsurprised.

"We have," Dad said. "Thanks to Mirasol here."

"And a little help from Van, it seems," Mom added. She nodded appreciatively at the helicopter. "I remember how much you wanted those fancy toys. But how about Eagle and I show you the future of travel? We're going to need your help in protecting it, after all. I'd say we can talk on the way, but we'll be in your office before we've even begun."

Mirasol clasped Van's hands in hers. "We did it!" She knew

she was grinning crazily, but she didn't care. "Now we can go on adventures again as a family!"

Cas has been writing since he was around twelve years old. One of his greatest passions is creating worlds and bringing characters to life in people's minds. This is Cas's first story published so he can't wait to hear what people think and do more in the future.

DAYS BEYOND RAGNAROK

BY ASHLEY NEWELL

Withered. Withered and hollow. Despite the passing years, it never got any easier to see. He was like a broken mortal soldier, the last breathing of his generation, where the words failed and the memories flickered in and out of focus, with no one left who knew how to stitch them back together.

The Lady brought the bowl to his lips and let him drink in deeply. Wine. Cheap, and weak, but it didn't matter. It was gift enough to bring a spark back into the icy eye of this broken spirit. Her slender hands were strong enough to keep the bowl steady, even as his brittle hands trembled at both the weight of the gift and his eagerness to appease the seemingly endless drought inside of himself. His tongue, looking more like a grey eel than warm, pink flesh, darted out greedily, spraying droplets all about his thinning white beard.

It should have brought tears to her eyes, but the Lady didn't have any tears left to shed for this shell of a Father. She cooed soothing words of encouragement, knowing that he probably hadn't heard a single syllable, but the sound, she knew, was enough—enough to ease the bursts of hostility that flashed up through a thick fog of confusion.

With the bowl drained, the Lady dabbed at his wet beard with a silken handkerchief that had long lost the beauty of its vibrant colour, uneven now in tone and texture. Still, it was what she had, and the Father, who in better days would have ridiculed or scolded her for putting such a rag towards him, now didn't care enough to even look at it; even if he did, she doubted that he would even see it.

"Thank you," he said distantly, as if his lips knew what he was supposed to say though his mind couldn't remember why. "Are you a daughter of mine?" he asked, looking her in the eye for the first time today.

The Lady smiled sweetly for him, knowing that the truth would take more words to say than his memory would allow.

"Yes, Father," she replied. It wasn't exactly a lie, so her heart let the statement go freely. After all, it was he who gave her away on her wedding day. Granted, he had arranged it, but the Lady was also eager. Her husband was planned for her, even his ... It was all planned, wasn't it? She had to believe it was so. Even the worst parts. Even the suffering. Even now, living a life of crumbs—worse than that: dust. The Father had given her everything, and for years she wrestled with her heart to blame him for all he had taken away. Her husband, her children, her very place in the world. But it had all come back to him now, hadn't it? The serpent who bites his own tail will eventually feel the piercing pain, no matter how great the serpent. And the greater the serpent, the greater the pain.

"What is your name?" he asked, the black of his eye flitting back and forth as if scanning through pages of memory.

This time the tears did well up, though they could not fall, could not roll down her cheek. Even still, the Lady quickly wiped her chin as if she could feel the flood that should have amassed there.

"It doesn't matter now," the Lady said softly, the words sticking to the sides of her throat.

How could she explain it to him? How could she explain all that was lost? He had known once. He had seen it all coming, watched it all play out. He could stand tall then—even then. His long beard thick, his hands powerfully strong, his eye seeing all of the world as it was and the horizon of what was to come. Even this he once knew was to come. And yet, there was nothing more he could do to stop it. Or so the Lady had been told countless times. Some days she believed it, while other times she cursed the fool for every step he took to drive them down this thankless path. Today her pity outweighed her anger.

"I would like to know," the Father said, his head nodding drowsily, though his eye did not leave her.

She swallowed back a lifetime worth of words.

"So would I." She didn't mean to say it aloud, but it slipped out in a whisper. She clasped her hand over her mouth, as if to push the words back in.

Then, unexpectedly, the Father smiled. Not a practiced twitch of a smile, but a wave of knowing passed over his face and erupted there at the corner of his lips. The wine, surely.

"You will," he said. "And so will I."

She looked away and bowed her head, her tears betraying her at last. Her body stiffened as the dry brush of the Father's lips pressed gently to her forehead.

"I know you," he said. "And you know me."

The Lady cupped his cheeks and nodded, crying through the smile.

"I know you," she replied. "Always. And you have always known me." *Even when you didn't care to think of me.*

"It will come," he said knowingly. "He will make it right."

Her eyes met his once again. And they both held each other for a moment, as if clinging to the world they once shared.

"He will. He is. He is doing his best," her voice shook.

"I have never lost faith in Him."

The Lady wanted to believe it. Wanted to believe it more than anything. *Please tell me that it was all part of the plan. Please say that it was all for something greater.* But she could not plead with him. Not now. She watched as the fog drew once again across his face. The wine was not enough to sustain him for long, and there was no more to give him.

She could do no more than hold his frail hand, remembering the strength it once contained. Remembering the feats it once accomplished. Remembering the day his hand held hers as he gave it to her husband-to-be.

"Is he any better?" the soothing yet sturdy familiar voice spoke from behind her.

The Lady looked first to the Father; he had heard nothing. Then she glanced over her shoulder. The burden seemed to ease.

"The gift helped. Thank you," she said, slowly releasing herself from the Father. She tugged at her dress, as if her husband would ever care about the creases in the clothes or the disheveled frizz in her hair. She fell into his outstretched arms, burying her face into his neck until she was blanketed in his warm red locks.

"I know it isn't enough yet," the Husband said, "but I am getting closer."

She remained in his arms as she breathed him in. "I know you are. I trust you. And somewhere, in there, so does he."

It was the Husband who broke the comfort of the nest she had made under his ear. He held her shoulders and kissed her nose. "And you, my love? How are you keeping?"

"Better than most," she said, smiling through the weakness inside of her.

He kissed her, hard. It was the sort of kiss they used to share when the world was whole and their passion for one another was limitless. In this kiss she felt the tingles of being alive, as if he were trying to fill her with every last drop of his own essence, to make her whole again.

The Lady wrapped her arms around him, and he held her all the tighter. Then it was his turn to nestle into her neck. Softly he whispered. And she closed her eyes and drank in the soothing remedy of his voice against her ear. Her name. Ten times he whispered her name. And at each repetition she felt her knees quiver.

"I know it's not enough," the Husband said, clutching her tightly, "but I ..."

"It is enough," the Lady replied, clutching him just as tightly. "It is enough for now."

Hand-in-hand, they approached the Father, slouched over in what was once a great oaken throne. Now it was more bench than chair, ravaged by fires of war and worse. They both kneeled down. The Husband held up the bowl in both hands, closed his eyes, and drained some of the fire from within him to fill the bowl again. He rolled out the pinch in his neck and shoulders, the ache from pulling where there was little left to pull from.

"Drink this," the Husband said, holding it up to the Father's lips, who lapped it up without hesitation.

The Lady placed her hand on her Husband's arm, having noticed it shake under the weight of the Father's pull.

"Let me do that," she said.

The Husband smiled at her. "You've held the bowl long enough for me. I am not too proud to do my part."

She didn't release him. She grounded her body to keep her arm steady against his. "You've traveled the worlds and back again. You are doing far more than I, my love," she said, and she meant it.

"I would have traveled nowhere if it weren't for you. And my whispers would mean nothing if you weren't here to receive them."

When the Father relinquished the bowl, the Lady dabbed his beard again, but his eyes fell through her and to the man still aknee.

"I know you," his dry voice croaked.

"You do," the Husband said, "or so you think." He could not help but add a wink, regardless if the gesture would be appreciated now.

It must have been, for the Father's teeth separated, and the faint echo of a laugh emerged from the hollow shell. "What is your name?"

The Husband grinned playfully, as though the two were seated at the mead hall once more.

"That is not for me to say, I'm afraid. But let me gift you yours."

The Father did not protest as the Husband approached, lifting the thinning long hair away from the greying ear.

The Lady could not hear how many times her Husband whispered the name, but she could see the Father drinking it in, eyes closing deeply, his chest rising with air it had not tasted in some time. Just watching it seemed to fill her again, too, and so she hugged her arms tightly to herself, hearing her husband's voice in her own mind.

When the Husband pulled away from the Father, they gazed into the eternities within one another's eyes.

"Brother," the Father uttered with such certainty.

The Husband grinned once more—or had he ever stopped? "That is name enough for me, Brother," he replied, holding tightly onto the Father's arms as in the good old days.

"So, it is not yet over?" the Father asked, small sparks rising within him.

The Husband shook his head. "I have crossed every world, whispering our names, our deeds, our stories, our songs. Some still hear. Some hear it differently than what it once was. But even whispers can make echoes when spoken in the right places. I have found places that echo. The end is at an end, Brother. Forgive me for needing to weave a new beginning."

The Father's face seemed to glow, ever so slightly, and the lines of the skeleton on his hands seemed to smooth.

"It was always you," he said, less strained, less searching. "It was always you who could do what I could not."

The Husband took the Father's hands into his own and kissed them deeply. "I will not fail you. I will not fail any of us."

It was the Father's turn to kiss the Husband's hands.

"You never have"—he took a breath, as if deciding his next words carefully—"Loki."

Hearing it aloud, not restrained by a whisper, the name he could never utter himself, the Lady watched as her Husband's flesh warmed, his back straightened, and even his hair seemed to fill out fuller. The Lady's heart felt fuller, too, and from the corner of her eye, she spied the bowl, set unceremoniously on the floor, fill once again. She knelt and picked it up, bringing it between both of the men before her. Both Husband and Father drank from it, remembering the old oaths, the old bonds.

"I knew you could do it," the Father said, wiping his own chin.

"I have more whispers to feed our people with," Loki said.

"And your wife," said the Father, looking now quite clearly at the Lady who held the bowl, "Sigyn, she too tirelessly toils to keep us dying flames alight. I knew she was the right choice for you. For all of us."

And the Lady's most inner stem was set aflame, starting somewhere unknown within her, like a seed in her belly she didn't know she had swallowed, and it sprang forth to her fingers and her toes. She felt younger, lighter, almost as if the end days had never been.

Loki winked. "As did I. Odin."

* * *

Ashley Newell is a teacher and mom from Calgary, Alberta. She writes speculative fiction, designs board games, and occasionally finishes a craft she thought would be a good idea at the time.

CONSTELLATIONS OF NAMES

BY CAITLIN HEAGNEY

Cool mists blanketed the babbling river as ethereal bodies leapt and danced across its rippling surface. The trees climbed high over the pool, creating a canopy to hold the stars at bay from its shores. Moonlight grappled with the branches, seeking to alight upon the ever-shifting bodies of the fae. They moved in intricate circles, making patterns in the water.

Within the shadows of the boughs, a young woman moved. Her sunken eyes scrutinized the scene before her. The dancers twirled in patterns inconceivable to the minds of men, yet she watched on, entranced by them. Slowly, the mists parted, revealing in the river an ephemeral gateway, leading to a world parallel to her own. The fae filed through the portal in a neat line and, splashing through the water, the Woman jumped to follow.

The Faywild was full of stars as bright as the Beltane fires, which lit a winding path. It was lined by wildflowers on either side, interspersed with swirls of lavender and violets. Overhead were arches of trees with doors carved into their bark.

Time moved like thick honey as the Woman walked, slow and nostalgic.

As she walked further and further into the Wild, away from the place she once considered home, the fae became stranger. At first, she saw those who would pass through portals to cause mischief in the world of men: pixies and brownies, who would trick and confuse. But as she pressed on, the fae became more untamed. Lakes seemed to stretch out to the very horizon and swam with kelpies and selkies—gorgeous creatures ready to strike the Woman should she step too close to the water's edge.

Scared and desperate, she began to walk quicker as ivory towers struck impressive silhouettes across the dark purple sky. She stumbled up the stairs to the gilded doors that guarded the entrance and stepped into a great throne room. The room held the atmosphere of a church but was overrun with divine chaos. Trees and vines covered the walls, stretching up to a ceiling of crystal, revealing the deep sky.

The Queen stood before the throne as the Woman entered, crowned in flowers and constellations, and shrouded by a dress made of the morning sky itself. The Woman fell to her knees in reverence, head bowed out of respect and divine fear.

"What brings you here, child of man?" the Queen asked. Their voice was woven of starlight and spiked with the poison of royalty. Elegant and venomous like a snake beneath a flower.

"I come with a deal."

"A deal? Did your people not tell you to never deal with a fairy?"

"Yes, my Queen, but I believe there are certain things worth the risk. I come offering my name in exchange for safe haven."

"What is your name, child of man?"

"I am no child. Am I granted safe haven?"

For the first time, the Woman's and Queen's eyes met. A delicate hand reached out and held the Woman's jaw, turning it gently to examine the purple distortions that graced her features.

"What is it you run from?" they asked, their voice softening.

"A man ..."

"The women of your world, they did not help you?"

"Why should they? He was so kind to them all. I was simply the exception."

The Queen considered this for a moment. A luminescent tear began forming in their eye, begging to fall to the Woman out of pity. To look closely at such a symbol of empathy was to see endless stars and galaxies not yet formed.

"Safe haven is yours. What is your name?"

"~~Audrie.~~"

The Queen lifted their hand to the Woman's lips and drew the name from them like a golden string. The string hummed with light, and a noise burst through the room. At first, the sound was beautiful, like gentle whispers from a mother to a daughter. But it quickly changed. It rusted and rotted, the gold falling away as the sound became that of gnashing teeth. They lifted it above their head and let it drop into their mouth like the nectar of the gods.

"Welcome to the Faywild, child of stars."

The Woman had entered the castle with the burden of a name, but she left free of such weight. The name was decided for her before she even breathed, and yet it had defined her life for decades. She was bound by it in earthly matters, in signatures and contracts, and to have it taken from her was a sweet release.

With her newfound freedom, the Woman became a citizen of the Fairies. She spent long days wandering with them in fields and flowers. She didn't know how much time had passed outside, but she knew she had grown far wiser than the outside world would have allowed her. Her days were full, as was her heart. She lounged in the pools of wine-dark water with the selkies, no longer afraid of their claws or speed. Her favourite place, however, was in the castle with the Queen.

The Queen and the Woman spent many afternoons together, sharing sweet foods and sweeter words. Evenings were full of dances and elaborate clothing that twirled with the very forces of nature and hummed with music. With every coming dawn, the sun shone above the world and welcomed the Woman into the day. Every day felt like sweet memories of childhood that she may relive again and again.

The Woman was part of the fairies' ecosystem. She taught them of the outside world, so they may better deceive and confuse those who lived there. In return, they taught her all manner of tricks. Her body shone with the light of the sun, and her mind became a field of wildflowers. She was at peace, and all was well. But a storm brewed on the horizon—a storm made of anger and of man. It crashed against the rocks that bordered her happiness, ever present and threatening. With every passing day she grew calmer, but the storm would not fade, and eventually, it had to arrive.

And so, He did. Cain stormed up the path that his wife had previously walked. He was clumsy and blind to the beauty of the Faywild. Beneath his feet, flowers died and were replaced by burning ash. Brownies scurried around after him, and kelpies whinnied as he rushed past their pools. Where his wife's time was sweet honey, his burned like lava, erupting from his anger and flooding the world around him.

His voice echoed through the realm, shaking birds from their roosts. The stars above glistened and, angered at the interruption, shouted down at him.

"Turn away!" they demanded. "Leave this place before you taint it further!"

But he continued. He cared not for the beauty of the flowers or the opinions of the stars. He was single-minded, his arrival in this realm serving only one purpose: to retrieve what he considered his property. The ivory towers shadowed him from the sky. Feet fell flat in front of the intricate doors that guarded the palace against siege.

"~~Audrie.~~" he demanded, the name lost and forgotten but heard nonetheless. "Come out here, you stupid girl!"

The Queen opened the doors and gazed upon the image before them, taking in the dishevelled sight. They sighed and turned away. It was not their fight. The Queen looked at the Woman who stood before them. She had lost so much and yet embraced even more, and now she had to confront the man who had stolen her previous life. It was a life she could have had, content in the world of men.

"What say you, dear?" the Queen asked. They brushed their hands up the Woman's arms, her skin prickled under the cold touch. The Woman could not meet their eyes, staring past their figure to the open door.

"I won't ever be free of him ... will I?" the Woman whispered. "Not unless I end it."

The Queen nodded reluctantly, unable to formulate a reply that felt any bit appropriate.

"Then I know what I must do."

Their bodies intertwined briefly, a comfort before the storm truly hit. In that embrace, they made space for themselves: the Woman and the Queen, two archetypes forging their own stories and shaping their world. Releasing the Woman, the Queen turned away and took an object from a bench. It was wrapped in a deep purple cloth, hiding its form from sight. Delicate hands held it out, an offering of support that could not be given any other way.

The Woman pulled the cloth away, revealing an elegant blade. It glimmered with power, crafted by Fairy Fire and adorned with intricate runes. Power, protection, prosperity, and everything the Woman wished for. This the Queen offered to her. She tore her eyes from the object and met the Queen's gaze. Her features softened, and a serene smile graced her face.

"Thank you," she said, taking the weight of the object into her hands. She turned to the door again, now full of righteous anger, never again fear.

"You," the Woman began, stepping down the stairs to meet him.

The man went to speak but was choked. His eyes scattered across the crowd and found the Queen, who stared down at him with contempt. The Woman continued towards him.

"You stole everything from me. My dignity, my humanity, my faith. You stole my very name, given to me by my mother, and branded me with it like a prize bull! Well, I am not yours, I never was, and I never will be!"

"How dare you!" the man started, biting against his invisible muzzle. "You are my wife, and you dare to embarrass me like this? I thought you better, ~~Audrie.~~"

The Woman's head snapped at the name. Before he, or any creature, could have reacted, the blade was at his throat. His posture was not yet shaken, the folly of men blinding him to the danger.

"Do not speak that name. It is not mine."

"Oh, you think yourself so mighty now! You are but a girl, a feeble-minded prize. Mine to mould and use."

"You moulded me into a creature of fear. But I have found salvation. You are no owner of mine, no artist or creator. You are but a man. And a horrid one at that."

Cain scoffed. Excitement buzzed through the fae, like

lighting seeking the Earth.

"What is your name?" The Woman asked, her blade lifting his chin towards her.

"You know my name! Or are you that lost in your fantasies that you forgot it?"

"Oh yes, dear husband, I am so lost. Please give me your name!"

"My name is Cain, you—"

Before he could utter another syllable, the woman whipped the sword away from him and pinched her hand upon the sliver of his name. Much like she had seen the Queen do however long ago, she drew the string up and away from his lips. It hummed with sound. Kind, quiet voices turned angry and forceful, gradually dissipating until it was only his voice singing out his name.

The Woman brought the string to her mouth. Whether it were Ichor or Ambrosia, it slipped down her throat sickly sweet. As she consumed it, her stature seemed to grow. The incomplete woman she'd been for so long was now gone, and in her place was a woman grown. The man sat at her feet, choking on his own name, trying again and again to spit it out one last time but failing. Smaller fae buzzed around his ears, teasing him and eager to drag him off.

"What shall we do with him?" A sprite asked, a wicked grin decorating his face. "Where shall he go?"

"Return him to the world of man," she said, "so he may suffer knowing he will never again have me nor any place here. I pray no name is ever gifted to you again, dear husband."

She turned from him as he was dragged away by a myriad of creatures who laughed at his plight. She moved back up the stairs towards the Queen. The sword clattered to the ground as she and the Queen embraced. The two separated, and soft laughter escaped their lips. The storm had passed; he could never hurt her again. The air cleared around the pair.

"Tell me, my dear," the Queen said. "How will you shape your new name?"

She considered for a moment, thinking of all the possibilities. A sea of choices expanded out before her, waves lapping gently at the shore.

"My name ... is Alvina, friend of the Fairies," Alvina said, grinning up at the taller figure.

"What a beautiful name. Mine is Titania, friend of Alvina."

* * *

Caitlin is a queer Aussie with a penchant for fantasy and mythology. She loves taking the chance to explore everyday experiences through the lens of magic and reverie. For her first ever publication, *Constellations of Names* is a Shakespeare-inspired journey into the Faywild.

THE PHOENIX AND THE FEY

BY ERIN CASEY

Quinn strummed her lute on the edge of Queen Favreh's nest while the phoenix nestled around two crimson eggs. Favreh kept a steady flame burning along her golden feathers to provide extra warmth to the fragile shells. Quinn couldn't blame her for her precautions. After losing her last clutch to a sudden frost, Favreh wasn't taking any chances.

Neither was Quinn for that matter. Her fingers danced across the strings and lent magic to her voice. She sang to the eggs, imbuing them with her fey power to help them grow big and strong. *Join us little brother and sister*, she thought to them. *The world is waiting for your fire.*

"Such a beautiful melody," Favreh cooed, swaying to the tempo.

Quinn smiled. Favreh was like a mother to her, and the rest of the flock was an extension of her family. After losing her village to fey hunters, Quinn had stumbled into one of the phoenix kingdoms, wounded and exhausted. It was Favreh, then a princess, who had taken her in, nursed her back to health, and given her the name Quinn.

"Quinn is a strong phoenix name," Favreh had explained. "And if you wish to be part of our flock, then you should have a name befitting a child of a phoenix."

Quinn had done more than that. She'd used her magic to transform her iridescent wings into flaming feathers. Sometimes she even transformed into a phoenix so she could join her adopted brethren in the sky, though it had been some time since she'd last done so.

Quinn leaned back as she resumed her song and looked around at the mighty phoenixes surrounding her. Her flock resided in a forest nestled on the edge of a cliff overlooking the land of Sylvaldia. A glistening blue river just shy of the mountain provided plenty of fish for them to hunt.

While some nests had been built on the cliff face or inside caves (for the quieter or more timid phoenixes), some nests, like Favreh's, were located in black-branched Shadow trees. Phoenix fire would have destroyed a regular forest, but the Shadow trees grew from seeds coated in phoenix ash to repel their flames. Thick, broad silver and green leaves filled the branches, sheltering them from rain and snow. A single leaf was nearly the length of Quinn's forearm and was used in nest making.

Favreh was positioned in the heart of the flock, where it would be harder for other phoenixes, fey, gryphons, or humans to reach her. Favoring safety, several flock members with eggs or newborn chicks had built their nests near Favreh's as well. Quinn's nest, located above in a nearby tree, meant she could also lend her magical protection. For now, though, she happily perched beside her mother and played for the nestling families.

A couple of talons pricked Quinn's skin, pulling her from her thoughts. She shifted one wing and glanced beneath it at the fledgling snoozing against her. The young phoenixes loved cuddling with her, especially when she sang. In fact, she was surprised more of the flock hadn't joined her. Still, most of the little ones were snoozing in the nests surrounding them, their mothers and fathers keeping close watch.

The fledgling peeked open a big brown eye before he buried his head further into her side.

Quinn laughed, causing her to hit a wrong note. "Akis, that tickles!"

Akis didn't budge. He ground his beak in contentment and flicked his wings before folding them down his back.

"Spoiled chick," Favreh teased.

Quinn reached behind Favreh's head and scritched her feathers lightly. "Happy more than spoiled, I think," Quinn said, chuckling. She shifted to get more comfortable and resumed playing, Akis's tiny beak grinds adding an accompaniment. She closed her eyes and lost herself in the peaceful moment with her feathered family.

"Mother!"

A screech shattered the quiet. Quinn jumped, and Akis squawked and scrambled backward until he fell into her lap. As Quinn righted him onto her knee, a brilliant crimson phoenix with golden accents flew up to the nest. The poor bird panted, her talons digging into sticks and branches to keep her upright. Quinn reached out to steady her.

Favreh sat up sharply. "Gala, what's happened?" She looked around, her eyes growing wide. "Where's ReiRei?"

Quinn's stomach twisted when she realized the younger phoenix sibling was indeed missing.

"I'm sorry, Mother," Gala keened, her head bowed miserably. "ReiRei and I were out flying, and we saw a zapfruit by some bushes. ReiRei landed to fetch it, but the moment she grabbed hold, a fey appeared. She said she could bring us to a tree with even more zapfruit, and then ReiRei—" her voice caught in her throat. "She told the fey her name."

A gasp went up around them as the other phoenixes heard

the news. Quinn gritted her teeth and held Akis closer. Zapfruit was a rare and special plant for the phoenixes. Not only did it nourish them, the fruit made their fire stronger, ensuring the wellbeing of their eggs.

No wonder the fey had used the fruit to tempt ReiRei.

Though Quinn felt a couple phoenixes glance her way warily, most trusted that she wasn't like her name-stealing brethren. It was dangerous to give a fey your name, as that was tantamount to giving her your will. And some fey never released their victims.

If ReiRei, the youngest daughter of the phoenix queen and king, had found herself trapped, the fey could do unspeakable damage to their flock. ReiRei was the perfect bargaining tool.

Favreh screeched in outrage and rose over her eggs. "Where was your sister taken? What did the fey look like?"

"Sh-she was pale blue and dressed in black. I found her in Bramble Woods."

Favreh threw her head back with another cry, fire bursting around her body until every feather glowed with barely restrained magic. "I will make that fey suffer for this!"

Gala whined and shrank pitifully beneath her mother. Quinn's heart ached for her. She knew the guilt of losing someone she loved and being unable to do anything about it. And if Favreh left to save her daughter, and something happened to her, the eggs would likely perish. Gala would blame herself for both the loss of her mother and siblings.

Quinn wished Malore, Favreh's mate, was there to help, but he wasn't meant to return from a diplomatic mission with a neighboring phoenix kingdom for another week. With ReiRei in a fey's clutches, they couldn't wait that long.

Quinn stood up, cradling Akis in her arms. "Favreh, wait," she pleaded. "I know you're angry and scared, but Gala needs you right now, and so do your little eggs." She gestured to the nest. "Let me rescue ReiRei."

Favreh's feathers poofed up in anger, fire snarling from the tips. "I should be the one to save my daughter. That fey needs to pay! I'll not let her take her revenge on my chicks."

Quinn frowned in confusion. "Revenge? What do you mean?"

But Favreh wasn't listening. She crouched, preparing to leap.

Quinn sprang across the nest in front of her, spreading an arm to make her stop while the other clutched Akis to her chest. "What if you get ensnared in her trap, what then?" She bowed her head deeply. "My queen, you brought me into your family when I had nowhere else to go. I live and serve you both as my queen, and as my mother, which makes ReiRei and Gala my sisters. *Please,* trust me to save her so you can be the strength our flock needs. Look at Gala. She needs her mother. And you can't risk losing those eggs."

Favreh slowly shifted her angry eyes to Gala, who huddled at the edge of the nest, inches from Quinn. Seeing the fear, guilt, and sadness encompassing her little one, Favreh's gaze softened, and her feathers flattened. She leaned forward and preened her daughter. "Come here, my chick. It isn't your fault."

"Mama," Gala wept and huddled against her mother's warm breast feathers. She peered at Quinn with one eye, the other hidden in her mother's chest. "What if she takes you, too? Or she doesn't come out because you're a fey?"

"She won't know what I truly am," Quinn said with a wink. She placed Akis beside Gala and stepped out of Favreh's nest onto some of the Shadow branches. She spread her wings and flew up to her nest a few feet above Favreh's. Several leaves were woven together with thread, creating a more private canopy for herself. Still, that didn't stop the younger phoenixes from flying or climbing up to snuggle with her.

After Quinn tucked her instrument away, she took a breath and spread her arms.

Fey magic rushed over her, causing her body to grow larger. Her arms sucked inside her chest as emerald and blue feathers, their tips dusted gold, washed over her breast. Talons formed where her feet should have been. As her face morphed, her lips grew hard and turned into a sharp, snapping beak.

"You're going as a phoenix?" Gala asked in surprise.

Quinn nodded and shook out her feathers. "The fey would keep her guard up if I went to her in my natural form." She leapt off the branch and flew down onto the edge of Favreh's nest. "I'll be swift, I promise."

"Be *safe*," Favreh said and draped a wing over Quinn. "Don't trust this fey. I banished her long ago after she stole eggs from us for her spells."

"She *what?*" Quinn cried, appalled. "She killed hatchlings?"

"No, but she prevented us from performing the soulfire ritual that would hatch them," Favreh explained. She looked down at her little eggs. "The eggs will only hatch under a noon sun and if they're bathed in a phoenix's hottest flames, ideally those of a parent. Without the ritual, the chick's soulfire never ignites. It's why the eggs are so precious; so few hatch. She took the eggs before the soulfire could be awakened and used the contents in what I can only assume were vile plans. For her crime, I banished her." Favreh glared off into the distance. "She won't be content until she has my head."

Quinn clacked her beak in anger. The only solace she found was that, without the soulfire, the chicks hadn't suffered when the eggs were broken. It also reinforced her decision that *she* should go and not Favreh. If Malore didn't return for *any* reason, Favreh's flames would be the best to ignite the soulfire. "Is there anything else you can tell me about her that may help us? Do you know her name?"

Favreh shook her head regretfully. "I never learned it, but some call her Monarch because of her wings and her rather matriarchal disposition. She's not someone to be trifled with. Come home. Both of you."

Quinn bowed, but that didn't feel like enough. Though she was confident in her skills, it was possible she wouldn't return. If this was goodbye ...

She leaned forward and nuzzled Gala and then Favreh—no, her mother—on the cheek. Favreh rubbed her beak affectionately along Quinn's feathers.

"Gala, where in the Bramble Woods did you find the fey?" Quinn asked.

"The southern entrance, beside the river flanked with juniper bushes."

Quinn jumped off of the nest and spread her fiery wings, carrying her past the other phoenixes who screeched their support. They were likely glad *they* weren't the ones flying off to face a fey.

Quinn wasn't foolish; even a fey like her could get caught up in another's spell. She had a name just like any other being, but there was far more to her name than most knew, something she meant to use to her advantage.

She flew over the crystal blue river and followed it to the juniper bushes. The entrance of the Bramble Woods, a place of mystery and danger, loomed over the foliage. Mist coiled in and out of the trees. Branches glistened with jade leaves, while others dripped with poisonous fruit.

Few ventured there for fear of never leaving.

It was said that, long ago, the Goddess of Night cursed the forest. One evening, she followed her chosen priestess into the trees and found her worshipping, and loving, the Goddess of Dawn. Enraged, the Goddess of Night turned her priestess into a twisted, gnarled tree that grew poisoned berries. Each berry that fell to the ground birthed bramble bushes from the seeds. Their roots tainted the trees and turned them into twisted ghosts of their former selves. The few living trees remaining contained some of the precious zapfruit the phoenixes craved. Phoenixes, especially, had worked for years on lifting the curse, but still the mist and poisoned trees lingered.

Quinn landed near the juniper bushes and folded her wings. She looked around at the beautiful foliage that gave way to dark trees and forbidden fruits at the entrance of the forest. Quinn clacked her beak in frustration.

"ReiRei? ReiRei, where are you?" she called. She stalked closer to the entrance, then stepped inside the Bramble Woods. The mist swallowed her up as she ducked her head beneath claw-like branches. Even the air felt colder.

Spiders skittered along tree trunks. Somewhere, a beast roared a vicious warning. This was a place of nightmares for young phoenixes; it was no wonder, then, why a deceptive fey would choose it as her home. Then again, according to Favreh, it hadn't exactly been a choice.

Quinn treaded carefully on the ground, searching for foot or talon prints that might belong to either ReiRei or the fey. She didn't dare jump into the trees lest the twisted branches snare her feathers.

Suddenly, magic washed over her, throwing her into a tree trunk. She crumbled to the ground with a pained squawk, dazed. Vines coiled around her and dragged her violently across dirt and stones. The entrance vanished from sight. With a hiss, Quinn dug her talons into the ground and burnt the vines to a crisp with her magic.

"Well, well, well. Queen Favreh sends someone else to do

her dirty work," a voice chimed in the darkness.

Quinn struggled to her feet and squinted. She found herself in a small clearing surrounded by trees and bushes. She searched the canopy until she caught movement.

A fey perched on a branch, her skin the color of a cool cloudy sky. Long, blue hair coiled in ringlets around her face, with some pinned behind her head with black butterflies, their small wings flicking every so often. An ebony snakeskin covered her chest and stopped at trousers made of blue butterfly wings and cobwebs. She offered a vibrant red-lipped smile.

A webbed cocoon hung on the branch beneath her, keeping ReiRei trapped. Only the young phoenix's head was left free, except for her beak, which was tethered shut with white strands. ReiRei whined when she saw Quinn, but there was nothing she could do to break free. The web somehow resisted her quivering fire.

"Am I too unworthy for the great queen to trade words with?" the fey—Monarch, Quinn presumed—scoffed. She glanced at ReiRei. "Or does she care so little about her daughter's plight she'd send someone in her stead?"

Quinn approached, keeping an eye on loose roots, vines, and webs. "I pledged to free her daughter. Release her. You have no right to keep her here."

Monarch laughed. "She gave me her name! Surely you know what that means?" She reached down and flicked ReiRei's beak. "She must obey my every word. If I ask her to attack you, she will."

"But you won't, because you need her," Quinn countered. "I've come to make a deal. Take me in ReiRei's place. If you let her go, I'll give you my name, and then you may do as you please with me."

The fey curled her lip. "*You're* not the one I want."

Quinn ruffled her wing feathers and stepped over a

branch. "You want the queen because she banished you, isn't that right?" The fey's murderous gaze was answer enough. "What do you hope to accomplish by luring her here?"

"Favreh must pay for the pain she's caused me," the fey growled. "I've been trapped in this cursed forest for a decade, unable to return to my family or tell them I'm even alive. All because I took a few phoenix eggs."

"You kept those eggs from the soulfire ritual," Quinn argued. "Because of you, those phoenix chicks were never born! She had to ensure you wouldn't do it again. And yet you still stole her daughter."

"Yes, because then I could bring Favreh to me and end her myself. Once she's gone, I'm free." Monarch looked up at the sky with longing. "I *want* to go home. I took *eggs*, ones unfertilized by fire. I didn't take chicks. And I've paid for my crimes. All I've done is wither away. I don't even know if my family still lives."

Quinn frowned as she listened. She didn't doubt the fey's words, and Favreh's warning corroborated the story. She understood what it was like to have her home stolen from her: the ache and longing to return to everything she'd known. But she'd found a new family, one the fey had invaded and desecrated. She had every reason to condemn Monarch, and yet, something about Favreh's story niggled at her mind. Favreh had said the fey had taken the eggs for what she could only assume were "vile plans." And yet, Monarch made it clear she'd taken eggs rather than chicks, so there had been some thought in her actions, some desire to preserve life.

In a hesitant voice, Quinn asked, "*Why* did you take them?"

Monarch squinted suspiciously at her.

"Shouldn't you know, little phoenix? Their shells are magical, and I needed them for my mother. She was stricken by a hunter's poisoned arrow. My magic wasn't enough, but the shells amplified it. The elixir *healed* her. I took more eggs to help protect my people, but Favreh caught me and banished me here with her magic."

Quinn grimaced. While she understood the reason for stealing the eggs, that didn't make it right. There were other ways; there had to be!

"I know you're cross with Favreh. And if you want revenge on her, fine. Take *me*. I'm her eldest daughter. You don't need to keep my little sister if you have me."

The fey's eyes lit up. "Favreh has *three* daughters?" She clicked her tongue and spread her iridescent black wings. She fluttered down toward Quinn and looked her over. "You would really trade yourself for your sister?"

ReiRei jerked in her cocoon, releasing muffled squawks of protest.

Quinn smiled lovingly at her then nodded. "I'd trade my life if I had to."

"Hm ... perhaps I *can* make a deal then."

"Release ReiRei," Quinn demanded. "Then I'll give you my name."

The fey shook her head. "No. You give me your name first, and then I'll release your sister." She tapped her lips. "A fey can't lie, so you know what I say is true."

Quinn studied her. She didn't like it, and it was obvious the game Monarch was trying to play by not designating *when* she'd release ReiRei. She meant to trap Quinn, if not them both. But Quinn could play a trick of her own, and it might be the only thing that saved ReiRei's life. The fey's magic was old, Quinn could feel it in her bones, which meant Quinn would be no match for her one-on-one.

It's a challenge of tricksters, then, Quinn thought. *So be it. Don't worry, ReiRei. I still have the upper hand.* With a grunt, she raised her beak.

"Very well. My name is Quinn."

The fey laughed and threw out her hand. Blue magic wrapped around Quinn, forcing her to walk toward the fey then bow in front of her. No matter how hard Quinn struggled, the magic kept her pinned. No, not just the magic, the fey's *will*. Her phoenix body, now named, was forced to obey.

"Ha!" Monarch crowed. "Now the queen has lost *two* daughters. If she doesn't come for me, then I can be satisfied knowing she'll never see either of you again."

Quinn's eyes flashed indignantly, adding to the ruse. "You promised to free ReiRei! You can't lie!"

"And I will." The fey leaned down and cupped Quinn's beak, smiling. "I just didn't specify *when* I would release your sister." She cackled and flew up into the sky. "ReiRei and Quinn. You both are mine."

Quinn grunted as she was made to bow her head to Monarch. She screeched in anger and tried to fight it, but the force was so *strong*, far stronger than she expected. For a moment, she feared she'd let herself get bested, but Quinn wasn't ready to give up yet. She was still a *fey*. "Who are you?" she cried. "Are we just supposed to call you master now?"

The fey chuckled and flew back up to the branch holding ReiRei. "I suppose there's no harm in telling you now, especially if I order you, which I do, not to say it to another living soul." She smirked. "I'm Atala."

Quinn felt a jolt inside her chest as the name reached her ears. With a cry, she shed her phoenix form. Feathers and fire fell away from her, revealing her crouched fey body, her old wings arched protectively over her. Quinn rose, free of Atala's magical commands. The shock on Atala's face would have made her smile if she didn't feel some pang of pity. They had both lost their family, after all, but this had nevertheless been the fey's own doing.

"Atala, I order you to release ReiRei unharmed."

Atala gaped, but surprise turned to outrage as she was

forced to do as she was commanded. The fey fluttered down to the captive phoenix and used a rusted dagger to cut the cobwebs except for a single strand. She lowered ReiRei gently to the dirt and yanked the last thread off of her. Freed, the little phoenix darted to Quinn's side.

"*How?*" Atala snarled, tears of anger and despair pricking her eyes. She landed and clenched her hands into fists. "You told me your name! I felt it in my chest!"

"I told you *one* of my names," Quinn replied. She bent and wrapped her arms around ReiRei. "But I wasn't born with that name. It was given to me by my adopted mother, Favreh. I never once lied about being her daughter or ReiRei's sister." She held out her hand. "I order you to release the name Quinn back to me."

Against her will, Atala shouted and drew her fingers across her chest. She pulled her hand back, taking with it a white orb. With a scowl, she tossed it to Quinn. Quinn caught the orb and pushed it into her own chest. Her wings changed once more, taking on their feathery and fiery glow.

"I don't understand. If Quinn *isn't* your real name, then how was I able to control you?" Atala asked with a growl. "I *felt* my will and yours collide, and mine was far stronger!"

"Because as far as I'm concerned, Quinn is as real to me as my fey name. It was given to me by a second family that loves me. As for you." Quinn pressed her lips together and studied Atala. The fey shied away as if waiting for Quinn to destroy her or, worse yet, order her to obliterate herself. Quinn squeezed ReiRei's wing gently. "Atala, I order you to return to your family. You will never touch another phoenix egg. You will never darken Favreh's or her family's nest ever again. You will bring no harm to others, and you will not *steal* names. You will live your life humbly with your family. As the holder of your name, I order this of you."

Instead of looking enraged, Atala's eyes widened in shock

then gratitude. She looked up to the sky and tentatively flew upward. She reached out a hand and slid it past the tree line. Atala released a joyful cry. She burst through the canopy and vanished from their eyes. Quinn thought that would be the end of it, but when she turned to guide ReiRei out of the forest, Atala reappeared in front of her, staring at her.

"*Why?*" she whispered. "You had every reason to destroy me. Why free me?"

"Because I know what it's like to lose loved ones, and I wouldn't wish that pain on anyone else. Besides," she said as she smiled at ReiRei, "I was lucky to find a new family. And I hope that, if you can't locate your old one, you'll find others to welcome you and love you. Remember this gift, Atala."

The fey sniffled and wiped at her tears. "Thank you," she said. Then with a burst of magic, she flew up into the sky and disappeared.

"You saved me," ReiRei said in wonder. "But ... but what if she'd trapped you forever, too?"

Quinn knelt and reached for her little sister. She pulled her into her arms and stroked the phoenix's soft feathers. "Well, then I would have been trapped with you, and I could have made sure you'd never be alone."

ReiRei nuzzled her. "Thank you, Quinn. I love you."

"I love you too, little egg." Quinn kissed ReiRei's head and gave her another warm squeeze. "Now, let's go home. Mother's waiting for us."

Erin Casey is a fantasy/urban fantasy writer and author of The Purple Door District series. She's a mom to six feathered kids, the inspiration behind many of her winged characters, including the phoenix and the fey in her story. Learn more about her at erincasey.org.

TANUKI TROUBLES

BY ODESSA SILVER

It happened in the fifth month of the year, or so the humans named it. The sakura had already fallen, the forest was bursting with new life, and now in our leaf-filled den lay six tiny tanuki pups, eyes closed tight to the bright new world. Shiki, my partner, had birthed them in the night under the watchful gaze of the full moon.

"What should we name them, Tanu?" she'd asked me, curling up around the pups with exhaustion.

I thought about it for a while, going through every name I could think of until I collapsed down on the leaves beside her. Naming children was very difficult indeed.

"For now, why don't we number them?" I suggested. "And think of names later."

However, 'later' never happened. And so that's how our children gained their names: Ichi, Ni, San, Shi, Go, and Roku.

Now, the forest leaves were clinging on to the last of summer before they burned orange and red. Together we'd raised the pups almost to adulthood, teaching them everything a tanuki needed to know: where to find the best frogs, which berries would upset a stomach, and most important of all, which way the humans lived. The forest was safe enough for tanuki, we weren't disturbed too often and kept ourselves hidden away, but children were far too curious.

One day, a travelling monk passed through. He was quiet enough, his steps soft in the grass, but the look in Roku's eyes told me everything.

"Father," she whispered, watching the monk settle down in a small clearing, under the warm sun. "Is that one of those humans you've talked about?"

"Yes," I replied, trying to usher her back into the den with my head. "Let's stay away from him."

"But Father, look at his strange face."

"Yes, humans have such a flat face, but let's go—"

"But Father, look at his strange fur—"

I grappled Roku with my paws and pinned her to the dirt. "Yes, humans wear strange things." I let out a huff. "Den time."

"But Father—" I placed a paw on her muzzle to stop any more words. Roku wriggled and wiggled until she broke free. "Ichi gets to go see the human. Why not me?"

"What?"

I spun around in panic to see Ichi, the bravest of the pups, charging into the grass, fearless and reckless.

"Ichi, Ichi!" I barked, trying to summon him back, but just like the other pups, Ichi did not listen. Instead, the rest of them joined him, brown balls of fluff bounding into the lush green grass.

I wanted to yelp and cry. How did Shiki keep them out of trouble?

Of course the pups chose the moment she left to find food to get up to mischief. I had never wanted her back more.

It was a disaster. Ichi pounced first, followed by San, both landing on the monk's lap with a soft plop. Ni decided it was more fun to bite his staff, and all three earnt a laugh from the surprised monk.

Eventually they all grew bored of their new plaything, except Roku. She stayed by the monk's side the whole time, right up until he finished meditating and left the forest as quietly as he'd arrived. And every single night since then, she asked question after question about humans.

At first I told her the scary stories, how humans used long metal weapons and drank very hot liquids, but nothing swayed her love. And then, finally, two nights ago, she told us what we'd expected since the day of the monk.

"Mother, Father," Roku said, dropping a half eaten frog on the grass in front of me. "Soon it will be time for us pups to leave you and find our own way before we hibernate. I have decided that I want to go into the human town."

I let out a long huff. I wanted to protect her and keep her safe. However, soon she would be old enough to live her own life. The other pups didn't want to leave at all; they preferred being cared for. But not headstrong Roku.

"You'll need to be really good at transforming," I said finally.

"I've been practising!" she boasted. "Yesterday I spent all day as a rock in the river."

"I hope you'll return to us from time to time," Shiki said, sniffing. She wasn't ready for the pups to leave us either.

Roku wiggled her brown tail with excitement. "I'll even bring you gifts!"

"What about a name?"

She stopped, puzzled. "What do you mean?"

"Well," I started, "you'll need a new name for when you're around the humans. They have names like *Hikoshige* or *Kazuyasu*. Your name would stand out."

"Oh," she said, stopping in her tracks. "I never thought of that."

Her big black eyes betrayed sadness, and guilt nagged in my stomach. I stood up. "Don't worry, I will find you a name perfect for a human."

"What?" Shiki and Roku said in unison.

"Yes, I'll go into the human town. I've done it many times before. I can hold a transformation long enough."

"Are you sure?" Roku asked. "You've always told me scary stories about humans. Won't they boil you alive and use your pelt to hammer the gold?"

I blanched a little. It certainly was a possibility if they realised what I truly was. "They won't catch me," I said. "If anything goes truly wrong, I'll just transform into a kitsune. They'd have to take a chance on if I was Inari's messenger or not. Nobody is going to risk angering a god."

They both stared at me, and I puffed out my chest. I knew what I was doing.

Exiting the den, I collected a pile of fallen leaves and a few pebbles and placed them down in a small clearing. I needed to be able to see the moon. Shiki and Roku followed and watched me carefully.

"First, I will need what the humans call money. They use it to trade for food and items." I reached out and placed a paw on the pile, and with a *poof* it changed to human coins. "Like this."

Roku gasped and ran over, inspecting the coins. "That's impressive."

"Of course it is! Not all tanuki can do this. Now for me too."

Looking up to the moon, I nodded. It was time. I sat back and placed a leaf on my head then started tapping my belly, creating a tune.

Pon pon pon pon went the light drumming.

Pom poko pom poko went the tune, changing as the transformation was near.

One, two, three, *poof!*

I changed my form from a tanuki to an adult human clothed in a forest green kimono. Looking at Roku, her eyes sparkled more than I'd ever seen them.

And so, that's how I ended up on my back, partially drunk, in the human town. I'd forgotten how just the smallest cup of sake was enough to send my head into a spin. The fishermen had found it hilarious and kept refilling my cup. I could hardly say no to their kindness, and so I drank and drank until I fell over.

"Kouji," one of them slurred at me. "Do you have a family? A wife waiting at home when you return from travelling?"

I'd told them I was a travelling merchant, looking for goods only found along the coast. Not that they cared too much; they were too busy enjoying how easily I got drunk.

"I do," I said, trying not to bring back up all the sake in my stomach. "A wife and children. They eagerly await my return."

"That must be nice," another chimed in. "I've always wanted a wife."

"Kouji, you should see how Jun scares away all the women with his stern face. Soon the only women he won't have chased away will be fish. Think they'll marry him?"

"Then I will be surrounded by many wives," Jun said with a laugh and drank another cup of sake.

The sky stopped spinning for a moment, and I sat up. "What about children? I've always wanted another child, but I have run out of names I like."

I watched the fishermen eagerly. Soon Roku would have a new name, much faster than I had anticipated.

"I've never thought about it before," Jun said before nodding. "How about Junichi?"

"Yes," the largest fisherman called Kyosuke added. "A

strong son to help with the fishing. We need some more youngsters."

"Little Ryuuma will be old enough to join us soon. We should bring him on a trip."

"Hey, how about a game of hanafuda?" A new voice interrupted.

"Oh, did you bring your cards?"

I sighed as the conversation shifted away from names and my chance was lost. Perhaps my answer wasn't with the fishermen after all. There were other places I could go tomorrow, when I wasn't so drunk. For now, I would try to keep the sake in my belly.

The second day of being in the human town started off better than the first. I walked the busy streets and took in all the new scents; it had been a long time since I had been amongst the humans. I hadn't told Roku how I learnt so much about them, hoping it would dissuade her from visiting. And she had turned out just like me anyway.

As a younger tanuki, I had visited this town many times, transforming into many of the strange objects I found and changing back to scare the humans. It had been so much fun —well, mostly. Once, after drawing too much attention by not wearing the right clothes, I changed into a tea kettle to hide and rest. But that had abruptly ended when I was placed above a fire. I had a bald patch for the next two moons!

I almost had the urge to check it hadn't shown in my human form somewhere. Long ago, my sister had fallen into a dye pot after being found snooping at kimonos. Her fur changed to a deep green, and when she changed into a human to get close again, her human hair was green too. She'd cried and cried and stayed in the river until it all washed out.

Being a human was difficult business. But so fun. Too fun, sometimes.

I happily passed by many different workers heading here

and there, the streets heaving with people busy with daily life. Nearby I could smell fresh foods being sold at a market, and further beyond that the burning smell of the blacksmith forges hard at work. As I continued on, the market came into view, along with stronger smells. I wandered over and looked at all the wares with interest. One man sold a variety of pottery, earthy coloured pots and jars, and a small selection of bowls. I had to fight the urge to transform into one of them to trick the owner. I could be bought by an unsuspecting person, and when they tried to use the bowl: *poof!* I'd surprise them by transforming back. It'd be hilarious.

The next stall held pots of brightly coloured powders. When I tried getting closer to smell the deep red one, it tickled and burnt the insides of my nose. I quickly grabbed hold of my nose as my eyes watered, but the smell was too strong. *A-A-Achoo!*

A cloud of red exploded. Everyone around me started coughing and batting away the air. One man brought out a fan, but that made everything worse, and then even the owner was bent over in a fit of coughs. I hurried away from the stall as fast as I could in the unfamiliar and restrictive kimono, trying to breathe once again. Angry voices started to call in my direction, so I quickened my pace until I couldn't see them. I slipped down a side street and hoped nobody followed me from the market.

"Sakurago, my son," a woman cried desperately, "how can you leave me such a letter?"

I spun around to try and find the source of the voice.

"I will find you and bring you home, where you belong. It is true that we suffer hardships with poverty, but I suffer more without you."

Spotting the source, I walked closer with intrigue. A crowd surrounded a raised open platform, and on it stood a woman with a painted white face, still and unmoveable. Even while she spoke, the lips didn't move. I couldn't stop watching her move, her heart crying out for her son.

"Sakurago, where are you?" she wailed, running to the back of the platform. "I must find you."

Music played, and a man walked to the front now, his face unmoving as the woman's. A monk, I decided, as his clothes were the same as the one we'd seen in the forest. He spoke now, but my mind was elsewhere. *Sakurago*—that was a nice name, but would it be a fit for Roku? I looked around at all the people watching. Everyone would know it. Perhaps it was a name too known and would make her stand out. Plus, she didn't remind me of cherry blossoms at all. Roku was more like the autumn, fiercely beautiful.

When I'd been to the human town before, I'd seen a similar act of humans wearing the still faces. I'd been curious and snuck into a nearby room where they dressed and transformed into one of the faces. Instead of copying the scary oni, I made my own: a brown tanuki face after my own. It had been funny at first, watching them all question where it came from. That is, until a man placed me on his face, where I was forced to stay until evening. His breath was foul, and I so desperately wanted to get away. He'd even taken me to his home, laying me carefully on a table with pride. I even began to feel sorry for him.

When he was finally out of sight, I transformed with a *poof* back to my tanuki self, so I could escape onto the roof and away from his rancid odour.

The third day exploring was a disaster. It had rained all day, and I'd huddled up on my futon, lonely and missing my family. I wanted to be back in the warm den with Shiki. We'd never been apart for this long, and I'd been too confident about coming here. The roads were the same as before, but the people were different, and there were so many things I just didn't understand. I'd need another lifetime to learn them all. I wasn't going to stop looking, though. Roku needed a name if she wanted to be successful, and I would do anything to give her that. I would make Roku's dream come true.

I'd also decided I would come back to the town in a few months to find her, secretly checking up on her. After all, I only wanted the best for my pups.

Days continued to pass with no luck. I'd talked to strong swordsmiths and nimble dancers, and nobody had the most perfect name. The swordsmiths named their children after the emperor, and the dancers named theirs after the wind and the sky. Roku wasn't these things either.

Dawn, the warm sun climbed higher in the sky as the tenth day began. The trees had started changing now, leaves shifted colour and fell, leaving branches bare and spindly. I had to go home. This was always the time that young tanuki left the den, and I couldn't miss it.

I sat on the edge of the town, staring at the trees, wishing I had found a name for Roku. Would she leave to see the humans now or go off like her brothers and sisters into the forest?

A sadness hit me: I'd spent nearly every day with the pups, raising them, teaching them, and now they'd go off on their own. No more chasing after mischievous pups, no running around and jumping in the river to catch frogs. A wetness filled my eyes, a strange thing only humans seemed to do. Even with my blurry vision, all I could see were the tall trees surrounding me.

"Sakurago," I said, remembering what I'd seen in the town. "Named after the spring blossoms. But what about autumn? The lingering warmth, the feeling of change and age."

I stared at the maple tree before me, and a word came

rushing to my mind. "Momiji. The beauty of autumn. That's her name."

Laughter filled my belly, and I quickly dried my eyes. I could return home triumphant. Jumping up, I rushed back as fast as my feet would go in the human sandals. Rushing down the road, I went past the lady with the stone face and turned down the street with the market and painful powder, and further still I ran past the docks and busy fishermen. I didn't stop until the forest welcomed me back with wide arms.

Poof! And, once again, I was tanuki.

"Shiki?" I barked, leaping through the grass and falling leaves. "Shiki, where are you?"

"Tanu?" a sleepy voice came from the den. "You're back?"

"Yes!"

"Father, Father." Out of the den popped the heads of sleepy and inquisitive tanuki, waking up quickly as they saw me. "The humans didn't eat you."

"Eat me? No, no. I was safe." I laughed and joined them in the den. "And now I am home."

Curling up next to Shiki, I breathed in her scent. I'd missed them all so much. The warmth, the cuddles—it didn't take much to make me drift away into a happy sleep once the pups had stopped hounding me for answers about my trip.

When I awoke next, the sun was high in the sky. The pups were outside playing already, and only Shiki remained.

"This is what it is going to be like again," she said sadly.

"Yes, but we'll see them another time. They won't stay away forever. And one day, there might be more pups to keep us company."

"I'd like that," Shiki said, stretching and climbing to her feet. "But will you be able to keep up with more pups? What if we had more next time? My sister once had ten pups."

"Ten pups?" I buried my muzzle into my paws. I could not

deal with ten pups. "I would find a way," I said, lifting my head back up. "Anything for you, my Shiki."

Shiki nuzzled her face into mine. "First, let's get these pups off on their paths."

Shaking her fur of clinging leaves, she left the den. I stretched my paws as far as they could go before I made my way out into the light of the forest again.

It was great to be home once more.

Today, the pups weren't jumping around in the grass and getting up to no good. Today, they stood calmly, fully grown with brown bushy tails. They weren't pups anymore.

"Mother, Father," Ichi said, looking between us. "I think today is the day I am ready to go off by myself. I searched deeper in the forest and found an old tree stump I want to live in. I'll be close so I can see you often."

"My son," Shiki said, embracing him. "I'll even bring you berries and catch you the fattest birds to make sure you are eating enough."

"Good luck," I said to him.

And off Ichi went, disappearing into the forest.

Ni spoke next, followed by San, Shi, and Go, and they too walked off into the forest like their brother. Only Roku remained, her paws dancing in a mixture of worry and excitement.

"Father? Did you find me a name?"

I embraced her tightly. "For days and days I searched for a name, speaking to all the people who live in the town. I even was attacked by a powder that hurt my nose! I searched everywhere I could ... until finally I found you a name. Momiji."

"Momiji ... Momiji ... I love it, Father!"

Unlike her brothers and sisters, Roku stayed with us until the evening, when the moon peeked through the leaves. Just as I had, Roku laid out leaves and drummed her belly and

—*poof*—transformed into a human. My heart was heavy, but I was proud.

Together, we all walked to the edge of the forest, where she finally left us, our human Momiji.

* * *

Odessa Silver is a fantasy author from the UK who is inspired by her love of Japan, the natural world, and the human mind. Always a dreamer, Odessa pulls ideas from the many thoughts which dominate her awake or sleeping mind. She has been writing since she was a young child, needing to get down the stories crafted in hours of daydreaming and has always written under the fantasy genre, finding it most freeing and able to explore each idea to its fullest.

AUTHOR SOCIAL MEDIA

Alex Masse
Instagram: http://instagram.com/fairythingflies
TikTok: https://www.tiktok.com/@fairythingflies
Website: http://alexkmasse.ca/

By Nicole L. Soper Gorden
Facebook: http://www.facebook.com/NicoleLSoperGorden/
Instagram: http://instagram.com/NicoleLSoperGorden
Twitter: http://twitter.com/NLSoperGorden

Arlen Feldman
Twitter: http://twitter.com/arlenfeldman
BlueSky: http://bsky.app/profile/cowthulu.bsky.social
Website: https://cowthulu.com

Ally Kelly
Facebook: https://www.facebook.com/AKFantasyWriter
Instagram: http://instagram.com/AKFantasyWriter
Tiktok: https://www.tiktok.com/AuthorAllyKelly
Website: http://akfantasywriter.com

E-mail: ally@akfantasywriter.com

Sara Kuzuoka

Instagram: http://instagram.com/sarakuzuoka

H. Robert Barland

Twitter: http://twitter.com/hrobertbarland
Instagram: http://instagram.com/h.robertbarland

Mika Grimmer

Twitter: http://twitter.com/mikagrimmer
Instagram: http://instagram.com/mika.grimmer
Website: http://www.mikagrimmer.com

Freya Bell

Facebook: http://www.facebook.com/profile.php?id=100087297279654
Twitter: http://twitter.com/FreyaEH
Instagram: http://instagram.com/darkneptune_19
TikTok: http://tiktok.com/@freyabellauthor
Website: http://www.freyabellwrites.com

Kathryn Reilly

Twitter: http://twitter.com/Katecanwrite
Instagram: http://instagram.com/Katecanwrite
Website: www.katecanwrite.com

MJ Pieloor

Facebook: www.facebook.com/MikePieloor

D.T. Powell

Instagram: http://www.instagram.com/dtill359/
Facebook: http://www.facebook.com/profile.php?id=100039385217526

Ashley Newell

Facebook: http://www.facebook.com/NewellBooks
Instagram: http://instagram.com/anewellauthor
Twitter: http://twitter.com/olanthea
Website: www.newellbooks.com

Erin Casey

Facebook: http://facebook.com/erincaseyauthor
Twitter: http://twitter.com/erincasey09
Instagram: http://instagram.com/erincaseyauthor
TikTok: http://tiktok.com/@authorerincasey
Threads: erincaseyauthor
BlueSky: http://bsky.app/profile/authorerincasey.bsky.social
Website: http://erincasey.org

Odessa Silver

Facebook: http://www.facebook.com/OdessaSilverAuthor
Instagram: http://www.instagram.com/odessa_silver
BlueSky: http://bsky.app/profile/odessasilver.bsky.social
Website: http://odessasilver.carrd.co

WORLDSMYTHS NEWSLETTER

Did you enjoy this anthology? Want to read more like it? Follow our monthly newsletter for updates on upcoming publications, monthly challenges and community milestones.

WORLDSMYTHS SOCIAL MEDIA

Worldsmyths is at its heart a writing community. These anthologies exist because of the robust group of unique writers we have from all over the world. Interested in joining a community with monthly challenges, weekly discussion questions and more? Join us on Discord!

Discord:
http://discord.gg/SvbpsdZ

Website:

http://worldsmyths.com

Facebook:

http://facebook.com/Worldsmyths

Instagram:

http://instagram.com/WorldsmythsWriters

BlueSky:

http://bsky.app/profile/worldsmyths.bsky.social

E-Mail:

publishers@worldsmyths.com

CALL FOR SUBMISSIONS

Fantasy, Sci Fi, and Horror Novels and Novellas

Worldsmyths is now open to novel and novella submissions for Fantasy, Sci Fi, and Horror novels between 10k and 90k words. We are looking for stories set in a secondary world (not our world) or the distant past/future, with fantastical worldbuilding. We accept sci fi but it will be a harder sell than fantasy, so send your strongest work.

What we don't want: Excessive violence and darkness. Stories don't need to have a happy ending, but they shouldn't be endlessly bleak. Nothing wrong with dark stories, just not our cup of tea. We also don't want religious texts or essays. For this call we don't want any urban fantasy or super hero stories. Stories below or over wordcount will be deleted unread. No AI generated or assisted stories.

Submission Period: Now to filled (2024)

Length: 10,000-90,000 words

Genre: Speculative fiction

Pay: $100 advance + 50% royalties paid biannually

Rights: Exclusive right for a year

Reprints Accepted: No

Simultaneous Submissions: No

Who Can Submit: Anyone

Where to Submit:
https://forms.gle/LRXF4PRnK8oMDgkR8

LGBTQ+ Fantasy Anthology

This Fantasy LGBTQ+ short story collection will feature ~10 stories (depending on submissions) between 2 and 10k.

This will be a **charity** anthology – This means we are paying only a token amount ($10USD), with all profits going to an LGBTQ+ charity (to be decided by members via a vote)

What we want

Secondary world fantasy: This means no stories set on planet earth, no matter the time period.

LGBTQ+ character(s): The story should feature LGBTQ+ characters, preferably as the lead character. The story doesn't need to be 'about' their queerness necessarily, but it should be an important facet of their character.

Edited work: Stories should have had at least one editing pass before submission – no first drafts please.

What we don't want: Excessive violence and darkness. Stories don't need to have a happy ending, but they shouldn't be endlessly bleak. Nothing wrong with dark stories, just not our cup of tea. We also don't want religious texts or essays. For this call we don't want any sci fi, urban fantasy, or super hero stories. Stories below or over wordcount will be deleted unread. No AI generated or assisted stories.

Submission Period: Now until March 31st, 2024 at 11:59pm EST

Length: 2000-10,000 words

Genre: Fantasy

Pay: $10 token pay

Rights: Exclusive right for a year

Reprints Accepted: Yes

Simultaneous Submissions: No

Who Can Submit: Anyone

Where to Submit:
   https://forms.gle/dMBi3CB8coVdrZTB9

AARON H. ARM EDITING

We'd like to thank our fantastic editor, Aaron H. Arm, for editing this anthology! If you're looking for editing, you can find his website link below.

http://aaronharm.com